AFTER THE SHIFT

Freezing Point

Killing Frost

Black Ice

This is a work of fiction. Names, characters, places and incidents either are the product of imagination or are used fictitiously. Any resemblance to actual persons, living or dead, events or locales, is entirely coincidental.

RELAY PUBLISHING EDITION, JANUARY 2019
Copyright © 2019 Relay Publishing Ltd.

All rights reserved. Published in the United Kingdom by Relay Publishing. This book or any portion thereof may not be reproduced or used in any manner whatsoever without the express written permission of the publisher except for the use of brief quotations in a book review.

www.relaypub.com

AFTER THE SHIFT SERIES BOOK THREE

BLACK ICE

GRACE HAMILTON

BLURB

Losses pile up like the snowdrifts of a never-ending winter in this post-apocalyptic series conclusion.

Nathan Tolley's wife is gone, leaving him adrift in a vast ocean of bitter white that promises nothing but heartache and despair. Yet, his weary band of travelers continue to look to him to secure their safety. But Nate's no leader. Every decision he's made on their dangerous cross-country journey has taken them from bad to worse. First Detroit. Then Chicago. Now, Wyoming, which proves the deadliest of all.

As circumstances continue to deteriorate like the weather, Nate turns their sights south, but the past is about to catch up to them in ways none of them will see coming. And in order to embrace an uncertain future, sacrifices must be made.

Survival of the fittest gets real—fast.

And, this time, it's personal.

THANK YOU

Thank you for purchasing 'Black Ice'
(After The Shift Book Three)

Get prepared and sign-up to Grace's mailing list to be notified of my next release!

You can also follow Grace on

Facebook: Fb.me/authorgracehamilton

Goodreads: Goodreads.com/gracehamilton

1

"You can move back or I can shoot your face off. It's entirely up to you, my friend."

The business end of the Remington Model 887 Nitro Mag pump-action shotgun was indeed pointed at Nathan's face, and it was being held in the hands of a petite, blonde-haired woman wearing a denim coat, a black Stetson jammed onto the back of her head. Her face was set, her sighting eye squinted, and the hood of the silver 2004 Cadillac SRX V8 across which she was leaning glinted in the weak Wyoming sunlight. Behind her, men backed her up with their own weapons at the ready.

Nathan had walked up from the horse-drawn wagon after they'd hit across the roadblock across the I-25 on their approach to Casper—four cars across the highway, placed end to end on each side of the interstate, and so he'd approached from just beyond them.

The grass on the central reservations was almost free of snow, and the air smelled damp and rotten, like fall, even though the first spring Nathan had experienced in the last four years had come in the middle of these summer months. The crust of the Earth had slid off its axis, the Arctic was now in the middle of the Atlantic, and America was one-third winter wasteland, one-third Siberian tundra, and one-third earthquakes and volcanoes. With that amount of natural confusion, spring could turn up any time it liked as far as Nathan was concerned.

Nathan had already raised his hands, and he spoke calmly. "I'm Nathan Tolley. We have two kids, six adults including me, and a dog. We were hoping to come into Casper."

"For what reason?" The woman's voice and the barrel of the Remington didn't waver. Behind her, men in checks and denim, shotguns over their shoulders, were looking out past the woman at Nathan. One plopped a brown spatter of tobacco juice onto the blacktop.

Nathan kept his voice level. "To stay. If you'll have us."

The woman didn't move, and Nathan dared not lower his hands. He was dog-tired, feeling like he hadn't slept in half a lifetime, and his heart was broken.

The only thing that had kept him going since the death of his wife, Cyndi, had been the thought of getting his family and friends to the safety of Casper. A town they had heard, from sources on what was left of the internet, was doing okay. It was on the edge of the new Arctic Circle. The prairies were cold and wet, but they would nurture hardy crops and sustain livestock in a way that the landscape east of Casper wouldn't.

And with Nathan and the others pretty much out of food, it felt like they were almost out of luck.

The woman still didn't lower her gun. "We're not authorized to let anyone through. You'll have to make an application."

Tobacco Juice snorted as he walked up closer to the woman and gave a wry smile. Nathan got the impression that making an application wasn't going to get them past the roadblock, however good it was, but he plowed on anyway. "Look, we heard Casper is a good place. We just want to come in and help. We're ready to work—I'm a mechanic, a good one, and we have another. We also have two tech wizards and a woman who makes the best Bloody Marys outside New York."

Nathan's attempt at humor didn't have the desired effect. It didn't take the tension out of the situation one bit.

Tobacco Juice spat again, then leaned in and whispered in the ear of the woman with the shotgun. Nathan couldn't hear what was being said, but the woman lifted her elbows from the Cadillac hood. She kept the gun trained on Nathan's chest.

"You got a medic in that wagon?"

"No," Nathan replied, playing his ace, "but I do have the next best thing."

"And what's that?"

"That will be in my application."

Tobacco Juice's face hardened. "You play games with us, mister, and we'll just shoot you all now."

3

"I'm not playing games. I have the next best thing, but I'm not going to tell you what it is until I get certain guarantees."

"Which are?"

"That I'll be given a fair hearing by whoever it is I need to talk to in order to get my family and my friends into Casper."

Tobacco Juice whispered to the woman, who at last lowered her shotgun, allowing Nathan to relax a hair. Since the coming of the Big Winter, there had been a lot of guns pointed at him, but he wasn't getting used to it. Even though he was wearing a Kevlar vest below his North Face jacket, he didn't feel any safer.

"Okay, you can come in," Tobacco Juice said. "But the rest stay here until we get the go-ahead to let you all in."

Nathan nodded, and with that, he turned and walked back to the wagon.

Tony clung to Nathan, coughing into his coat. "Don't go, Daddy, I don't like it."

Since Cyndi's death, Tony, Nathan's eleven-year-old, hadn't exactly descended into any traumatic well of sadness, but Nathan had noticed the boy wasn't as confident as he had been. And now Nathan heading off without him into the unknown was sending even his diminished level of confidence spiraling down.

To lose one parent could be seen as tragic, but to lose another…

"It's gonna be fine, son. I'll just go in, talk to whoever is in charge, and then I'm sure they're going to let us through. I'll be back by the morning. Maybe even sooner."

Tony relaxed his arms and looked up at Nathan with Cyndi's blue eyes. "If you're sure?"

"I am."

Nathan squeezed his son, ruffled his hair, and left him to scratch at Rapier's, their malamute sled dog's, ears, joining Freeson, Lucy, and Tommy at the wagon.

Free and Lucy were as unlikely a couple as it was possible to imagine. Free, a gnarled and grumpy, mid-thirties mechanic from New York State, and Lucy Arneston, just a squeak under forty, a millionaire socialite and Bloody Mary expert with a nice line in waspish putdowns and a fine eye when out hunting deer, had been thrown together in adversity and had stuck.

"You sure this is a good idea?" Free asked, eyeing the roadblock and huddle of Casper residents.

"I don't see what choice we have. They're not going to trust us if we don't trust them."

Free shrugged. Lucy crossed her arms across her mink coat and sighed.

Tommy, his immoveable US Marines baseball cap permanently reversed no matter what the weather, was someone Nathan could only describe as a Texan who'd fixed a redneck mask over his Native American body, sucked in his cheeks. "You sure you want to go alone? I could follow cross-country, keep my head down…"

Nathan held up his hand, "Tommy, no. Come on. You heard what I said about trust. They're just scared of strangers is all. If they wanted us dead, they could have killed us all where we stand. If I were running Casper, these would be the hoops I'd make people jump through to get in, too. I'll be okay."

By the sour look on Tommy's face, Nathan could see that he wasn't convinced. "We're nearly out of food and getting low on ammo."

Nathan didn't have time to argue this out. They needed to get into Casper stat, and if that meant going in alone, then he would. "Where else are we going to get to if we don't at least try?"

Tommy shrugged. "Just don't let them use you like a doormat."

"I won't."

The chilly silence that descended between the men was cut through by Brandon. Nathan's baby son, as if amplifying everyone's hunger, started to cry from within the wagon. Lucy, who'd willingly become his de facto nanny since Cyndi's passing, pulled the canvas aside and climbed up to see to him. The wails hung in the air with a grim finality, causing Nathan to set any other concerns aside.

Dave and Donie, the two twenty-one-year-old techno whizzes, jumped down from the wagon once she climbed in. Dave was a clean-cut African American, Donie an edgy punk-goth with crazy red hair (which she'd recently colored after a score at a half-looted drug store). Now, she reached into her biker jacket, all zips and studs, pulling out a compact digital walkie-talkie. "It's got about three-quarters' charge and should reach from here to Casper. The land is flat enough."

"Say the word and we'll come running," Dave added. Not a natural warrior, the boy had been through a torrid time in Detroit, and he was growing into a hard-muscled, canny combatant who Nathan could rely on to have his back.

Nodding, Nathan pocketed the walkie-talkie, feeling it settle against his side just below the hard edge of the Kevlar vest. "Right. Let's do it," Nathan said, setting his jaw.

The Cadillac was rolled back as Nathan approached; Shotgun introduced herself as Mary Woolston, and Tobacco Juice as Cal Temper.

"Hope you've got your walking legs on," Mary said as they set off along the blacktop of I-25 heading west into the city.

To the south, the dark blue face of Casper Mountain rose like a wall into the blustery, cloud-scudded sky. Even though the wind was bitter and the prairie bleak, it was still an improvement over the conditions of Big Winter that Nathan had experienced in the preceding months. This weather was near tropical compared to what he'd been used to, and it grew the first shoots of optimism in his thinking.

What he didn't expect, as they came into the Casper suburb of Evansville three hours later, was another roadblock, and it seemed Mary and Cal didn't expect it, either. The highway was obstructed next to a huge, modern-build *'Ev'ry-1-Welcome'* Inn. Behind the barrier, a porcupine back of rifles, shotguns, and pistols sprouted over the hoods and trunks.

"What the hell is Blaine playing at? Wait here," Cal said over his shoulder as he approached the cars.

"I don't understand," Nathan said to Mary. "What's happening here?"

"As soon as we know, you'll know," Mary said under her breath. There was a sudden tenseness in her voice, which led Nathan to conclude that the new roadblock wasn't just unexpected, but presented a particular new threat to Mary as much it did to him.

Nathan's eyes moved down to the entrance hall of the inn. There were bullet holes in the glass, and scattered window shards on the floor, which suggested they were recent. Beyond the doors, he could see a smear of blood on the marble and red footprints leading into the gloom of the building, stopping at a thick puddle of crimson. There were no bodies he could see, but unless someone had sacrificed a bull to the gods of spring in that entranceway, there was someone beyond it who was very dead, or close to it.

"I think we're a tad exposed here," Nathan whispered to Mary, and she nodded imperceptibly. In the corner of his eye, he saw her index finger moving into the trigger guard of the shotgun resting on her shoulder.

"Are you carrying?" she asked, still at the level of a soft whisper.

"I have a knife in my boot. I thought it would be a good idea to trust you guys if you were gonna trust me."

"Well, I have a fair idea we might have to shoot our way out of here. Be prepared to duck and run. Blaine has been promising something like this for a while; I guess when I thought he didn't have the stones to carry it out, I was wrong."

This situation had gone south far too quickly for Nathan's sensibilities to have caught up just yet. There was a surreal, dreamlike nature to the scene—the cars across the highway, and the forest of guns which were not necessarily pointing at them yet, but ready to be dropped into position if the mood took the guys on the other side of the roadblock. "Internal problems? Rival factions? Civil war?" Nathan whispered wearily.

"You from the United Nations?"

"No," Nathan said with a deepening sadness. "I've just seen it all before, and recently. Here. New York, Detroit, and Chicago. Everything's falling apart."

Mary nodded. "And Blaine is the kinda guy who would bring the wrecking ball. He's wanted more power and influence since day one. I guess he got tired of waiting."

Cal had reached the cars now; spitting tobacco juice onto the tarmac, he kept his rifle high on his shoulder, ready, but clearly trying not to show any obvious signs of threat.

The wind was still present, and it whipped some of the words spoken away from Nathan's ears, but he got the gist of what was going down.

"There's been a change, Cal," said a gruff voice behind a beat-up, gray 1999 Ford Taurus LX wagon. A huge, middle-aged man with hands like river dredgers and a wild-bearded face surrounded by a riot of blond curls came out into the open.

"What do you mean a *change*, Blaine? We went up to the roadblock last night and everything was settled." Cal didn't move his gun off his shoulder, but Nathan could see the straightening in the man's back. The screw was tightening on the anxiety in the air. Nathan didn't need to be a fortune teller to divine the chilling of the already cold atmosphere.

"We had a reorganization, Cal, that's all." Blaine's hands moved into the pockets of his parka. It was a natural move that wasn't in and of itself threatening, but Nathan could see that everyone else behind the cars was armed. Why would this Blaine character come out without a weapon? It didn't make sense.

Nathan got his answer as Blaine's pocket exploded and Cal went down, dropping his shotgun in a fashion that sent it clattering to the tarmac. Cal groaned, his hands clawing at the blood pumping from his opened thigh.

Mary cursed, and Nathan started to back away, hands raised. Blaine kicked Cal's shotgun away to the curb and pulled a snub-nosed Colt from the pocket of his parka, pointing it back and forth between Mary and Nathan.

"Put your gun down, Mary. I don't want to have to shoot you. And you, Mister *I-Don't-Recognize-You*, keep your hands where I can see them." Blaine called over his shoulder, "Baxter! Reed! Check them over."

Baxter and Reed turned out to be a joyless, fat-thin double-act with stony faces and a putrid line in bad breath. Fat, who Nathan decided was Baxter, frisked him, pulling out the walkie-talkie and finding the bowie knife in his boot, holding both items up for Blaine to see.

"Guys, this isn't my fight. I just came here to see if we could join up. My name is Nathan Tolley and I don't want any trouble," Nathan offered, still reaching for the leaden clouds, the cramp of the position starting to encroach around his shoulders. Lack of food and sleep had poured gritty fatigue into his frame, and the march from the first roadblock had sapped what energy he'd had.

Blaine eyed the walkie-talkie Baxter had passed to him and then pocketed it himself. "I'll be the judge of who is or isn't trouble, boy," Blaine said, his voice thick with menace. "Okay, get them inside."

Baxter and Reed pushed Mary and Nathan toward the inn while other men came from behind the cars, lifting Cal in order to take him down the slope to the entrance.

Cal moaned softly, applying his own pressure to the wound in his leg, but as he was manhandled into the building, thick rivulets of blood seeped between his fingers and left a drip trail behind him.

"He's gonna bleed out if you don't let us help him," Mary said to Blaine as they entered the building.

Blaine looked at the trail of blood and Cal's whitening face. "If I wanted him to die quick, I'd have shot him in the head."

Mary didn't respond. Nathan's throat tightened and his guts twisted. Was nowhere a safe haven for him and his family? They'd come here with a sense that it might be somewhere better than Detroit. But, as ever, it seemed human nature in these desperate times was constantly defaulting to the violent rather than the cooperative. He had no idea what Blaine's beef was with Cal, but this kind of factional conflict seemed like it was becoming the norm in Big Winter America. Was the gun the only regulator now? The gun and the brutality behind it?

Whatever notions Nathan had harbored over getting his family and friends into Casper had dissipated like smoke on the wind. The priority now was getting away from here, and getting away soon.

Inside the *'Ev'ry-1-Welcome'* lobby, it was clear there had been a short and vicious battle which had resulted in a lot of bullet holes in walls, a smashed receptions desk, floes of smashed glass, Jackson Pollock-type sprays of blood, and a pile of corpses both male and female, which had been constructed into a stack at one end of the lobby.

Blaine pulled a cloth-covered lobby chair back onto its legs and sat down. Then Baxter, Reed, and the others—a motley crew of men with grizzled chins, winter coats, Stetsons, and baseball caps—arranged themselves around their big, blond-haired leader.

Cal was placed on the floor in front of Blaine like a tribute to a chief or a king. Cal's eyes were flickering now, blood loss and shock taking over. If Blaine's bullet hadn't severed his femoral artery, then it had certainly nicked it. His pale hands had fallen from the ragged wound now, so blood was weeping and welling over the material of his jeans, drenching the denim a rich purple.

Blaine placed the Colt on his knee and then leaned back in the chair with his hands laced behind the back of his head like he was waiting for someone to bring him a coffee. Nathan eyed the routes to the exit and then the three corridors which radiated from the lobby into the deeper confines of the gloomy, unlit inn. Nathan knew he wouldn't make it five paces before he was shot. Whatever happened now, he was going to have to ride this out and see what Blaine was planning to do with them.

But if it came to a choice between definite death and a sporting chance at suicide, Nathan knew which option he would take. The nearest corridor was fifteen feet away to his right. There were two of Blaine's men who he would have to go through to get there and they both had shotguns at the ready.

The options for survival were short, but at least he knew that he would try, and he had the basis of a plan.

"We took over City Hall last night. There wasn't what you might call much of a resistance from Stewart and the others."

Mary's bottom lip trembled. "You killed them?"

"What choice did I have, Mary? Come on, you know he wasn't interested in sharing Casper with us."

"You mean letting you run it."

"Someone has to take charge. Stewart wasn't the man for the job."

"So, you shot him," Mary spat out, a solitary tear working down her cheek.

"Of course we didn't shoot him," Blaine countered, as if his feeling were hurt, but Nathan could feel the follow-up coming hard on the keels of Blaine's first sentence, before he ever heard the words. "No. We lynched him."

Baxter sniggered, cricked his neck, and stuck out his tongue and mimed a rope behind his head.

Blaine grinned. "Which, Mary, because you're such a fusspot and because I can't trust you to be on our side under the… what shall we call them… the new, uh, prevailing conditions of Casper's governance, is exactly what we're going to do to you and your friend Nathan here."

The wide grin came again, with the relaxed attitude in the chair and the voice which was soft, level, and calm. "Reed. Get the ropes."

2

Blaine's calm was shattered at the same time as his kneecap.

It wasn't the sudden movement from the collapsed form of Cal on the floor in the widening pool of blood that caused everyone to look at Blaine. It wasn't even the yell of desperate hatred from Cal as he kicked out with the solid boot heel of his uninjured leg, catching the side Blaine's knee smartly and with maximum force, that made everyone turn. No, it was the sickening crack and crunch of Blaine's leg collapsing like a clapperboard snapping closed in the first shot of a film that drew all eyes toward him, wide with horror.

The noise was sharp, final, and it stilled time in the lobby.

Nathan, who had already been checking which was the best route out of the area, was the first to react. He grabbed Mary's arm and dragged her to their right as the first screaming howl from Blaine's mouth erased the cracking bones from Nathan's immediate memory and gave time permission to start up again.

Nathan barged into the nearest man and bowled him off his feet like the last pin in a bowling alley. The unbalanced man crashed into his nearest counterpart and they both went sprawling over the upended furniture, smacking into the beige, marble-tiled floor, their guns skittering away.

The guns, unfortunately, slipped so far that Nathan knew there was no time to bend and pick either of them up before the other men in the room tore their eyes from Blaine's destroyed leg and raised their guns toward him. Instead, Nathan tightened his grip on Mary's hand and dragged her into the gloom.

The corridor wasn't wide, and had doors along either side, leading into what Nathan guessed were rooms or suites. Mary ran hard beside him, still holding on to his hand. Behind them, the bellows and shouts followed fast on their heels as Blaine's men cocked their weapons and peppered fire down the corridor after the fleeing escapees.

The first bullets and sprays of pellets burst into the floor behind them, ricocheting upward, carving arcs along the walls or bursting the dead lights in the ceiling.

If Nathan and Mary had still been in that first corridor, they would have been zeroed in on where they ran, but before the men in the lobby had mustered the wherewithal to fire, Nathan, hearing the weapons being readied, had already kicked a door open on a room and dragged Mary inside.

He kicked the door closed behind them, too. "Chairs. Tables. Anything. Put it all in front of the doors!" he shouted at Mary.

The woman didn't need to be told twice.

As Nathan upended the room's metal bedframe and slammed it into place against the door, Mary began dragging a hefty, two-seat sofa across the carpeted floor and pushed it hard against the bed frame.

"That's not gonna hold them for long," she said, eyeing their makeshift barrier suspiciously.

"It doesn't have to," Nathan said as he lifted a leather-bound armchair above his head. "They only have to *think* we're still in here."

Nathan hefted the armchair, put his head down, and ran with it toward the window at the back of the hotel room. The rear window overlooked an enclosed central courtyard in the center of the complex.

The window burst open, glass dropping from the frame like melted ice. Nathan pulled the drape across the window sill so as not to catch his hands on the shards of broken glass which remained, and then he vaulted into the courtyard, landing at the bottom of the five-foot drop in a bed of soil that might have once held ornamental flowerbeds.

Mary dropped down beside him.

"What now?" she asked, looking up at the windows around the courtyard. Nathan looked, too—there didn't yet seem to be anyone watching them.

"Follow me."

Nathan grabbed the armchair, hefting it up over his head again and running now on pure desperation and bitter adrenaline. His heart was beating hard in his ears, his mouth tasting like metal and blood. He ran across the courtyard's fifty or so feet and launched the armchair into another window. The glass split down the center with a crazy, star-crash pattern and the chair tumbled back to Nathan's feet. He yanked the armchair up again and hurled it against the already weakened glass. The ice-dusted window broke open like a frosted merengue and the armchair disappeared into the dark.

Mary brushed past Nathan and made to start climbing.

"No!" Nathan hissed. "This way!" Nathan dragged her back across the courtyard to the window they'd just come from and prepared to pull himself up. From the room came sounds of banging and pushing as the men on the other side of the door tried to force it open.

"Are you mad?" Mary spat.

"Quite possibly," Nathan said as he hauled himself up over the window ledge and back into the room. The door was starting to come open. There was no way anyone beyond it could see into the room yet, but it was only a matter of time before they did.

Nathan reached back out through the window, laying across the drapes and holding his hand out to Mary—whispering desperately, "Come on! We've got seconds!"

Mary's face wasn't sure, so her body made her mind up for her. She grasped Nathan's hand and let him haul her back up into the hotel room.

Nathan didn't wait for Mary to get her breath after all the exertion; he pulled her toward the room's bathroom situated in the space immediately adjacent to the doorway, and just after their sofa and bed-constructed barrier. Once inside, Nathan closed the door quietly behind them with a soft click.

The bathroom had no light and no window. They were in complete darkness. Nathan felt for Mary's face and put his fingers across her lips to remind her to keep quiet.

In the room beyond the bathroom door, the heaving and the crashing was starting to bear fruit. The tortured crunch of the bed frame, scoring a deep gouge into the wall as it was pushed back, cut across the air. There was a crash and a yell, and the door came free and crashed against the door behind which Nathan and Mary now cowered.

Nathan had made the calculation that their pursuers would clatter into the room without noticing the obscured bathroom door, and instead establish the smashed window and the connotations of a swift exit it implied—and once they spied the broken window across the courtyard, they would act accordingly.

It had been a huge gamble, but it paid off.

"They've gone through the window!"

"Reed! Get back to Blaine and tell him they're in Block C across the quad!"

"Baxter! With me!"

There was a scrambling of feet over the window ledge and a curse or two as egress was made over the broken glass, accompanied by the sounds of footsteps running across the concrete beyond it toward the other smashed window.

Nathan counted to ten, then opened the door a crack. He sneaked a look through. The crack in the doorway brought thin gray afternoon light from the broken window into the bathroom.

The room was empty.

Indicating for Mary to follow him, Nathan came out of the bathroom, keeping his head low. He could hear the men across the courtyard scrambling up into the far room through the second window he'd broken.

Nathan moved gingerly to the doorway into the corridor and ventured one eye forward to look along it. It was lit only by light coming in from a frosted window at one end and the illumination bleeding up from the lobby. The guy who'd been charged with going back to Blaine, a thin, black-haired man with a padded yellow body-warmer over a denim jacket, was already jogging out of the corridor to report back to his boss.

As the four guys at the end of the corridor heard what Yellow had to report, they took the safeties off their rifles and shotguns and hared off down the middle corridor. Nathan assumed that the route they took would take the men all the way to Block C, where Nathan and Mary would absolutely not be found.

It gave them one hell of a slim chance to escape, but it was one he was willing to gamble upon.

Nathan's scrambling brain tried to assess what forces might be ranged against him still in the lobby.

Two men had gone across the quad.

Yellow and four others had taken the corridor. Nathan racked his memory, trying to figure out how many people would be left in the entrance hall after all that. He'd been too interested in finding an escape route to worry about an accurate assessment of the forces. Now, he figured that on top of Blaine, there was just Cal —probably with a bullet in his head now—and two other men. Surely, they'd be dealing with Blaine right now, not expecting Nathan to show up exactly where they believed he wasn't…

It was worth a shot.

"Wait here," he whispered to the shock-eyed Mary, and with that, he set off down the corridor toward the lobby. His feet moved as quickly across the carpet as he dared without overtly announcing his presence.

The first things he heard were Blaine's moans and cursing. His voice was a low rumble, and Nathan inwardly winced when he imagined what pain the man might be in. Cal's kick had collapsed the leg like a house of cards. Apart from a few cracked ribs and a dislocated thumb playing football in college, Nathan had never experienced a fully dislocated fracture of a limb. The way Blaine's moans and curses were ripping through the air, Nathan thought that he definitely didn't want to. Especially in this world, where the majority of hospitals were closed, society had broken down, and doctors were rarer than a hen's teeth.

Nathan reached the end of the corridor, leaning his back against the wall and weighing up what he firmly believed were his only two options. If he wanted to make it into and out of the lobby alive, he was either going to have to attack like a cornered cougar or walk in like he owned the place.

If he rushed in, he'd not have much time to assess the situation, but if he caused enough confusion by selecting the second, but much bolder, course of action, he just might pull this off.

"Try not to move, Blaine... Ralph's getting splints."

"Don't touch my leg!"

"I've got to, man. It needs to be straight. Here, bite on this."

"I'm not biting on anything! Leave my leg alone!"

Nathan listened to the conversation, thinking on what it told him. Ralph was gone. Gone where? Out to the roadblock. How long had he been gone? He could be back any second, but right now there were only two voices. Blaine and the guy offering him something to bite on for the pain.

You can do this.

You can *do* this.

Nathan took a breath so deep it almost popped open his jacket, and then he walked out into the lobby, unarmed and fully exposed.

Cal was on the floor looking like there was more blood outside his body than in it. His eyes were closed and there was no time to see if he was breathing. Blaine had been laid out on a three-seat sofa, and a short fat guy who looked like all the hair on his head had migrated to his chin was bent over the injured man. Short-Fat's hand was on Blaine's shoulder, and there was a matte black Beretta 1301 tactical pump-action shotgun laying by Short-Fat's feet, the stock wallowing in the spreading pool of Cal's lifeblood. Blaine's Colt was on the seat where he'd been earlier, and of Ralph, there was no sign.

Short-Fat's back was to Nathan, and he was also obscuring Blaine's line of sight to the corridor from which Nathan had emerged.

Nathan had already committed himself to his forward trajectory—if he stopped in his plan now, there would be more than enough time for Short-Fat to turn, see Nathan, and pick up the 1301.

In for a penny...

"Blaine, Baxter and Reed say they can't find them in C Block, so they're gonna sweep back to B," Nathan said levelly and firmly. Short-Fat was trying to keep Blaine still. Blaine for his part was bucking with pain, and still not able to see beyond his subordinate. Nathan had guessed that he was in too much pain to differentiate voices at this point, and he was right.

"I don't care! Just find them, you moron!" Blaine screamed hard enough to rattle the lobby windows, but it was enough. Nathan pocketed the Colt, lifted the 1301, and then began to turn to get out of the lobby before Short-Fat looked around or Blaine managed to find a sliver of focus through the shattering pain.

It would have all worked out fine, too, if the guy Nathan assumed was Ralph hadn't come back into the lobby right then with two short planks of pine under one arm, holding a SIG Sauer in his other hand.

"Dammit! It's him!" Ralph shouted as he fired.

Nathan was already diving to his left, and the 9mm bullet smashed into a picture frame already skewed awkwardly on the wall. Nathan hit the floor, crunching his shoulder hard into the marble, and this had the effect of jouncing the muzzle of the shotgun in his hands up—he pulled the trigger reactively.

Ralph's face bloomed with blood and his head snapped back so hard that a crack not unlike the one that had accompanied the breaking of Blaine's knee became the starting pistol shot marking the beginning of his slow pitch backward.

Short-Fat was reaching for the 1301 that was no longer there, Blaine screaming in a mixture of panic, rage, and agony.

Nathan leveled the 1301 on them both, fixing them with a look that he hoped would chill their hearts as he got first onto his knees and then to his feet. "Reach, boys. I don't want to have to shoot you like Ralph now—and please, Blaine, do not under any circumstances shout again or I will, so help me god, end you here and now."

Ralph and Blaine raised their hands. There was a sweat of shock and pain over Blaine's face, but Ralph was pure scared. He had the face of a man who was ready to give out as much fear and terror as he could, but when the boot was on the other foot, he turned into a teetering pile of anxiety with a backbone deficiency.

"Now, boys, I have nothing to do with this. This isn't my fight. I have no idea what trouble has been going on back in Casper, and quite frankly I want nothing to do with any 'who can pee the highest' contest."

"Why should I believe you?" Blaine asked through gritted teeth. "When my men get back here, I'm gonna have you strung up in the parking lot."

"For a man with a broken leg on the wrong end of a shotgun, I'm not sure how you're going to manage that, Blaine, but I hope not to give you the opportunity to make good on the promise."

Blaine winced as his loose knee shifted on the sofa and screwed his eyes up as the wave of pain rushed through him. "I am going to enjoy watching you swing, boy. I'm going to enjoy it immensely."

"One more word out of you and you won't be enjoying anything ever again."

Blaine managed a smile. "You shot Ralph by accident. I can see it in your eyes; you're not a killer, Nathan. You might try to pretend you are, but if you're so fixed on making me stop talking, why don't you blow me away?"

Blaine might not believe that Nathan would shoot them, but Short-Fat looked like he believed it from there to kingdom come. Blaine was warming to his speech, though, and he wiped his cuff across his sweating forehead as Short-Fat looked askance at his boss, cold terror in his eyes.

"Blaine…"

"Shut up, you lousy puke! Nathan, in three seconds, I'm going to start shouting for my men. I'm going to scream at the top of my voice and they are gonna come, and I am going to tell them to shoot you in the legs so you can't run away, and then I can watch you take the drop, boy. No one does this to Blaine Peebles. No one."

Nathan knew his bluff had been called. There was no way he'd wanted to shoot Ralph in the first place, and he wasn't going to start shooting unarmed or injured men now, however much one of them deserved it.

So, he stepped forward, turned the 1301 around, and brained them both where they stood and lay. Unconscious Short-Fat crashed to the floor and Blaine sighed, rolling over so that his arm hung limply down into Cal's blood.

Nathan looked down the corridor that Yellow and the others had gone down not more than three minutes before. They weren't yet returning—the inn was a big building with many rooms, and a systematic search was going to take them some time, especially if they had to kick down every door to check beyond it. They hadn't looked like the most fit guys Nathan had ever seen, and he could imagine they were breathing and sweating hard by now.

He looked out of the lobby windows, up the slope to the road-block. There was a chance that if those cars had been put there today or last night, that at least one of them would have enough fuel to get him and Mary back to the wagon and the others. *Maybe.*

Further thought or planning was interrupted as a woman's scream ripped the air apart behind him, just down the corridor from which he'd emerged. Tracking back, 1301 at the ready, Nathan sneaked a look down the corridor.

Mary was being dragged by her hair along the floor by Baxter. He had her blonde locks in one hand and a Remington, short-stocked shotgun in the other. Mary was screaming and struggling. Baxter dropped her to the floor and backhanded her across the chops, busting her nose in a spray of blood before he grabbed a meaty handful of her hair and began dragging her again.

Nathan stepped out into the corridor, his 1301 leveled at Baxter's midriff. Baxter looked so surprised at seeing Nathan that his first reaction was to pull the shotgun trigger rather than raise his hands. The blast seared past Nathan's right ear as he moved, pellets ripping the shoulder of his jacket but not drilling their hot lead into his flesh.

Nathan came down in a crouch and tried to return fire, but Baxter pushed his advantage and, instead of pointing his Remington at Nathan, had the presence of mind to point it to where Mary had fallen and push it into the back of her skull.

"Put it down!" Baxter screamed at Nathan. "Put it down or I swear I will paint the walls with her brains!"

Even if Nathan fired and his aim was true, there was more than an even chance that Baxter would pull his trigger and Mary's blood and gray matter would be spread over the carpet and up the walls of the corridor.

You don't even know her! She pulled a gun on you! Why are you risking your life to save her? Why?

Nathan couldn't answer himself. He just couldn't allow Mary to be shot dead in front of him. He couldn't. Nathan put the 1301 down, raised his hands, and got to his feet.

Baxter motioned him to walk backward. "Get in the lobby. Now!"

Nathan moved back, and Baxter stalked him, still dragging Mary by her hair as she crawled at his feet.

Moving evenly, Nathan side-eyed Short-Fat and Blaine where he'd left them.

Baxter emerged from the corridor with Mary and got his first view of the carnage there: Ralph's dead body and Short-Fat unconscious, adding to the pile of bodies of the people they had already cut down. "My god…" he breathed, keeping his Remington trained squarely on Nathan's body.

Blaine's eyelids were flickering; he took a ragged breath, groaned, and opened his eyes. There was a trickle of blood running down his forehead from where Nathan had hit him hard with the shotgun. As Blaine lifted his head, that trickle of blood ran into his mouth.

"Well, well, well…" He smiled at Nathan and Baxter, "Well, well, well, indeed." As he smiled, the blood trickle stained his teeth red and turned his whole mouth into a maw of horror.

3

Blaine was carried out to the parking lot of the *'Ev'ry-1-Welcome'* on a chair like a South Sea Island Chief from a 50s B movie where, at any moment, you'd expect King Kong to appear over the horizon. The men carrying the chair were straining and sweating under the weight of the huge man, but Blaine himself had ordered them to carry him out so that he could witness the execution.

For a man with a badly busted leg which dangled uselessly from the chair, he was doing remarkably well. The half-empty bottle of Jack Daniels he was taking for *medicinal purposes* was obviously helping to numb the pain, but it wasn't softening his resolve for showy violence any.

Cal's body had been dragged from the inn by Baxter and Reed. They held him by the feet, affording him no dignity or respect. Cal's head was lolling and bumping sickeningly across floors, down steps, and across the rough tarmac. If Cal wasn't actually dead, his body was so deep into shock from the blood loss that he might as well have been. Nathan considered it a small mercy that Cal was so out of it.

Man, I wish I was, too.

Nathan and Mary had been pushed out into the wide blustery expanse of the lot, their hands tied with rope behind their backs. Nathan's right eye was swelling and closing from a punch that Short-Fat, now identified as Riley Peach, had hit him with once he'd woken from unconsciousness and gotten his bearings. The fist that had hit Nathan had landed just a glancing blow, but the thick wristwatch on Peach's left arm had snagged his eye with considerable force. Nathan figured he would have a beauty of a shiner if he lived long enough to find a mirror.

Mary walked with her head down—resigned, it seemed, to their fate as they approached the forty-foot-high *'Ev'ry-1-Welcome'* sign by the side of the I-25. Two of Baxter's men were up ladders, attaching ropes to the high gantry in the air. The ropes were thick blue nylon tow lines on which rough nooses had been fashioned to their dangling ends.

There were *three* ropes.

Cal's body was going to be hung alongside those of Mary and Nathan. "If you're making a statement," Blaine had said before he'd been carried out into the parking lot, "you might as well do it properly."

The delight Blaine had taken in pointing that out to Nathan chilled him completely. It stopped the breath in his throat and sucked any hope from his bones. He was tired and alone, three hours of hard walking from what was left of his family and his friends, and there was nothing left in the tank to help him.

The men sat Blaine down with a good view of the makeshift gallows—near enough so he could have a good view, but not so near that he'd have to crane his neck back too far. He swigged at the whiskey, his gnarly Adam's apple bobbing like a grizzly yo-yo, then wiped the back of his hand across his lips. "By the power vested in me…" he began.

Mary snorted, throwing Blaine off his stride. "Power? You've always been a bully and a coward, Blaine. You couldn't get any power or influence in Casper because you were smart or kind. No, you had to take it. Stewart is fifty times the man you are."

"*Was*. Get your tenses right, Mary."

Mary began to talk again, but Blaine held up an emphatic hand. "Be quiet. I can't sit here all day watching you die. I need to see a doctor about my knee."

Mary wasn't being quiet for anyone. "You need to see a psychiatrist, Blaine. You're a weak psychopath, and I'm going to my death cursing you with all my might."

Mary had lifted her head now, and was spitting the words at him. Nathan had seen some things since the fall of the Big Winter, but this ranked as one of the most remarkable. That Mary could draw on such righteous anger at such a moment gave him at least some comfort, in that there were still strong, able, and good people in this horrific world. People who his two sons, now to be left without either of their parents, would have a chance of meeting as they grew up.

A tear welled in the eye Peach had punched. Anyone looking might have thought the tear was because of the injury, but Nathan would know differently. Even at this time of maximum hurt and danger, there was something here to salve his worn spirit. And Mary was that something.

"Baxter," Blaine said simply.

Baxter nodded and came up behind Mary. He pulled a dirty handkerchief from his pocket and hoiked her nose back like he was a league bowler lifting his favorite ball. As Mary yelled in pain, he stuffed the cloth into her open mouth.

Mary's eyes blazed with all the anger in the world, but her tongue was stilled.

Blaine nodded, took a swig from the open neck of his bottle, and continued, "By the powers vested in me during the emergency session last night in City Hall, I hereby sentence the three of you to death."

Electricity leaped from Mary's eyes directly into Nathan's heart. "On what charge?" he asked.

Blaine thought about it, and then nodded to himself and grinned. "No charge. It's a freebie."

Baxter, Reed, and the others laughed and clapped. Like every extra-judicial lynching in history, there was only need for a cursory nod to the idea of due process or justice. This was pure bloodlust brought about by the dereliction of morality. Nathan knew there was no point arguing this out with Blaine along logical lines. He wouldn't be interested in that. All he wanted was to see Nathan swinging and his legs jerking.

"So, for the third, and last time, of asking—powers blah blah blah, defense of the City of Casper blah blah blah, sedition, mutiny, blah blah blah, and aggressive jaywalking without due care and attention, I decree we get this party started. Get 'em up the flagpole, boys—let's see who salutes!"

Nathan and Mary were pushed to the base of the sign. Reed and Baxter dragged Cal's corpse behind them.

"Start with the dead boy first," Blaine ordered. "Let them see what's coming. They'll enjoy the instruction."

Cal's body was lifted high enough to get the noose around the neck, and then the men on the gantry hauled him up hand over hand until he was dangling five feet above the tarmac.

Nathan looked away as Mary began to sob through the handkerchief. Nathan's arms were being held from behind by hard hands which bit like claws into his skin. Even if he bothered trying to run, there was far too firm a grip on him.

"I'm trying to decide whether it should be ladies or gentlemen first," Blaine crowed. He snapped his fingers as if he'd had an idea. "No, I have a better notion. Two for the price of one. Take 'em up together!"

Two more men from the gathering swarmed up the ladders to join the other two on the gantry. Nathan and Mary were pushed under their nooses, Nathan's eyes coming level with Cal's gently swinging boots. He'd shown no sign of resisting the lynching, and that at least was a now confirmed blessing. The drag across the parking lot had apparently finished him off.

Nathan was surprised at how clear and precise his thinking was at this moment. He'd faced death a dozen times since leaving

Glens Falls, but seen nothing on the scale and finality of this. Perhaps it was freeing, knowing the end was coming and there was no obvious route of escape. There was no point to being angry or giving Blaine the satisfaction of seeing him panic and lose it.

"Can we just get this over with?" Nathan asked. "I'm freezing."

Blaine looked angrily at two of his men, who laughed appreciatively at Nathan's wisecrack. It suddenly looked like all the fun had gone out of the process for Blaine, though. His face deflated like a punctured balloon. "Get on with it!" Blaine ordered curtly, and Nathan felt he could at least go to his end knowing he'd scored one last satisfying field goal.

The nooses were placed around Mary and Nathan's necks and tightened at the back, and then the men charged with pulling them up took the strain into their hands.

Nathan felt the rope bite into his skin, and his throat constrict. He shook his shoulders and tried to pull his hands apart, thinking that perhaps even at this late stage there was a chance the knots around his wrists might have slackened.

But they had not.

Nathan was pulled up onto tiptoe and then lifted off the ground. His eyes felt like they were deforming, and his head was filled with images—Cyndi laughing. Tony smiling; Brandon in his arms. The house in Glens Falls. His daddy.

Family first, son. Family first.

Nathan's feet smacked to the floor, and such was the unexpected shock of it happening that he continued all the way down to his knees. The rope attached to his neck snaked down around him like an Indian Rope Trick gone wrong.

Mary was also back down, but still standing, trying to cough the handkerchief out of her mouth as her rope fell around her, too.

Blaine was screaming, "Get them! Get them!" to the men left on the ground. Peach had begun looking around wildly, trying to get a bead on something.

"Where are they? I can't see anyone!" Peach fired blindly in the direction of whatever threat was bringing a halt to the lynching.

Nathan didn't know exactly what was happening, but he got a pretty good idea of what it entailed as a body fell from the gantry above, smashing into the tarmac face-first.

A second body thumped into the tarmac behind the inn's sign and Blaine howled, "Get me inside! Get me inside!"

But the men around him were already running for their own lives. Peach was backing away, firing into what seemed like empty space at the top of the slope of brush lining the highway. A bullet punched a hole through his forehead and blew the back of his skull off. He spun backward and crashed to the ground, the brisk wind flapping his clothes with thrumming vibrations. Two more men who were running and firing as they did so were felled before they made it to the entranceway of the inn.

Shots rang out from the gantry above as the last man able to fire tried to get some idea of where the killshots were coming from.

Nathan, keeping his head down, got to his feet. He didn't know if he was next on the menu, if this was retaliation for Blaine's takeover in Casper or a rescue mission. Whoever was firing on the group was doing so with the impunity of deadly accuracy. Baxter was shot on the steps to the inn's entrance. Reed made it to the door before he was felled.

One more body plummeted with a scream from the gantry above the sign, and suddenly Nathan, Mary, and Blaine were the only ones left in the parking lot, the wind cutting down out of an iron gray sky that was threatening rain across the Wyoming prairie, or something even colder.

Mary had finally gotten the handkerchief out of her mouth and spat it to the ground. "Who the hell is firing at us?"

Nathan shook his head. "No idea. But I'm not complaining. Thought it might be friends of yours."

Mary shrugged. "Not a clue."

An agonized yell from Blaine made Nathan immediately think that man had been shot, but as he looked back at him, he could see why he'd called out. The pain in Blaine's leg had come back like all the angels in hell.

Blaine, terrified that he'd be the next victim of the sniper, had thrown himself off his Chieftain's Chair and was trying to pull himself over the tarmac. His nails were already bloody and broken, his chin grazed and his broken knee lagging behind. He didn't have the strength to get up on his good knee, and so he moved like a dry swimmer in a desperate miming of movement. His breathing labored, his eyes full of tears, whispering to himself, "Don't shoot me, please don't shoot me…"

A screech of tires took Nathan's attention away from the pathetic sight of Blaine trying to drag himself to safety. As long as he wasn't shot any time in the next hour, the man might make it.

The gray Ford Taurus LX from the roadblock up the highway skidded in a wide circle to take the shortest route toward Nathan and Mary. The windshield was reflecting the sky and burgeoning clouds, and there was no way to see who was driving, but within ten seconds, the car had negotiated the low-curbed strips of scrub that had once been the grassy areas between the parking areas and bumped to a stop.

The door opened and Free hopped out with a SIG in his hand. He covered Blaine and the building across the roof of the Taurus and shouted, "Come on! Get in!"

He fired two shots toward the inn and then hooked open the rear door of the Taurus.

Nathan and Mary, still tied and with ropes around their necks, sprinted toward the car. In the back, Donie was waiting with a knife. As Nathan bent his head, she cut the blue nylon around his neck and threw it to one side, doing the same for Mary as the other woman slid in behind Nathan.

Nathan looked up as Free got back in the car and pushed it into drive. The car growled, the tires squealed, and they were off. A bullet twanged into the roof, making everyone duck, and Free turn the wheel savagely, but the car kept moving forward, making for the ramp back onto the highway.

Nathan was breathless. His mouth felt stuffed with questions about how they had found him, or known that he needed rescuing, but there would be time for that later.

On the highway proper, Free stamped on the brakes again. The Taurus slew to a halt by the top of the slope leading down into the parking lot.

Lucy was there, laying in the grass, a Winchester XPR bolt-action long-range hunting rifle still pointed into the parking lot. She slammed the bolt back and forward, putting the next round in the chamber, and then put the telescopic sight to her eye.

"No!" Nathan yelled from within the car. So loud it made Lucy look up. Nathan had seen that her next shot was going to be Blaine, still crawling across the tarmac at nearly no miles an hour, his huge backside working, his spine twisting, his hands grasping at the ground.

Lucy looked at Nathan as he leaned across Donie to the window. "Wind it down!" he said to Donie, and the punk-goth complied.

Harsh blustery weather blew in, sending the first of the flakes of new snow into Nathan's face.

"Leave him! Let him be!"

Lucy's face formed a pretzel of confusion. "He's the guy who gave the orders to increase your height, Nate; surely, like any mean dog, you'd be fine with having him put down?"

Nathan shook his head. "No, Lucy. Let him live with the shame. It'll hurt him so much more."

It had been the walkie-talkie that had alerted the others to the danger Nathan was in.

Dave held up his walkie-talkie counterpart. "When they took it from you, they accidentally turned it on, or maybe they were just checking that it still had a charge. I dunno. But we listened to what was going on best we could. Heard someone talk about a lynching at the *'Ev'ry-1-welcome,'* so Donie found it on the map and we came to get you. Had to explain to these guys that we weren't taking no for an answer, I'm afraid…"

Dave pointed at Mary's friends, who were laying in the road back at the first roadblock. They were trussed up like joints of beef, and not at all happy. Mary released them and took them to one side to explain what had happened back in Casper.

Nathan was still rubbing at his wrists, and trying to peel Tony off of his body—the boy being stuck to him like a hard-glue limpet. "Well, I can only thank you guys. I thought… well… you can guess."

Free nodded, and Lucy, having taken Brandon from Tony as he'd rushed toward the returning Nathan, squeezed the top of the mechanic's arm in a rare show of public affection. "We didn't plan on only showing up in the nick of time, believe me. But once we got to the second roadblock and I saw the Winchester in the Taurus, I knew I could take them down like deer."

"Remind me never to grow antlers."

Lucy threw her head back and laughed. She'd lived a life of high privilege and had married well several times. Longrifle hunting was just one of her skills, and Nathan was more than grateful for her ability. It was a skill that had saved the day when everyone was hungry, many times, but now it had saved him from his own death. He didn't think this sparky, spiky woman would ever stop impressing him.

"What's the plan, Kimosabe?" Tommy asked. His heritage was Texan and nothing else—whatever anyone said, he would insist on this, even though he was of the Diné people, a Navajo by birth; it was a heritage he didn't identify with. A recent addition to the party, Tommy was boldly pragmatic and utterly no-nonsense. There wasn't an ounce of waste on his frame or in his demeanor, and there was also nothing PC about Tommy, especially when it came to his own heritage. In fact, Nathan often got the impression he said things like that because he enjoyed the reaction more than he would like to admit. "If they have half a brain, whoever's left back there is going to be after us, and pretty soon."

Nathan wiped the flurrying snow from his cheeks and hair. "Depends how much gas we have in the Taurus, I guess."

"Half a tank," Tommy replied.

"You can siphon anything else you want out of the other cars if you want." Mary was coming back from her conference, her neck still red raw from the rope. Being much smaller and lighter than Nathan, she had been taken up higher and faster than him. She rubbed at the skin and then hugged Lucy, hard.

"Thank you."

Lucy smiled. "My pleasure. I'm only sorry I couldn't save your friend."

Nathan explained that Cal had already been gone by the time they'd strung him up, and that seemed to make Lucy less regretful. Mary went around to all of them, giving them hugs of gratitude. She finished with Nathan. "We're going to go back to Casper, to see to Cal's body and then figure out a way of getting things back to how they were before Blaine happened. It might be rough there for a while. I wouldn't recommend it for you or your family and friends for a while."

"Yeah, I get that," Nathan said. "You're all welcome to come along with us, once we decide where we're going."

For a moment, it looked like Mary was considering the idea, but in the end, she shook her head. "No, Nate, my friends and family are back there. We'll go back, and take Blaine with us and show them what a scumbag his men have been following. You were right to leave him alive. His situation now will tell a more convincing story than we ever could."

And so, when the Taurus' tank was full, and what supplies they had all transferred into the back of it, they prepared to leave. Mary also let them have a warhorse 2015 Ford F-350 with an enclosed utility body from the roadblock. It came with a near full tank, too, and space in its aluminum utility body for more supplies and Tommy riding shotgun. Lucy, Free, and Rapier would take the Ford with Tommy. Nathan, Dave, Donie, and Tony with Brandon in the boy's lap would be in the Taurus. The gas would get them far enough from Casper in the short-term to outrun anyone coming after them from Blaine's gang. From what Mary intimated, they'd have too much to deal with holding on to power to worry about Nathan and his crew.

But which way to go?

The snow was coming down heavier now. It reminded Nathan more of the Big Winter than anything had for many weeks. Was the Earth's crust still slipping? Was the Arctic Circle encroaching ever westwards? When would this rolling disaster settle down and allow people to plan for even an uncertain future? A future that just a few hours ago Nathan had been convinced he would never see.

Which direction?

West into Casper was out, but so were north and east. Going back into the Big Winter would be a chilly suicide. That left south.

South it would be.

4

For the third time, Nathan dropped the battery connector from his freezing fingers.

The air was blue with cold. His breath billowed like smoke from a dragon whose fire had been extinguished, and his jaw chattered his teeth in a winter tattoo that had not been played on Nathan's body for several months. The Big Winter was hauling its blanket back over America, further south than it had before.

Nathan and his party had been moving down the country from Casper for a week now. The gas in the two vehicles Mary had gifted them had taken them well on their way to Denver—over 220 miles over the border and on into Colorado. The F-350 had dried up first, three miles outside Wellington on the I-85. Nathan had taken the Taurus with Tony, Brandon, and the others onto the forecourt of an abandoned Shell station. He'd left them there to build a camp inside the abandoned Burger King, and worked his way back up the highway to fetch Tommy, Lucy, Free, and Rapier.

The wind was scything across the prairie now, bringing frost and billows of icy snow that stung the face like needles. It wasn't a full-on ice storm yet, but Nathan had experienced enough of them since leaving Glens Falls to know that one was brewing in the volcanic dust-chilled sky. Their journey into Wyoming had been one of near optimism, but the race out of it had been one of pure pessimism.

Whatever hope Nathan had felt about temporarily moving out of the grasp of the Big Winter had totally dissipated now. Somewhere beneath the grinding tectonics of the Earth's crust, the slippage that had moved the Arctic Circle to cover half of America and most of the Atlantic was continuing. The ice was moving south at a rate you could almost see before your eyes.

As they had traveled west from Glens Falls, first to Detroit and then on past Chicago to Casper, the evidence had suggested a population who had mostly fled south, like migrating birds in winter—but that winter was following them hard now. It wasn't going to let them go easily.

Nathan's fingers slipped again, and he came up from under the hood of the Taurus, cursed, and stuffed his hands into his pockets to warm them. In a service block attached to the Shell station, Tommy had scored a new battery which had been missed by the usual looters and ne'er-do-wells. Those usual suspects who descended like locusts, taking anything and everything they could. Tommy had been pleased to hand the opaque cube over to Nathan after sloshing the contents around next to his ear to make sure it was full and hadn't leaked. Meanwhile, Free had siphoned enough gas from the Taurus and trudged back to the F-350 to bring it into Wellington.

Nathan had taken the battery, gone swiftly to the Taurus, and popped the hood.

Anything to be on his own.

Nathan took the old battery unit from the Taurus and tried to fix the new one into place. He'd charged it enough to start the Taurus—when it was in place—with Dave's portable wind turbine setup, which he used to charge the mapping laptop and connect to the satellite system for patchy internet information. But the cold was biting, even with the Taurus out of the wind and snugged against the side of the Burger King.

Cyndi wouldn't have put up with Nathan pushing himself like this. She would have insisted that he come inside where the others were fixing food on the camping stove and get warm and fed before attempting to change the battery. She would have swiped him playfully across the arm, dragged his body inside, and made him sit and eat and laugh and…

Nathan shook his head, wiping at a tear that had threatened to turn to ice on his cheek.

There were days when he could cope with the loss of his wife and best friend, Cyndi. There were times when he could huddle up in a sleeping bag with Tony in the car, while Brandon snored and breathed like only a baby could, and Nathan could sleep soundly. Then there were times like today, with the constant shadow of anxiety and grief playing across his gut, when he just needed to be on his own, away from the Dave-and-Donie/Free-and-Lucy love-in axis. Times when there would be a secret tear, a hollow at his very center, and a blackness waiting at his shoulder to tell him dark things about his many failings.

Free and Lucy were developing a deep love and understanding with each other. One that Nathan often had to check himself over, so as not to get covered in splashes of envy. Cyndi's end hadn't been easy or pleasant, and it hollowed him even deeper when he saw Free and Lucy, the two of them so easy and comfortable together. Because Dave and Donie were so much younger—near kids, really, who kept the party connected to the internet's mapping systems, via satellite uplinks powered by wind turbines and police-issue laptops—Nathan was less troubled by their outward shows of love and affection for each other. He still got a pang sometimes, but he also got the impression they'd been toning their demonstrable expressions of love down around him since Cyndi had died. He could at least appreciate them for that.

On days like today, though, Nathan would throw himself into whatever needed to be done, and he wouldn't stop until the task was completed. It was his defense against the horror of losing Cyndi. Remembering holding her dying heart in his hands in her freshly opened chest. No man should have to do or see that. And sometimes, in his head, it was the only thing he *could* see.

Head down. Get it done.

Nathan sighed, blew ineffectually on his hands, and began working again on the connectors. No amount of dwelling was going to get the new battery in the Taurus.

But…

Why this? Why this damn battery? Surely, there were other more pressing things to do before changing a battery that was old and cranky starting in the mornings as the cold encroached south, but which was *still* working. Why insist on making the change now?

Why so stubborn, Nathan? Why?

He wished the run of thoughts would just race on past without catching in the filters of his head. Lately, Nathan couldn't help second-guessing himself. Questioning his own decisions and plans. If he'd learned one thing since this whole venture had started, though, it was to make a plan and stick to it. Your first instincts were usually the best ones in any given situation. And now the only decision Nathan felt he could make firmly and correctly was to stay out of everyone's way while he tinkered under the hood of the Taurus, in a killing wind, when he absolutely didn't need to.

The new battery in place, Nathan had to reach into the guts of the engine with a 5/16th socket to secure its locking clamp. Twice, the socket slipped before it bit into the metal, and twice, Nathan had to close his eyes, count to ten, and try to get the socket in place before starting to twist. It was on the second try that a cough came out of nowhere and racked his chest.

So surprising and deep was the explosion of ragged breath in his body that Nathan dropped the socket. It clattered on down through the engine, coming to rest against the base of the battery. Nathan's chest heaved again, and he felt his eyes bulging in their sockets. His knees weakened and his calves felt like lead.

"I told you to take a break, didn't I?"

Nathan looked up, covering his mouth as another cough ripped out through his lips.

Lucy was standing next to him, holding out an enameled, blue-rimmed camping mug full of steaming coffee. "I've put brandy in it, natch." Nathan took the mug with trembling fingers. "You're so stubborn, Nathan. You're not going to make it to your next birthday at this pace. You have to slow down. I've been telling you about your chest for days."

Has she?

More evidence, if it were needed, that Nathan was in his own little world of grief and withdrawal.

"We're out of antibiotics. We've got some of Elm's witchcraft nonsense, and the universal medicine of brandy mixed with coffee, but that's it. Look at your forehead, Nate. You're sweating like a guilty man waiting to be searched at the airport. You need to come inside."

Nathan ran his hand over the skin above his eyes; even in the cold, it was damp with sweat. The warmth in his cheeks might well have just been a reaction to the stinging wind, but Lucy was intimating that he was ill. Or at least not one hundred percent. But it just wasn't important right now. The car wouldn't start without the battery fully in place, and that's what Nathan wanted to get done, and get done *now*.

"Lucy, come on, I'm okay. The car needs the battery."

"And you need to recharge yours. I'm worried about you. Free's worried about you, and it's only because Tony doesn't want you to think that he's talking behind your back that he's not saying he's worried about you…"

At the mention of his son, Nathan looked up and around. He could see the boy across the concrete with Donie, going through some broken crates to see what they could salvage. Rapier, Tony's huge, furry fury of a sled dog was sitting patiently by, head cocked, looking at the boy expectantly. The dog wanted to play and have some fun with his young master, but Tony was intent on other things. Things that would allow him to keep his eye on his father.

Before Cyndi had taken the bullet meant for Nathan, Tony had been happy to play alone with the malamute. The hound had been a part of the dog teams which had pulled them out of Detroit. Once the snows had eroded in the rising temperatures and the improving ground conditions had meant that sled travel was no longer a viable method of transport, Rapier had become a pet, Tony's closet friend. But even that connection wasn't sufficient to keep the boy feeling safe or self-assured. Nowadays, Tony didn't seem to want Nathan to be out of his line of sight. Which was understandable under the circumstances.

There was a rising warmth of anger now in Nathan's belly. He didn't need this now. He just wanted to get on with the damn car. "Don't put words in my son's mouth."

"I'm not. I can just see them unspoken in his eyes. You might think all that my head is full of is Jimmy Choos, features in *Cosmo*, and which Caribbean island I plan to winter on next year, but I *know* men. God, I've married enough of them, and over the time we've been together, I've come to know *you*, Nate."

Nathan didn't want to hear it. He took a mouthful of brandy-infused coffee and then passed the mug back to Lucy, shaking his head. "Thank you for your concern, but I have things to do."

Nathan turned away, expecting that to be that, but Lucy's stubborn streak could give Nathan's a run for its money and then do a lap of honor.

"You don't have to listen to me, Nate, but I'm telling you your boy is worried. You're too wrapped up in yourself right now—and yes, I get why, Cyndi was your life as well as your wife—but she's only memories now, Nathan. You've got two boys who need you to not only be well, but operational, too. How are you going to protect them if you're falling apart?"

Nathan would have thumped his fist down on the Taurus' engine if his lungs hadn't buzz-sawed up his throat and brought a fresh mess of tears in to smear his eyes and degrade his vision.

Lucy put a hand on his back. "Please, Nate. Come inside, out of the cold. Free can finish this off later. We're staying here tonight and you need a rest."

Nathan wiped at his lips, the cough leaving the taste of blood in his mouth where it had sandpapered the insides of his windpipe. There was no point arguing with Lucy when she was in this mood, and he had to admit to himself she was right, especially if he stopped for a moment to think about the reality of his situation, rather than sticking his head into the past where Cyndi now dwelt. Or by blocking everything else out by elevating less than important jobs to being vital to their continued survival.

Nathan knew he was sick. His chest had had a background rattle for two days, though he had pushed it from his mind and papered over it with thoughts of Cyndi. His joints were stiff and achy, which he'd told himself was just a reaction to the increasing cold, but if he hadn't been so set on jettisoning any sense of his own needs from those of the people around him, then he might have acknowledged that the dryness in his mouth was caused by more than just his not having drunk anything for a couple of hours.

"Okay, okay. It's just a cold. That's all. Just a cold."

Lucy's eyes were squinted with the strong transmission of *Oh really?* "Come off it, Nathan—you might be able to lie to yourself, but I'm far too smart for you to lie to me." Lucy hooked her hand through Nathan's arm and began to pull him away from the Taurus.

Nathan slipped her grip and she yelled at him, but Nathan held up a hand before another cough jumped up his throat. Just shaking his head at his own weakness, he pulled the prop rod from its mount in the Taurus' hood and let the metal clang down. Then, still trying to catch an elusive breath, he put his arm back through Lucy's and let her walk him toward the entrance to the trashed Burger King.

"I'm sorry I've been such a grouch," Nathan managed to say as he leaned on Lucy's arm. A sudden dizziness, probably caused by the severity of the cough, swam through his head, and he stumbled. That was scary. It was almost like the ground had been rearing up to whack him in the face. Not a pleasant feeling at all… but something odd had happened. Lucy was on the floor next to him. Holding on to the ground like she was about to slide right off of it.

The cough wasn't shaking Nathan—it was the ground beneath him. Bucking and yawing, he suddenly felt like there was a soupy sickness running through his innards. Lucy was screaming, and below the yell of her distress was a low rumble. Almost out of the range of human hearing… a rumble that was more a physical presence than a sound. It was boiling beneath the surface of the Shell station's concrete forecourt. As Nathan looked out through teary eyes, he could see Donie shepherding Tony, who in turn was holding Brandon to his chest, swaddled in blankets, out of the building.

The building was shaking like the walls were made of paper, not brick. There was a crash somewhere out of sight, and then a rending of metal as the roof over the now defunct gas pumps slid backward on its legs like a stack of playing cards toppling. The crash of it hitting the ground sent a gust of dust and concrete chips over Nathan's face.

Tommy was following Donie and Nathan's boys out of the burger joint, his baseball cap gone—strange, what you think of in a moment's crisis—but it was the first time Nathan had ever seen the Texan without it. He was surprised how much older Tommy looked with the hat off, revealing a balding head covered in iron gray stubble. Behind Tommy came Dave, panic painting his face with terror.

Dave got one foot outside the door before the building crashed down around him. He disappeared like a magic trick in a gust of dust, crumbling masonry, smashing glass, and tearing aluminum.

Tommy was thrown clear, his arms outstretched with trying to make sure in the tumult of crashing brickwork that Donie and the boys were shielded. This had the effect of him barreling into all three of them and sending them sprawling.

"Daddy!" Tony was yelling.

The baby was bawling and Tommy had taken a three-brick chunk of masonry in the back of his legs, the projectile having been spat out of the demolition cloud.

The ground was still thumping up and down.

Nathan couldn't move. He was just riding the wave of the world as it rippled and rodeoed, the grinding from the twisting clatter of Colorado's underlying geology shaking the breath from his lungs and frothing the blood in his veins.

The Shell station was utterly destroyed.

As Nathan hauled himself to his feet, the smoke and dust clearing, all he could see of Dave's body were his jeans and boots sticking out of the rubble.

Nathan allowed himself just a second to see that both Tony and Brandon were alive and unencumbered by the collapsed gas station. Tony was sitting up coughing and Brandon was still crying in his arms. Their faces were covered in dust in a way that, at any other time, might have looked comical, so caked and pale were their faces. But not now.

Nathan yelled at them to stay still and ran past Tommy's groaning form to where Dave's feet emerged from the rubble, deathly still. There was a Burger King sign digging into the material of Dave's jeans, but there was no visible blood.

"Hold on, buddy, I'm gonna get you out of there!" Nathan began getting some purchase on the plastic sign with the aluminum edges. It was lighter than he'd been expecting and came up almost too easily, raising Nathan's hopes of a quick rescue, but beneath the sign were a whole bunch of wooden struts, ceiling tiles, and a boa constrictor of dead electrical cabling. The cables snaked through the shattered plastic casings of fluorescent lights, which had, in turn, burst open like fat, glass snowflakes.

Through the wood and the glass and everything else, Nathan could see Dave. His face, like those of Nathan's sons, was smothered in white dust.

Nathan reached down through the smithereened tubes and felt at Dave's neck for a pulse, but he was prevented from registering it as another monster cough doubled him over and threatened to tear the spine out the back of his body.

As soon as the cough subsided, Nathan was back and reaching for Dave, but it was no longer necessary to find a pulse—the boy's eyes were flickering and his face was curling up with the first pulses of pain.

If Dave was in pain, that was a better sign than him not feeling anything at all. Nathan began pulling at a length of pine, thick with dust and sporting a row of rusty nails that were now exposed, trying to release it from whatever it had been fastened to before the earthquake.

Earthquake?

The very word felt wrong in Nathan's mind. Since the crustal displacement had changed the world seemingly forever, there had been many desperate transformations to the natural conditions of the Earth… the bone-breaking winter cold, the sunlight-shrouding volcanic dust in the upper atmosphere shortening the days and clogging the skies… but Nathan had yet to experience an earthquake. The one thing that had been a constant in Nathan's life so far, however many miles he'd come from his home in the valley outside Glens Falls, was that the ground beneath his feet was solid, and one of the only things that could be relied on to stay the same. And now even that certainty was gone.

"What…?"

Nathan snapped back to the present from where his mind had wandered, but his hands continued their autonomic movements, dragging and clawing at the pieces of collapsed gas station covering Dave.

Dave's lips moved again, and this time Nathan caught the faintest of words. "My arm… my… arm."

Nathan moved two bricks that were holding down a thick, surf-board-sized piece of plasterboard from the Burger King's walls. Nathan heaved the board away and it slithered down the pile of rubble, dragging a scree of broken glass in its wake.

Beneath the plasterboard was the blood Nathan had been glad not to have seen around Dave's legs. A girder, maybe ten feet long and twelve inches wide, iron brown and orange with patches of rust, was pinning Dave's left arm like a seesaw across a brick pivot. The force of the roof beam landing on Dave's forearm had snapped it clean across. White bone drenched in redness was sticking out at an oblique angle from his flesh. Blood was welling thickly from the wound around the bones, and Dave was trying to move his shoulder to pull the arm out from under the iron, but all he was doing was snagging the exposed bone ends against the metal. The girder would have to be lifted.

Nathan got to his feet, hooked his hands underneath the metal, and heaved. His lungs exploded, his chest rasping and his tongue forced out of his mouth. Bent over, he felt his hands slip from the metal, coming away thick with cold rust.

"Stop! Wait!" Lucy was beside him, pulling at his shoulder.

Nathan shrugged her off and yelled, "Get off! If you want to help, get the other end and lift! We can't leave him!"

Lucy was back yanking at Nathan's coat, her fingers digging into the flesh of his arm. Nathan roared in frustration, let go of the girder, and pushed Lucy firmly in the chest so that she sprawled onto her backside, arms and leg splayed. "I don't care about my damn cough! We've got to move the girder. Tommy! Tommy! Help me!"

He yanked hard, straining and growling with his effort. The girder began to shift.

"Don't touch it, you fool! Leave it!" Lucy screamed, pointing past Nathan's shoulder.

Nathan finally followed where Lucy's finger was indicating.

Cold water splashed over Nathan's innards.

A three-foot-high brick pier, which had been kept in place by the girder Nathan had moved, had begun to topple toward Dave's exposed head and chest.

5

A shadow moved out of the reach of Nathan's field of vision. There was a crunch of feet on glass and metal, and strong hands caught the brick pier with a harsh grunt of effort. The three-foot-high column falling toward Dave's head slew sideways and crashed into the rubble a good twelve inches from the top of Dave's skull.

Freeson Mac was looking down at the dots of blood growing in the center of both his palms where the torn masonry had cut into his flesh as he'd first held and then pushed the pier away from Dave.

Free took a squint at Nathan and then shifted into position at the end of the girder. "We moving this off his arm or what, Nate?"

Nathan was still too stunned to move. He felt as if his feet had been glued to the floor, his knees turned to rock. A cough spluttered out before he could form any words.

They left him there to catch his breath. Tommy brushed past, taking the end of the girder nearest to Nathan, and he and Free took turns lifting each end while Lucy slid a brick at a time beneath it to either side of Dave's arm so that, as the girder came back down, there was less and less pressure, and then zero pressure on the fracture.

Donie had crawled through the wreckage to sooth Dave's cheek, to kiss him on the forehead and tell him, "Everything is going to be okay, baby."

Nathan was still frozen while they worked on moving Dave out from under the girder to lay him on the ground, and then cover him in blankets taken from the Taurus to protect him from the cutting wind. In fact, Nathan didn't move until a small hand slid into his and Tony, face and hair still caked with dust, holding Brandon to his shoulder, looked up and said, "It's okay, Dad. It's okay."

Wellington had been flattened by the earthquake.

Where they had seen neat rows of houses coming down off the ramp of the I-85, now there was a desolate field of rubble with slews of wreckage caused by the collapsed dwellings. There were no residents left in Wellington who they could see, all of them having, as in many other towns along the route from Casper, left to go south. The lack of people in the moonscape that had once been a town only added to the desolation Nathan felt inside and out.

The wind cut across the newly destroyed landscape—flapping dog ears of plastic reaching up through rubble, swirling grit into mouths and eyes, creaking through shifting wreckage. Nathan looked at the broken town like someone beholding a mirror image of themselves, occasionally coughing and hacking up thick phlegm from his ruinous chest. Tony and Brandon sat with him while the others saw to Dave, who was now fully conscious and groaning sporadically on waves of face-creasing pain.

Free told them that he had been coming down the highway off-ramp when the quake hit. He'd slammed on the brakes and ridden out the shaking with a ringside seat to watch as the town fell over.

"Ain't seen nothin' like that in my life. Don't want to see anything like it again."

When the shaking had stopped, Free had gotten out of the F-350 and jogged to where the Shell station had been chewed and spat out by the Earth's tectonic nervous breakdown. He'd reached the spot where Nathan had been trying to lift the girder while Lucy screamed at him to stop, and there he'd caught the pier at an angle of forty-five degrees and averted a second disaster.

Tommy's leg had been deadened by the flying bricks from the falling building, and there was no way he could have reached the pier in time. As it was, he'd barely limped to the girder, and worked with Free and Lucy to get Dave out.

Nathan had tried twice to get up to see how Dave was since the others had been tending to him away from the girder, and twice Lucy had firmly pushed Nathan down to the ground and refitted the blanket around his shoulders. "Stay there. We got this," she'd said with increasing frustration in her voice. And so Nathan had stayed put, with Tony and Brandon next to him, watching as the bright white wrongness of Dave's compound fractured forearm made his guts ache and his bile rise.

When Dave was as comfortable as they could make him under the circumstances, Lucy went to the F-350 with Free and brought the truck down as near to the Shell station's remains as they could. From the enclosed utility body they used for storage, Lucy took Elm's ledger and the bag of Native American remedies he'd let them take from his home near Chicago.

Elm was, or maybe more accurately he *had been*—because Nathan had no idea if he was now alive or dead—a Lakota Indian who'd run a hardware store in Brookdale, Illinois. As well as trading and bartering with people in the surrounding area and suburbs of Chicago, Elm had been an expert in Native American remedies and folk medicine. He'd gifted Cyndi a ledger containing all of his known cures, remedies, and medicaments, as well as a large stock of ingredients to keep them well in the months ahead. It had been Cyndi's plan to spread Elm's knowledge far and wide—to get Dave and Donie to find a way to make paper and digital copies of the ledger and disseminate them where they would do the most good.

Cyndi being shot by Stryker Wilson, instead of Nathan being killed, had put a finish on that notion for the moment, but Nathan was still determined to find some way to spread the word. The ledger had been his trump card to play to get them into Casper... if he'd gotten past the *'Ev'ry-1-Welcome'* lynching party.

Lucy consulted the ledger, rummaged in the back, and gave Nathan something to chew on that tasted of strong warming licorice. "Osha root. Chew it. It'll help, according to Elm's grimoire."

Lucy was a *practical gal* who hadn't truly believed in Elm's *Witches-of-Eastwickery* nonsense at the start. But as Cyndi had said to her on many occasions when the subject had come up, this had been how pretty much all drugs had started out. Just because they grew in the ground and were picked by hand rather than their same chemicals being cooked up in a big pharma laboratory didn't mean they were any less effective. Lucy had said finally something about "sticking to her aspirin," to which Cyndi had said, "made from willow bark," and that had been the start of Lucy's conversion. Now she was the go-to gal for Elm's ledger when a problem arose, and that was why she'd been nagging Nathan about his chest for the last few days.

If only Nathan had been in the right place to listen to her, he thought, with a bitterness tempered by the taste of licorice in his mouth. If he had listened, perhaps he wouldn't feel so damn ill right now.

Lucy knelt by Dave and gave him something from the bag for pain, and then she spoke to Free. Nathan couldn't pick out what was being said, but Free made a face, shook his head, and then nodded when Lucy pointed at Dave's arm and made a cutting gesture with her hand that looked like it would brook no disagreement.

Lucy pulled a bandage from the bag, rubbed an ointment onto it, and then said calmly and clearly to Free, "Now."

Free bent, took hold of Dave's wrist, and then pulled. With a shiver of disgust, Nathan watched as the broken ends of the bones slid back into the flesh and Dave screamed a high-pitched yell of anguish. Even Donie, who was resting Dave's head in her lap, smoothing his forehead, had to look away as the snapped bones disappeared back inside Dave's arm. When Lucy was satisfied, she made Free hold the arm up while she cradled it.

"Glad I didn't get my breakfast today," Tommy said, plonking himself down next to Nathan on the blanket. He rubbed at the back of his thigh where the brick had hit him, wincing. "There but for the grace of the Big Fella," he breathed out as Lucy finished tying the bandage.

"He's gonna need painkillers, antibiotics, a cast, and a hospital, stat," Tommy continued, putting his USMC baseball cap, recovered from the wreck of a Burger King, back on his head.

Nathan felt it difficult to process what the Texan was saying. He was still trying to put the pieces of his head together—feeling guilty because he'd nearly caused a further accident that might have given Dave ever more serious injuries or even killed him.

Internally, his lungs rattled and popped like an old moonshine still, and his head was rapidly filling with the cotton wool of fever. Added to that, Nathan felt wretched and not a little embarrassed about his pig-headed refusal to listen to Lucy's warnings right away. And even though she had given him the root to chew on, he'd felt—or imagined, he couldn't be sure—a change in her attitude toward him. Just the way she'd avoided his eyes had left the warmth out of her usual expression when she'd looked at him. Nathan figured she had the right to be angry and disappointed in him, but it would never match how disappointed he felt toward himself.

Tommy at least had not changed, and the fact that he'd chosen to sit with Nathan was at least a sign that not everyone in the party would have an overtly negative view of his behavior.

Tommy stared ahead, but he seemed to be picking up on Nathan's mood. "Don't fuss yourself none, Nate. You were trying your best. Dave'll get it. It's not like you knocked the town over, is it?"

"I guess not. I just… Tommy, I don't know. I don't know anything anymore. I'm not the leader this party needs anymore."

Tommy whistled and snorted. "You're the leader? Man, no one told me!"

Tommy's smile was as welcome and warm as the Osha root soothing his throat.

"We're a bunch of capable people, compadre. I know, since Cyndi went, you've been trying to protect us all, and you've been leading from the front. But you gotta understand, you can't do it all. Only one guy can do it all, and that's the Medicine Man in the sky. The rest of us… well, sometimes we gotta understand what our limitations are, you get me?"

The words made sense to Nathan's head, but his heart was resisting—too many good people had died since they'd left Glens Falls, and Nathan didn't want to add to the pile.

"I get you. But it's not easy letting go."

"Man, that sick chest is peeling your fingers off one by one."

And Nathan couldn't argue with that.

The Taurus had survived because, by some miracle, the wall it had been parked behind, which held an ancient carwash beyond it, had fallen away from the Taurus rather than on top of it. It had taken a few dents to the hood but was otherwise okay.

Free finished off fitting the battery while the others made space in the utility enclosure at the back of the F-350 for Dave to be transferred in. Nathan had voiced concern because the precise reason they'd pulled into Wellington had been the F-350 running out of gas. How were they going to move him now if they had no fuel?

Free had just smiled and tapped the side of his nose. "Gas, we got."

"I don't understand," Nathan said, looking at the devastated town and wondering where the hell Free had sourced any fuel.

"On the walk back to the truck with the can of siphoned gas, I saw a wreck half-buried in a ditch by the side of the highway. You'd only see it if you were walking, and if you were traveling north. Musta been there three or four months. Nothing I could do for the driver—he was killed on impact, I reckon. But the tank was full, and when I popped the trunk with my knife, I found *four* more ten-gallon cans. Three full and one half gone. It was like Christmas, man. I got the Ford, filled her up, collected the cans, and high-tailed it back here, and that's when the quake hit."

Thirty gallons of fuel between the two vehicles wasn't the greatest reservoir for potential travel, but it would probably get them as far as Denver, and there was a good chance they'd be able to trade or work for more gas there. Tommy stuck his head into the conversation with a grin. "I reckon we make Free the leader, Nate. He's the gas king!"

Free guffawed, "I ain't no leader, Tommy. I wouldn't even follow myself."

Lucy strode over, looking between them. "While you boys talk about who's gonna be in charge, let me just put your mind at rest. Right now. It's me. The tanks are filled, Dave's in the F-350 with Rapier keeping him company, and as soon as you've gone through the wreckage of the gas station to see what of our supplies you can salvage, we're moving out. *Capiche*?"

Nathan, Free, and Tommy simply looked back at Lucy as she finished giving her orders. When they didn't move immediately, Lucy clapped her hands like she was annoyed with her butler, gardener, and driver for having a crafty cigarette break on her time.

"Don't make me repeat myself," she said with a twinkle in her eye and steel in her voice.

And so they didn't.

On the road, they drove in silence.

The brief respite Nathan had been allowed from feeling like the world's biggest heel for pig-headedly endangering Dave turned back to face him. Lucy had given him more Osha to chew on, and Nathan knew that even if she hadn't given it to him, he'd still be working his jaw, grinding his teeth in frustration. The root cooled the burning in his throat, but it couldn't take away the thoughts burning in his head. Nathan couldn't work out if he was just being a self-pitying wuss or if there was something more going on. A lowering of his mood that coincided with so many emotional hits as of late.

For the first time in his life, Nathan wondered if he was suffering internal psychological problems. His thoughts were grim, he was beating himself up, and he had been over-compensating like crazy to try to be everybody's shield.

Even the toughest shields have a breaking point.

Nathan hated the idea that he could be suffering in this way. A broken rib or a chest infection, he could get his head around completely. You just waited for the body and the antibiotics you pumped into it to do their stuff, and then, after a while, the body was fine.

But the head?

He couldn't just go online and find a therapist, or a med-psych. He couldn't just make an appointment and sit on a couch talking about the relationship he'd had with his father. Or whatever it was psychiatrists asked people about.

Nathan only had the comedy realm's idea of what it was like laying on a shrink's couch to go on. No one he knew had ever had mental health problems... no, scratch that—no one he knew had ever *admitted* to them. Even when he thought about Free and the way he'd withdrawn after the crash that had killed his wife, and the way, at least until Lucy had come along, he'd been more morose than not, and been so quick to anger, Nathan remembered well that his friend had never once taken him aside to talk about how he was feeling.

Guys don't do that, right?

Since Free had gotten with Lucy and they had worked out, he'd become lighter and *way* less intense. And now Nathan could suddenly see in himself the same traits that had initially appeared in Free. He'd become withdrawn, serious, and wouldn't listen to reason—or even to being shouted at, as Lucy had discovered—and now it felt like he was slipping into the dark well.

Not even Tony could draw him out, his boy sitting next to him in the back of the Taurus, with Lucy feeding Brandon milk powder they'd mixed with water and warmed on the engine block in a metal pan.

Nathan had never felt more alone. Just sitting there. Aching for Cyndi.

Tommy was driving the Taurus, with Free following behind in the F-350, Donie and Rapier riding in the back with Dave.

The quake had ripped great cracks down the highway for a good ten miles, and they had to drive slowly and carefully to avoid dropping a wheel down one. They also came across two collapsed concrete bridges that were, luckily, only clover-leaf-on-and-off-access ramps to crossroads beneath.

Twenty miles from Wellington, there were no signs that the earthquake had ever happened at all. The telegraph poles which had been at crazy angles or fully overturned back near the epicenter of the quake were now standing tall as if nothing had happened. Sleet spat against the windows of the Taurus, though, causing them to smear with slick ice, and the roof of the car rattled like Nathan's chest.

"How you feeling, Dad?" Tony asked, looking up from the comic book he'd been carrying in his pocket when the quake had hit.

"Like the Incredible Hulk just stomped on my chest." Nathan's attempt at humor was thin and forced, but Tony didn't seem to mind.

He smiled, and said, "You wouldn't like me when I'm angry," and put his nose back between the pages. They'd done their best to clean the boy up, but his hair still held traces of dust. Elm's remedies had kept Tony's asthma pretty much at bay for some time, at least—Nathan was glad Tony hadn't suffered a recurrent attack and was able to just sit by his dad in the back of the car and read. Tony loved reading, and as he'd lost all the books they'd taken on their first journey from Glens Falls over the months, he'd been able to get his fix with scavenged comic books.

Tony liked Spider-Man and Batman, and wherever they stopped to look in any derelict store, he would whoop with joy if they found any magazines he could liberate. You can't eat comic books, which is why they nearly always found a few even in a well looted store, but they were sure feeding Tony's mind. In the absence of a school and a teacher, as the Big Winter had descended, Cyndi had homeschooled Tony as best she could, and Nathan had to admit that her schooling had been up to a pretty good standard.

The boy whose eleventh birthday had come and gone on the road, between where they'd buried his mother and the roadblock outside Casper, had been given a stack of comic books by Free as a present. He'd managed to keep them out of Tony's line of sight until the morning of his birthday, and then produced them from his jacket with a mighty *Ta-Dah!* that had gotten Lucy howling and clapping. It had also delivered an icy pang to Nathan's heart because *he* hadn't thought to do it. He'd been too concerned with getting the food, lighting the fires, checking the horses, and making sure the axles on the wagons had enough grease.

All work and no play…

"What about there?" Tommy piped up from the driver's seat, bending forward over the wheel to look through the sleet-smeared windshield. Nathan looked up and was surprised to see seven giants standing proud and gray against the darkening sky.

Huge turbines moved in the air like the propellers of impossibly large aircraft. That they were moving fast, spinning with mechanical grace while facing into the wind, wasn't even the most wonderful thing about these huge, majestic machines.

It was the buildings at their base, at one end of the line of turbines. These buildings were solid and square, and perhaps in the past, they'd been service stations for the wind farm, but around their eaves, blazing in an afternoon falling toward winter dark, Nathan could see rows of lights—twenty or thirty of them. All alight and ranged above a flickering pink neon sign that declared the largest of the squat buildings to be "*Caleb's Bar!*"

Lucy rebel-yelled. "A bar! An honest to goodness bar! Civilization at last!"

6

"Well, *howdy-doody*—hold on. Back up a tad. Do people really say howdy-doody? Do I sound like an idiot from a 60s sitcom yelling howdy-doody at strangers? How about I just say: Welcome to Caleb's Bar! And, *come on in!*"

The dapper black guy with a pencil mustache, an exquisitely arranged, slicked-down kiss-curl on his forehead, a precisely geometrical bow tie that looked like it had been cut out with razors, and a scientist's standard-issue white coat, had been waiting for them as their two vehicles had run up the curving stretch of gravel track that led from the highway off-ramp up two hundred feet of ridge, to where the wind farm hummed, swooshed, and spun in the settling dark.

He opened his arms expansively by way of underlining the welcome. "I'm Caleb, and this is my joint."

As the words left his mouth, the expression on his face changed in the same way that it had when he'd questioned his own use of "howdy-doody."

"*Joint* does make it sound a rather down-market establishment, I'm sure you agree, and I can tell from your shapely frame and noble bearing, young lady, that down-market is just something you will *not* tolerate, *amirite*?"

Lucy and the others just stared at the little man who couldn't have looked more out of place if he'd been painted purple and had a blue flashing light on top of his head.

Nathan finally stepped forward from the semi-circle of the party to take the lead, but Caleb took one look at him and shook his head vigorously. "Oh no no no no no no no *no!*" Caleb reached up, touched Nathan's burning forehead, felt both his cheeks, and then, in a move too surprising for Nathan to have time to react or step back, Caleb hugged him gently and placed his ear against the mechanic's chest.

"My friend, you need to sit down before you fall down. *Amirite*? Of course, I'm right. Everyone inside now; this boy needs help."

Lucy raised a hand. "We have another injured man in the Ford. We'll need to bring him in, too."

Caleb waived a dismissive hand and said, "Come one, come all. Everyone is welcome at Caleb's Bar."

Caleb put his arm through Nathan's and started to lead him toward the door. "I need to help the others with Dave…" he began, before his cough reared up again, antagonized by the freezing air and the dampness left after the sleet fall. Caleb was having nothing of it. "I'm sure your friend will cope."

Caleb threw his head back to the others. *"Amirite?"*

"Get inside with the kids, Nate; we got this." Tommy boomed, and so Nathan let the little man in the white coat, who looked like Little Richard transformed into a scientist, lead him past the buzzing neon sign in the dark doorway of the building.

Tony followed with Brandon, and Nathan heard the others going to help Dave get out of the F-350. His head was swimming, the backs of his eyes felt thick in his skull, and there were the stumpy thumbs of illness pressing hard into his ears, but what he found inside the building set all that aside and filled Nathan with the sense that he'd walked from a harsh reality into a dream.

While the others had been outside securing the vehicles and helping Dave toward the building, Caleb had taken Nathan, Tony, and the baby along a short, dark corridor with nondescript, tan-colored brick walls that reminded Nathan of a modern school building. Caleb then pushed through a set of green double doors which took them on through into a glittering impossibility.

Once, the room had been a refectory area that would have seated thirty or forty people comfortably. There were rows of steel tables and attendant benches, and at one end of the room was an area with a countertop that led to an area that had once been a kitchen.

Now, the room was lit by what seemed like a billion tiny lights sparkling off two rotating glitter balls hung from the ceiling. Brandon's eyes sparkled in wonder at the illumination. From the corners of the room, Vari-Lites blasted harsh white beams at the mirrored spheres. Caleb reached into his pocket, brought out a small remote control, and pointed it into another corner.

A booming soundtrack kicked in. Jungle rhythms and glacial synths. The Vari-Lites changed and warped their beams in time with the music. Nathan felt his aching chest vibrating with the subterranean sounds and his ears all but crackled with the beat. Tony looked around, amazement washing over his face and his cheeks blowing out with shock. Nathan could see that the jolt of the noise was starling the baby but couldn't hear the howl that was coming from his wide open mouth. Tony pulled the child to his chest and began to comfort him.

Caleb left them standing near the entrance and took up the beat of the music. He went dancing across the floor of the refectory, past benches and tables decked out in red feather boas, and tall, stainless steel, tubular art installations that had a simultaneous mid-80s and fallen-from-an-unknown-future vibe.

Caleb reached the counter and picked up a DJ's headset with a small microphone which sat in front of his lips as he turned, swirled, and clicked his fingers to the incessant beat.

"Cool, huh?" Caleb's voice was coming from speakers around the room. "Who said the apocalypse couldn't be fun? *Amirite*, boys?"

Nathan waved his hands at Caleb, calling uselessly, "Turn it off... the baby... I can't..." It was all too much for him. The fuzz in his head, the vibration in his guts, and the flashing lights, and so he stumbled to the nearest bench and sat down, the room spinning.

The music came to an abrupt halt and the lights stopped spinning, the glitter balls no longer reflecting a billion sparkling lozenges of light.

"Daddy, are you okay?" Tony asked, putting a small hand on his father's wrist in the sudden silence, his voice sounding loud and harsh in Nathan's ears. The baby, now settled, was again mesmerized by the lights, his eyes sparkling with reflections. Tony's voice sounded like it was coming down a long tunnel, though, or out from the mouth of a well. Nathan tried to focus on his son, but his eyes were wonky as hell.

"Of course, he's not alright," Caleb said, appearing at Nathan's shoulder and once again placing a cool, dry hand on his forehead. "Larry!" Caleb called out into the ether, and Nathan sat frozen—his chest now felt like his lungs were duking it out with each other in the mother of all bare-knuckled fistfights and began to tighten and constrict. Nathan's breathing hurt, and it was as much as he could do to blink his eyes with any sense of normality.

From behind the counter, a plump white guy in overalls, with smuts of grease on his face and hands that looked like they were made from walnuts, appeared. He lifted the countertop and ambled companionably across the space. Not in a hurry, but not in an attempt to be slow. This was a man who got to places at his own pace, not at the diktats of others.

"Cal, I'm halfway through the generator maintenance on stack four. You know I'm busy. I know I'm busy. Can't you just… ooooh."

Larry had stopped in his tracks about seven feet from Nathan and was looking at the mechanic with a pained expression on his face. "He's not well."

"Ten out of ten," Caleb said with a tinge of sarcasm that was affectionate rather than harsh. Nathan got the impression these guys had been more friends than work colleagues right from the off, even though Caleb was obviously the one in charge.

"I'd like you to go back and ask Miriam if she wouldn't mind making up a bed in the infirmary…"

"We don't have an infirmary, Caleb. I know that; you know that. In the same way this canteen isn't a disco, that storeroom isn't an infirmary. If you'd like me to go ask Miriam to make up a bed in the storeroom, then I'm your guy. Otherwise, let's keep the delusions of grandeur to a minimum, yeah?"

Caleb arched an eyebrow and straightened his bow tie with precise fingers. "Larry, you have no poetry in your soul."

"Very much like we don't have an infirmary."

"Shoo now. Shoo. Go speak to Miriam."

Larry turned and ambled away at his own pace, back toward the kitchen.

Sitting, as well as the shutting down of the lights and the music, had helped Nathan a lot. The pain when he breathed was still front and center, but being at rest was a vast improvement. "I don't need… a bed, Caleb. We just… we just…"

Speaking was proving to be a problem, however, as catching enough breath to form words was still something Nathan would have to work at, taking account of the reduced capacity of his lungs.

"Nonsense, Nate… I may call you 'Nate,' mayn't I?"

Nathan nodded and Caleb barreled on, "Diminutive forms are much more friendly, don't you think?"

Nathan didn't have enough breath to answer, and luckily Lucy, Tommy, and Donie, supporting Dave, trooped into the room so that he didn't have to. Dave's face was creased with pain. And he was favoring his shattered arm as best he could, but at least he was standing.

Free and Lucy held their guns in a way that wasn't necessarily threatening, but their fingers weren't far away from the triggers. They had met situations which had gone south far too quickly for them to not be automatically on edge when entering a new domain. Especially one as odd as Caleb's Bar.

Free looked around with some astonishment, and Lucy's greedy eyes took in all of the enhancements that had been made to the place, nodding with approval. "Nice place you have here, Caleb," she said as her eyes came back around to the white-coated, dapper little man. "Now, what can you offer a nice girl in a place like this?"

But Caleb had already zeroed in on Dave and come forward to meet him. Dave looked like he would fall down if Tommy and Donie didn't keep holding him up, and so Caleb settled Dave down on a bench on the opposite side from where Nathan was sitting. Then he peered at the bloody bandage Lucy had fashioned for the wound.

"I think we're going to need two beds," Caleb said, whistling. He felt Dave's forehead. "There's a fever cooking here, too. You people are not in fine fettle, are you? Not even a little bit." Caleb got up and addressed Lucy. "I can offer beds, medical help, food, and liquor, my dear."

"In exchange for what?" Free asked, his voice as suspicious as it needed to be in this changed world.

Caleb affected a wounded look, placing a hand over his heart. "Sir, you do me a disservice. All we ask for here at Caleb's is that a contribution be made—a fair contribution made in exchange for our largesse. If you don't have goods to trade, then we will take services, work in kind, or if you prefer, gold, diamonds, or any other precious materials. This situation will not last forever, and I'm sure you understand that fair exchange is no robbery."

Free looked like he'd heard it all before, but accepted that this was the way of things now.

Across the room, Tommy had begun looking around, assaying the odd combination of clashing styles in the space—utilitarian simplicity overlaid with nightclub opulence. "So, what's the setup here, Caleb? You want us to be honest with you, then you're gonna have to be honest with us. I've seen enough horror movies that start with strangers finding their way into seriously weird places in the wilderness, just before they got turned into lunch. And, man, this place is a bunch of weird biscuits covered in mighty peculiar gravy. You've gotta know that the last thing we expected to encounter beneath a wind farm was the Ross Avenue Sunset Lounge transplanted all the way from Dallas. You get me?"

Caleb nodded, but opened his arms expansively. "I assure you, sir, this room is just a glorious affectation. Something to remind us of the world that has passed. Yes, we're profligate with our use of power, but what else can we do with it? The power lines to the cities are down or out of commission, and the cities themselves are almost empty, with everyone going south."

"Why haven't you gone south?" Lucy asked, sure enough that they were not in any immediate danger to flick the safety back on her weapon and point it to the floor.

"My good woman," Caleb began, an edge to his voice that hadn't been there in all the sparkling bonhomie up until now, "it's our firm belief that some people should stay at their posts. One day, one day in the not too distant future, this facility might be a vital component in getting civilization back on firm footing. Power is *power* after all is said and done. We've decided to stay here and keep up a maintenance schedule on the turbines, and keep the generators in serviceable condition."

Caleb grasped his own lapels and sighed. "Not everyone has run away, madam. And we'll be waiting for those who have when they deign to return. Waiting for them with the energy they'll need to rebuild. We're not going to be able to transport fossil fuels in large quantities to the power stations, and who knows what has happened to the nuclear facilities in these turbulent times? The fracking derricks are silent, and oil is a thing of the past. Places like this are the only future we have right now."

Caleb's eyes sparkled with something Nathan might have recognized as the pride that comes with fulfilling a duty to one's fellow citizens, while at the same time acknowledging some true personal sacrifice in doing so.

"We're a small band here," Caleb continued. "Just eight of us, living, working, and, as you can see from my bar, having a little fun downtime when the opportunity arises. Surely, you wouldn't begrudge us that? I assure you, if you could carry the electricity away from here in barrels, I would give you all you wanted. Suffice it to say, for as long as you stay, you're at liberty to enjoy the fruits of our labor, and to contribute in any way we can all agree on. We're no threat to you. You are, after all, the ones with the weapons. All I have is a bow tie and a smile."

Nathan had just enough breath to say, "That's… fine… Caleb. We'll work… and we'll pay… what… we owe."

Caleb clapped his hands together and smiled brightly.

"Then I think, Nate, we have the basis of a beautiful friendship."

Miriam Slone was plump and ruddy, and had quick eyes thumbed deep into a doughy face. Her hair was braided with a ton of gray through what once might have been a reddish chestnut but was now just a standard brown. She moved with a lumpy determination around the room in her nurse's uniform, plumping pillows, checking on Dave's temperature, and doling out painkillers and antibiotics to both Nathan and Dave.

Nathan hadn't been able to sleep in the twelve hours he'd been in the infirmary—the place Larry had called a storeroom—such was the cough that wracked his frame. Any moment he felt like he was getting close to sleep, his throat would rasp, his eyes bulge, and his mouth fill with a gritty sludge of phlegm that he would have to spit into a bowl by his side on the bed.

He'd become concerned upon seeing there were tiny strings of pink blood in the foul material he was bringing up from his lungs, but Miriam assured him it was perfectly normal with the amount of coughing he was experiencing.

She'd been a nurse before the Big Winter, she'd told him, working mainly in theaters in various Denver hospitals. She was proudly single, too, she'd told him while bustling around Nathan and Dave—her patients were her children, and she cared for each and every one without fear or favor.

"How did you wind up... on... the... wind farm?" Nathan had asked as Miriam had given him the thumbnail sketch of her life and career.

"How does anyone end up anywhere in these troubled times?" she asked in return, putting a fresh jug of water on the table next to the bed. "Caleb and I had a fortuitous meeting, and I decided to stay. He's a little odd, as I'm sure you've realized, but his heart is in exactly the right place. He was the lead managing engineer of Dillinger Power, the company who owns the facility. Everyone else lit out south, except Larry and a few others who share Caleb's sense of duty. I think he's a rather fine man. Don't you?"

Nathan had tried to answer in the affirmative, but suddenly his throat had felt like he was trying to cough up a dog as bear-clawed and razor-toothed as Rapier. He'd just wanted the pain and the cough to leave him alone. Miriam had smiled compassionately, made him comfortable, placed a clean bowl next to him, and then left him to try to get some sleep.

That had been twelve long, painful hours ago.

A huddled conversation was beginning in the corner of the storeroom/infirmary, held between Caleb, Miriam, and Larry over the best thing to do about Dave's shattered ulna. Nathan hadn't been asleep but lay as still as he could to get the gist of what was being said. Dave stirred gently in his bed, but seemed asleep, or at least zonked out on pain medication.

Miriam said she'd seen the operation to pin broken forearms many times in her operating theater but didn't know if she had the skills to carry out the procedure herself. Caleb was flicking through a book of surgical operations and pointing at the glossy pictures which Nathan could only see as a blur of green scrubs and red blood. Caleb didn't seem to be sure if he could do it, either. It had been Larry, with his walnut fingers, who'd scratched at his head, sucked in his cheeks, and said, "Pinning those bones back together ain't gonna be much different from playing with my Erector set as a kid. Few screws and bolts, a couple of steel struts, and I reckon we can stabilize the break enough to have it knit."

Nathan had had to stifle both a gasp of shock and almost a laugh of amusement at the way both Caleb and Miriam had turned their heads toward Larry, there in his overalls with engine grease on his cheeks—where it seemed to be a permanent fixture—and looked at him as if they'd just gotten a visit from a Martian.

"You think you can do it? Truly?" Caleb asked, and Nathan tried to keep as still as he could, suppressing a savage cough that was growing in his chest.

"If Miriam can help me get the things we'll need clean and sterile enough, I don't see why not. It's gonna be a lash-up, whatever we do, but really, what's the alternative?"

"There isn't one," Miriam agreed. "If we don't go in and clean it up, see what's happening infection-wise, and at least try to isolate the fracture, there's a good chance that boy might lose the arm altogether."

Caleb nodded gravely. "And we all know what that might mean in the long run."

The three nodded, and that's when Nathan was no longer able to keep inside the cough that had been mountaineering up his throat using crampons and an icepick.

Miriam bustled over to Nathan's side and moved him gently to a more comfortable position, then took his temperature and tutted at the thermometer as it came out of his mouth. She showed the glass tube to Caleb, whose face wore a veil of concern.

"How are you feeling, Nate?"

"Terrified... A nurse, an engineer, and a mechanic"—Nathan had to stop to catch his breath and wipe at his eyes—"are planning surgery on that boy's arm. The very notion of that is... killing me."

Caleb nodded. "I can assure you, Nate, we're not enjoying the idea ourselves."

Caleb bent in closer, so that Nathan could see the pores in his skin and the individual hairs in his pencil mustache. "But the alternative is that we leave him to die of infection or saw the whole arm off altogether. You tell me, Nate... what would *you* do?"

7

Preparations were being made for the operation.

In a room across the hall from the infirmary, Nathan could hear the low voices of Miriam and Larry as they cleaned, scrubbed, lay down plastic sheeting, and moved furniture. Occasionally, Caleb or Miriam would look into the infirmary with serious faces, check out the forms of Nathan and Dave in their respective beds, and then go back to whatever it was they were doing.

Nathan hadn't seen his sons, Free, Lucy, or Donie since last night. Free had brought Tony and Brandon to the door to wave, but Caleb had suggested they keep the kids outside while there was so much infection in the room.

Tony had called from the door that he loved Nathan and couldn't wait for him to be better. He'd even picked up Brandon's little hand and waved it toward Nathan. It had been all Nathan could do to lift his arm to wave back. If he tried to talk, his ribcage would explode in a barrage of sickening coughs, spraying the air with spittle and God knew what bacteria. Miriam was still feeding him regular amounts of antibiotics, but as of yet, they weren't touching the infection.

Dave had been asleep most of the time. Although Miriam had stayed in the room in case she was needed, stretched out on a poolside lounge chair during the night before going to assist Larry in setting up the makeshift operating theater—or, well, she was more of a director than an assistant if Nathan read the intonation of her voice correctly.

Although there were no windows in the room to look out over the landscape, there was a dirty, plastic skylight that rattled in the wind, which had a fuzzy layer of ice across it. Through the opaque frozen water, Nathan could see a huge turbine thrumming and revolving in what seemed to be a pretty constant level of breeze. The power company had chosen well to place it here in this part of eastern Colorado. The ridge was wide open to the elements, and now that what had passed for a tiny break in the Big Winter this far west was over, the turbines would have to be kept moving lest they freeze up completely.

As Nathan listened to Miriam and Larry across the hall, he could see through the skylight—there were small, black, silhouetted figures up on the maintenance deck behind the turbine. They were dwarfed by the size of the machine. The turbine came slowly to a halt, and presently, eye-hurting white blasts of welding light threw crazy shadows against the superstructure. Keeping the windmills in working condition must be a full-time job.

It was as an arc of light sparked and splashed against the fast-moving sky that the idea hit Nathan. He blinked, tried to catch his breath, and then crashed into another fit of savage coughing. A sick feeling in Nathan's gut complicated the pain in his chest. If anything, his breathing was getting worse, and there were moments of panic, like now, which he assumed must be exactly the same sensation felt by Tony when he was in the middle of an asthma attack.

His body felt leaden, and his head thick with fever, but he wasn't going to lie there and not offer Dave any comfort that he could. The idea burned in his head like the white arc of light above.

He would have to go speak to Dave and tell him his idea. Calling across the infirmary would alert the others and would probably send him into another painful episode of coughing, though. Nathan forced himself to sit up. He did it as slowly as he could, but he was still slammed by the wet, soupy cough and a roiling wave of nausea.

Dave was awake in his bed, but he looked sick. His forehead showed a sheen of sweat and his eyes were rimmed red. His broken arm, with its now hideously swollen hand, lay on a wire frame to keep it steady. The wound, which Nathan could smell as he approached, was covered in gauze and a crust of dried blood. The smashed bone was still inside Dave's forearm, but the awkward angle at which the limb was resting told Nathan all he needed to know about Dave's earthquake-related injury.

Nathan just made it to the chair next to Dave's bed before his knees gave way. He thumped down onto the faux leather seat and had a thirty-second coughing fit that made speaking impossible.

When it finished, Nathan was left skirting the perimeter of colossal exhaustion.

Dave used his good arm to squeeze Nathan's wrist as the coughing reached its crescendo and then retreated.

"It's okay, Nate, take your time... I ain't going nowhere."

Nathan grinned. "I... came all the way... over here... to see if I could... help *you*... not have you comfort *me*."

Dave smiled back, but the expression was soon lost in a wince of pain. When the wave of agony receded, Dave flicked his eyes at his gauze-covered forearm. "Man, it hurts. I've never felt anything like it in my life. It's worse... than... you know. What happened in Detroit."

Nathan remembered that all too well—coming into the freezing tenement room and finding Dave crucified to the floorboards with six-inch nails through the centers of both his palms. The victim of a vicious gang leader, Dave had been left to die in the cold, unable to free himself.

He'd recovered well from the trauma of that experience, and for him to now be on the verge of allowing amateur surgery or losing his arm completely seemed to be the most unfair turn of events.

"You sure... you want... to go through... with this?" Nathan's ragged breathing punctuated his words like an angry rattlesnake hissing from his lungs.

Dave nodded. "I don't see how I have any choice."

"I'm no surgeon... and I don't have the experience to argue... with someone like Miriam... but there might be a better way than a mechanic going in, and bolting pieces of... Erector to your bones."

Dave's face lit up. "You think?"

"I... do... but..."

Nathan's head began to swim, deeper and harder than it had before. The pressure was building up. It felt like rubber stoppers had been forced into his ears, and the room lurched like it had been hit by a vicious undersea current. Nathan leaned forward, putting his head on the bed to steady himself.

He shouldn't have gotten out of bed; he shouldn't have been trying to get involved with Dave's treatment. His own health was shot to pieces, and he was putting himself through the wringer. Why did he have to get involved—why didn't he think of himself instead of everyone else?

It took a second for Nathan to realize that those words, words that he wouldn't ever have normally thought, weren't his thoughts at all. They were the product of someone else's voice.

"God, Nathan! Why can't you just rest and let us help you both? You don't have to keep playing the damn hero all the time!"

Lucy.

She'd come into the infirmary behind them and had overheard what Nathan had been saying to Dave. Now she was putting her hands under Nathan's arms and trying to get him to stand.

"Come on, you big stupid lunk! Get back to bed before I throw you on it!"

Nathan rose on pipe-cleaner legs with the gyros out in both his hips. He staggered forward, and Lucy arrested a potential fall by putting a hand on his chest and putting her other hand in the collar of his shirt, pulling him upright. It would do no good to argue now; she was determined to move him back across the room. Nathan tried to conserve what breath he had so he could at least explain his idea to Lucy. But as they shuffled slowly back to Nathan's bed, she read him the riot act and threw the book at him at the same time.

"Nathan, rest. For the sake of your sons, *rest*. Get *well*. You've got pneumonia. You're drowning in your own body! Stop trying to fix everything for everyone else. You are only making things worse for yourself! You driving yourself to your death will make it worse for the rest of us, but especially Tony and Brandon! Life isn't an internal combustion engine! You *can't* fix everything!"

They had reached the bed, and Nathan sank toward it like a wrecked ship touching bottom—all broken spars and collapsing rigging. He lay back on the sheets, raising a hand toward Lucy. "But... I've... Dave..."

Lucy took Nathan's hand and put it back on the bed—she clearly wasn't in the mood for listening. "Nathan, so help me, if you don't shut up and get on with healing yourself, I'm going to knock you out myself. We got this. *I've* got this. So have Tommy, Donie, and Free. I've given them the last of my gold—oh my, that *so* hurts, saying that—but I have. We're good to stay here until Dave's arm is fixed and you're better. Now shut up and rest!"

But Nathan couldn't rest; he needed to tell them about the idea he had for Dave's arm—one that wouldn't need surgery, and one that would give the bones in his arm time to knit, but the words were stuck in his chest. Kicked down by the cough that burst up on ragged ropes of phlegm.

It was the worst bout of throat-hacking pain he had yet experienced. His neck felt like it was going to split open on all sides and deliver his lungs onto his chest to steam and roil in their own blood. His hands clawed at the bed, his eyes becoming pools of pneumonia-enhanced tears; his head was filling with foam and his nostrils were blocked as surely as if he'd been holding them closed himself.

The breath left him with a thump, his chest banging and groaning. His heart trip-hammering through his torso. Blackness washed up behind his eyes so that Lucy and Dave were rubbed out of his vision as the lack of oxygen, and the pressure of coughing so hard as this, delivered him panicking and crying through the well-mouth of darkness into a deep drop of unconsciousness.

"Hey, honey, you're home early." Cyndi appeared from the kitchen, wiping her hands on a cloth. There was a thin dusting of flour on the front of her red sweater. She'd been baking, and Nathan had been able to smell it as soon as he'd walked through the door. The house was warm, and the bright day was spilling its summer light through the windows that fronted the house. Nathan closed the front door on the insect buzzing valley and heeled off his work boots before he could traipse in any oil that might have stuck to them from his morning in the auto shop.

Summer in Glens Falls was hot and beautiful—and so, Nathan thought with an inward smile, was his wife.

"Yeah. Decided I could cope with only half a Saturday today. Free's working on a couple of things for me, and pretty much pushed me out and home."

Cyndi came up to Nathan, put her now clean hands on his cheeks, and kissed him long and hard on the mouth. He could smell the warmth of the kitchen on her, the flour and the underlying aroma of her perfume. He hadn't been expecting the kiss, and took time, as he responded, to make sure Tony wasn't in the vicinity.

Cyndi broke the kiss, tutted, and then put Nathan's hands deliberately on her waist. "He's over at Stanley's place, playing video games. Nan picked him up at twelve. We have the whole afternoon to ourselves."

Nathan suddenly got the idea that everything was going to Cyndi's plan. Tony at his friend's house five miles away, and Free pushing to get rid of him early for the last two hours…

"You've been working me by remote control, haven't you?" he asked.

"Isn't that the best way?" She winked and brushed the flour off the front of her sweater with the cloth she held. "We haven't had any *us* time for too long, baby. Sometimes it's worth pulling a few strings to make sure I get you to myself for a few hours. And, after that… there will be cake."

"Today is just getting better and better."

Cyndi smiled, threw the cloth onto her shoulder, and frizzed her blonde hair with quick fingers. "So, you shower and I'll make some icing."

"You're the icing," Nathan said with a smile so wide that the top of his head might have lifted off.

Nathan went to shower as Cyndi went back to the kitchen. The water pressure felt incredible against his skin as he washed the morning's work from his skin. As he got out of the cubicle and started to rub himself down with a freshly laundered towel, he heard Cyndi jogging up the stairs and heading along the hallway to the bedroom, with a joyous shout that she expected him within the next three minutes or she'd start without him.

Nathan laughed.

Stryker Wilson laughed, too.

Nathan spun around, and Stryker, his old friend from college, was standing in the bathroom—his long, straggly hair, dirty surfer blond, falling onto the shoulders of his heinously busy Hawaiian shirt. Stryker held out Nathan's bathrobe.

"Looks like you've got a hell of an afternoon ahead of you, my friend!" Stryker said as Nathan took the robe and used it, without putting it on, to cover his nakedness.

"Stryker… dude… what are you doing in my bathroom?"

"I honestly don't know. One minute, I was shooting your missus' heart out all over the tarmac; next, I was here. God, man, that cake smells delicious, doesn't it?"

Nathan took a good few seconds to parse out what Stryker had said, and then… "You shot… Cyndi?"

"Yeah, man. Bullet was totally meant for you, but the plucky woman got in the way. Aren't they adorable when they do that?"

Nathan could smell burning... no, not burning, but something like it... it was a smell he thought he recognized. Not one that, thankfully, he'd had to smell that often, but one, now he identified it in his nostrils, that made him more than uneasy.

Cordite.

Stryker held up a pistol. There was smoke coming from the barrel as if it had just been fired.

"It's not cordite," Cyndi said.

Nathan turned, and there she was in the doorway, her blue silk robe hanging around her body. What it revealed was almost as interesting as what it concealed, but Cyndi seemed not at all concerned to see Stryker in the room.

"What?" Nathan asked. "What isn't cordite?"

"What you can smell after a gun has been fired. Anyone who calls it the *smell of cordite* doesn't know what they're talking about—unless they're talking historically." Cyndi walked into the bathroom and took the gun from Stryker's willing hand. "There's hasn't been cordite in gunpowder for seventy years. These days, it's sawdust soaked in nitroglycerin that you can smell when a gun is fired. Schoolboy error, really."

Cyndi squinted down the barrel of the pistol, a chunky black 9mm SIG Sauer, cleared the mag, checked it, and then snapped it back in.

Then she did something that Nathan could not comprehend.

Cyndi smiled, turned the gun around and, putting her thumb through the guard, placed the muzzle of the gun on that crinkly piece of skin at the apex of her breasts, the silk of her robe falling open slightly—maintaining her modesty, but revealing the gun placed there in the center of her chest.

"No!" Nathan shouted as he stepped forward waving his hand, hoping to knock the gun away from Cyndi. But his fingers didn't reach her. Even though he was just two feet away, his arm was not long enough to reach her.

He took another step.

His fingers moved uselessly through the air.

Stryker had moved, and he was behind Cyndi now. His face was set in a grimace, and there was a bullet hole right in the center of his forehead. The ragged wound was open and illuminated, and Nathan could see the damage it had done to Stryker's inner skull. But it didn't seem to affect him in any way at all.

In fact, he was *still* smiling.

In a near blind panic now, Nathan took four more steps forward that should have carried him past Cyndi and Stryker into the shower cubicle… but he was still in front of his wife.

"So, remember, Nate. When you smell the powder. It's not cordite. It's nitroglycerine, okay? It's important to get this stuff right."

Nathan felt his throat burning in a scream that was threatening to tear apart his head and explode his brain.

"Love you," Cyndi said, just as Stryker gave a cute little wave from behind her.

Cyndi pulled the trigger.

Nathan screamed, and it was the worst thing he could have done. It was a full minute before he could return his body from the excruciatingly twisted position he'd bent into to simultaneously cough out his insides while stopping himself from rolling from the bed. He snapped out a hand against the headrest and tried to steady himself.

Miriam was sitting on the edge of the bed waiting for Nathan to stop coughing, waiting with tablets and a glass water.

The room was gloomy and the skylight dark, but there was enough light to see that Dave's bed was empty. The panic and fear Nathan had felt in the dream washed through him.

"Dave… where… is…"

Miriam soothed Nathan's brow and popped the tablet into his mouth with quick fingers. "Now, don't you worry about David. He's fine, up and about and doing well."

Nathan blinked, the residual upset yo-yoing up and down between his gut and his head.

"But… I have to tell you… I have to stop…"

"You don't have to stop anyone or anything, Nathan. It's done. Free made the immobilizer and we fitted it two days ago. Brilliant idea, by the way. Absolutely brilliant."

Nathan didn't understand. It had just been morning—seeing the welding sparks above on the turbine had given him the idea. He hadn't been able to tell *anyone*, though. Miriam was talking in riddles.

Was he still in the dream? Nathan looked wildly around the infirmary, half expecting to see Cyndi's corpse at Stryker's feet in the corner. But other than Miriam, the room was empty.

"What... what are... you talking about?"

Breathing was hard, but it definitely felt easier. The pressure in his head had lessened, too. Lessened to the point where thoughts weren't lost in a stew of feverish pain.

Miriam stroked Nathan's cheek and smoothed the rumpled collar of his pajama jacket. "Nathan, the pneumonia hit you extremely hard; in the end, we had to give you antibiotic shots. Lucy, Free, and Donie have been here when they could, sponging you down and keeping you company."

Nathan had no memory of this at all. It was like someone had cut a huge blank hole right in the middle of his memory.

"Keeping... me company...? How... long have I...?"

"Nathan, you've been unconscious, apart from a few minutes here or there, for the last three days."

8

The news hit him like a steam hammer.

Three days? He'd been out of it for *three days*?

Sure, he felt like he hadn't eaten since the world had been made, and his mouth felt claggier than a mud pie cake. His muscles were badly frayed ropes and his eyes felt like they'd been rolled in sand, but still... *three* days?

"That's... not..."

"I'm afraid it is, Nathan. You woke up enough and just about dragged Freeson onto the bed with you to tell him about your idea for David. Freeson talked it over with Caleb and Larry, and the three of them made the tube and we fitted it to Dave's arm two days ago."

There was nothing in his memory that even came close to explaining any of this news. The fever and the pneumonia had sucked the life out of him. He looked down at his chest, rising and falling in a pair of Paisley-patterned pajamas that he didn't recognize, and which he certainly hadn't been wearing the last time he'd been awake.

The bedsheets looked clean and fresh, and there was a hand-drawn card with a smiley face on the bedside table. Someone had drawn a big red truck and a bright yellow sun with the words *'Get Well Soon Daddy'* across it. He had no recollection of ever being given it by Tony, or by anyone else, for that matter.

The last things he really remembered were the surgery conference, the arcing lights through the skylight, and Lucy shouting at him.

Anything else was lost to him.

The immobilizer idea had come to Nathan as a compromise between radical surgery and doing nothing at all. A hinged metal tube that would go snug around Dave's arm when the bones had been put accurately into place. Sponge rubber at both ends to stop the edges of the metal from chafing Dave's skin. The hinge would allow it to be opened periodically so that the wound could be cleaned and the stitches monitored. The arm would be kept in a tight sling against Dave's chest—immobilized in a secondary way—and all that would save Dave needing to have a major operation that could have exposed him to even great risk of infection and nerve damage.

"It worked… then… the tube?"

"It certainly has for now. You missed your vocation, Nathan. You should have been a doctor! That kind of thinking would have sent you quite a way up the ranks." Miriam seemed genuinely impressed and pleased enough to compliment him.

Nathan just shook his head. "I can't remember telling anyone at all about it. Not one thing."

"Believe me," Miriam replied, "for the few times you were awake, you couldn't stop telling us about it. Even after Freeson had made it and we had fitted it to David's arm, you wouldn't stop. In the end, we just let you babble on."

Although the horrific dream about Cyndi and Stryker was still a kernel of horror in the center of his thinking, Nathan allowed himself an incredulous smile.

See, Lucy? I can fix everything!

Tony holding Brandon, with Dave in tow, came to visit Nathan a few hours later in the so-called infirmary. Tony's face was wide and bright. Brandon gurgled happily and watched Nathan intently as he sat up on the bed.

Dave pointed to his immobilized arm. "Tony keeps asking me when the rest of me will change into Tony Stark," he said with a grin, ruffling Tony's hair.

"Iron Man has a nuclear heart, too," Tony said, tapping Dave's steel-covered arm.

"Your daddy's good, but I don't think he's that good, and right now, my heart's doing just fine."

Dave reached down to the bed with his free hand and shook Nathan's. "Thanks, man. Really… it's genius. How did you come up with it?"

"Genuinely… it came… to me… in a… flash."

It felt good to smile, and it felt even better to see his sons. Tony perched on the edge of the bed, cradling Brandon in his arms. His eyes were brimming with joy and his voice was full of excitement. "Uncle Free took me up one of the turbines, Daddy. They have a ladder all the way up inside…"

That cut through Nathan's thinking like a wrecking ball. His eyes flicked up to the skylight, to the turbine turning above the building. At almost three hundred feet from earth to blade housing, the windmill was an impressive, and when he really thought about it, scary height. Tony, *his* Tony, had been up there?

"Wait, you… went all the… way up?"

Tony nodded, wide-eyed, and not at all seeing a problem with the trip he'd made. "It's okay—there's a safety line, and I didn't look down. There's metal floors every fifty feet. It was amazing. When you get to the top, in the…"—he thought for a moment, trying to get the right word—"the *nacelle*… there's a hatch that lifts right up, and you can see the blades and all the world. All of it."

Nathan didn't like the sound of that at all. He'd certainly have vetoed the idea if he'd known it was happening, and he resolved to have words with Free as soon as he saw him, but the raw enthusiasm from the boy was infectious. It was the first time since Cyndi had died that the boy from before had peeked out of his shell. Perhaps Nathan should be grateful to 'Uncle' Free for helping his boy have what seemed to have been the experience of a lifetime. Nathan knew that, when he'd been Tony's age, his head had been full of engines and carburetors and axels and timing chains. Mechanics had been his life, mainly because of his daddy before him. And it seemed that, if nothing else, his love of machinery had rubbed off on his eldest son.

He just wasn't so sure of him expressing his love for these machines three hundred feet in the air.

"I stayed in the nacelle while Uncle Free and Larry went out to fix the, uh, adjuster vane... this spinning thing that tells the machinery to turn the blades into the wind. It's like the old-time windmills, Larry said. But they're running out of parts, and when a vane goes wrong, they have to go up there and fix it real soon. Because if the blades don't turn into the wind enough, then the whole thing might blow over! Dad, it was super cool. When you're better and can climb, can we go again? Please?"

The tumble of words from Tony's mouth were the most Nathan had heard from his son in months. He didn't want to transmit his worry about Tony going to the summit of one of the turbines to the boy yet, either, and so all he did was smile and stroke the baby's head.

Miriam hustled in at that point and sent the visitors on their way. "Your daddy still needs to rest. He's not out of the woods yet, boys. Come back and see him in the morning."

Tony was yawning anyway—it was near eleven-thirty at night, and he sleepily kissed Nathan on the cheek and left the room with Dave.

"He's a good boy," Miriam said, straightening the sheets around Nathan and tucking him in. "I'll be in the chair over there if you need anything. Just call."

Nathan nodded. "Thank you."

And with that, Miriam tuned off the light.

Three days later, Nathan was fit enough to leave his bed and join the others in the bar for breakfast. Miriam told him not to exert himself. Although the antibiotics had done their job, he was still weak and would be easily tired out.

And Nathan, although he was feeling a million percent better, knew that even his level of improvement was still a long way from him being fit and well. It took him a long time to get out of his pajamas and ease back into his clothes without causing another fit of coughing. And before he left the infirmary, for what it was, he had to sit back down on the bed to gather himself before traversing the corridor outside.

The slow walk he took down the corridor proved to him comprehensively that he was still vulnerable and kitten-weak. Before he got fifty feet, he had to rest his hand against the wall and catch his breath. He was still only able to take shallow respiration at this stage; otherwise, he found that his lungs had been so compromised by the pneumonia that any attempt to fill them fully felt like a harsh stab to his ribs.

Determined to carry on, Nathan made it to Caleb's Bar, finding all of his party, and also the wind farm occupants, sitting together beneath one of the glitter balls. The mood seemed companionable between the two groups, and Larry was serving pancakes, syrup, and eggs from the kitchen behind the bar.

"Nathan!" Caleb called out happily as Nathan came slowly and deliberately into the room. Faces both familiar and not turned to greet him with a variety of nods and waves.

"Daddy!" Tony ran from the bench and, checking himself just in time, gingerly hugged the mechanic, burying his head in Nathan's chest. Nathan kissed the top of Tony's head.

"Hey, scout… how you… doing?"

"I'm great, Daddy, really great," the boy said, taking Nathan's hand and leading him toward breakfast. "They've got eggs. I've had eggs! Every day!"

Nathan couldn't remember the last time he'd seen an egg—fried, boiled, or scrambled—and he lost himself staring at the glistening, steaming plate

"Of course, we have chickens," Caleb said in response to Nathan's amazed look. He pointed to a small Hispanic woman wearing overalls, her hair pulled back into a tight ponytail. "Rosa here is the chicken whisperer in the facility."

"And lead ITEC guru," Rosa added with a smile, "although Dave and Donie are giving me a run for my money."

Donie high-fived Rosa and Dave gave her a thumbs-up with his good hand.

Nathan sat down and tucked into the eggs as Caleb handled the introductions. "Me and Larry and Miriam, you know. Next to Rosa, that's Bill, our welder and general maintenance guy; Tyrone is cables, so is Michael, and Crane is our turbine expert. We all double-up on everything else where we can. Which is why Rosa is in charge of the chickens."

Bill, in his mid-fifties and beefy; Tyrone, black as midnight, quick to smile; Michael, wildly red-haired with constellations of freckles and somewhere in his thirties, like Crane, who was a thin, bird-like man with fingers too long for his hands. All of them nodded and welcomed Nathan to the table.

The eggs could probably have been the best thing he'd ever tasted in his life. He didn't know if it was because they were just damn fine eggs or if it was because of their scarcity, but to have them in abundance was something special indeed. Coming down the corridor, Nathan would have told himself that he didn't have an appetite at all, but now, with the aroma of the breakfast and good coffee filling his nostrils, he was completely ravenous.

Nathan's fellow travelers all looked easy, relaxed, and as if they were among friends. All except Tommy, anyway, whose face was set, and who was stabbing at his pancakes with what seemed like an angry fork. Nathan made a mental note to check on the big Texan at the earliest opportunity.

Stop. Trying. To Fix. Everything.

Lucy's words echoed through Nathan's skull. She was right—he rarely gave anyone else time to breathe before he waded in with his fixing tools and mending gear. Maybe this bout of pneumonia would give him a good opportunity to change his modus operandi. To take a step back. Lucy had already, from what he remembered of the journey here after the quake, become the de facto leader in his absence. Maybe he should let her deal with whatever Tommy's beef was.

But as it turned out, Nathan didn't have to wait too long to find out what was eating at Tommy.

"I'm no expert on your generators," Free was saying to Larry and Caleb at the table as the conversation drifted from introductions and greetings back to whatever they had been discussing before Nathan arrived. "But you're gonna run out of parts soon enough. That much is clear."

"Unfortunately, I have to concur," Caleb responded sadly as he sipped at his coffee. "We just don't have the fuel or the transportation to go searching the wilds for suitable parts. And even if we *could* find the things we needed, it's a full-time job keeping the wind farm going. If we went out to find the materials we need, by the time we got them back, the turbines might already be beyond repair. I think we can keep this facility going for at least the next year if we're careful. After that… well."

Free used his fork as a pointer as he spoke, his eyes lit up with possibilities. "Well, that could be where we come in. We can give you the time. We've got two good vehicles, which Nate and I can keep going. We've been lucky finding fuel so far, and I reckon, given how quickly people have moved south, that we shouldn't have too much trouble finding more. We could pool our resources; we'll go out, find your gear, and bring it back here, you keep the props spinning while we're away."

Caleb and Larry began nodding. "An equitable division of labor," Caleb agreed.

And that's when it happened.

Tommy threw down his fork onto his plate and got up and stalked from the room without a word, dragging the eyes of everyone with him.

Tony tugged at the cuff of Nathan's shirt. "Why did Uncle Tommy leave, Dad? Is he mad at someone?"

"Sure looks that way, son. Lucy? Free?"

Free shrugged. "Time of the month?"

Lucy patted Free's arm. "Don't make things worse."

Nathan's ears pricked up. "What things? What is he making worse?"

Lucy looked down at the table and sighed. After a moment, she'd collected herself enough to speak, but before she could answer, Caleb clapped his hands and stood. "Well. I think we should leave Nathan and his friends to sort out their difficulties without us around," he announced. "And I'm sure we all have plenty to be getting on with."

Caleb and the wind farmers got up from the table, taking their coffee cups along with them—and in Tyrone's, case a thickly draped plate of pancakes—and left the bar.

Before he went through the door, though, Caleb turned to Nathan and the others. "I'm sure it's not a catastrophic problem. One that will be easily solved by judicious application of diplomacy." With that, Caleb closed the door behind him.

Nathan looked around the table. Free was avoiding his eye. Donie reached out and held Dave's hand. Tony put Brandon in his carry cot and stroked his head as he listened.

Lucy sighed again. "Tommy doesn't think we should stay here. He thinks we should still continue to go south. The winter is worsening and he thinks we're too exposed, too far from safety up here on the ridge. Free and I… well, we think we can make this place work out for all of us. Once we build the shelters."

"Build what shelters?"

Free looked up from his plate for the first time. "You're not the only one who comes up with ideas, Nathan. You're not the only one who knows how to fix things."

Undoubtedly a direct quote from Lucy. Every day in every way, they were becoming a stronger couple. A single unit who thought with one mind.

In this case, Lucy's mind.

It seemed that, while Nathan had been out of action, there had been quite a lot of action going on.

Dave piped up. "I think Tommy would rather be our go-to guy instead of Lucy."

Donie said something under breath that might have been *sexist pig*, but it was lost to Free thumping the table with his fist, making plates and cutlery bounce.

"Dammit, Nathan, we wouldn't have got you out of that silo without him, I get that. But he's Lone Star State through and through. And he wants his way. I guess he respects you for whatever reason…"

The words dried up in Free's throat, and his cheeks colored with embarrassment. "Sorry, no offense…"

"None taken."

"But he's been throwing his weight around, making work schedules, negotiating with Caleb without consulting Lucy or any of us first, and generally getting on our backsides. He just wants you and Dave to be ready to travel before we hightail it out of here."

There was only one way for Nathan to proceed now that he'd heard one side of the story, and that was to talk to Tommy. Although the Texan had only been with the party for a few months, he'd put his neck on the line for all of them, not least of all Nathan when he'd been trapped and brainwashed inside of an ex-nuclear bunker by a whacky religious cult.

Tommy was good people. Nathan knew that. But then, so was Free, who he'd trusted with his life on several occasions. Tommy wouldn't want to get out of Dodge unless there were good reasons, and Nathan felt sure that, given time, Tommy would tell him.

"Okay, okay, forget Tommy for a moment," Nathan said after the moment's thought. "What are these shelters you're talking about?"

Free's tension drained away as he set about telling Nathan his big plans. "We get ourselves an excavator; I've seen plenty abandoned on the road between here and Casper. We dig ourselves a shelter in the hillside. Concrete the walls, power it from the turbines. Gives us a place to get insulated against the worst of the winter—this place won't stand up to a succession of ice storms—but keeps us close enough to the generators to ensure everything going okay if something breaks. Power is the future, Nate, and this place is the future right here."

Nathan could come up with a thousand reasons why the shelters were a crazy idea, not least of all what it would take to haul the materials and machinery up here to the ridge. But he didn't want to come out and dampen Free's spirit from the get-go, either, and receive a response like the one Free had given Tommy.

Maybe Tommy had seen the inherent problems in the plan, too. Couple that with thinking he should be, to quote the others, "the go-to guy" for the group, not to mention his natural lone wolf personality and his force of will, Nathan could easily imagine all the reasons that Tommy had gotten up from the table and left.

"Okay, we need to *all* get our heads together and make a plan about what we're going to do."

"That's it, Nate," Lucy said. "We *have* got a plan. We're staying here. And that's that."

9

Nathan didn't feel he had the strength to tackle Tommy for at least another twenty-four hours or so.

He was healing, that was for certain, but he felt transparent with fatigue, and he spent most of the next fifteen hours after breakfast sleeping. Thankfully, he wasn't visited by the Cyndi dream again, but it had sure made him reluctant to turn off the light in the room he now shared with Tony and Brandon. He would have happily stayed awake all night if guaranteeing not having his wife and ex-friend in his dream wouldn't have also meant being utterly wasted for the next day.

When he was eventually ready to go speak to Tommy, he found him in the facility's modestly equipped gym—Tyrone and Michael had salvaged the majority of the equipment from the nearest town's private residencies—bench-pressing prestigious amounts of black iron weights on his back.

Nathan sat on a nearby bench and waited for Tommy to acknowledge him. Sweat was breaking out all over Tommy's forehead, and there were dark patches of it already around the chest of his gray tee-shirt.

Tommy kept pressing much longer than was polite to do so. Nathan reckoned he was gauging how Nathan would employ his opening gambit. Perhaps expecting to be scolded or at least argued with, it was obvious he wasn't going to invite the confrontation. If Nathan wanted one, he was going to have to take the initiative.

Not feeling he wanted to be corralled into making the opening bet in this game of interactive poker, Nathan also waited. So, Tommy kept pressing, and Nathan kept waiting.

The exertion was making Tommy's face red with the effort, and Nathan wondered how long the other man would go on lifting the weights before he reached the point when his muscles gave out and he'd be forced to talk.

Surprisingly to Nathan, it was much longer than he'd been expecting, proving that Tommy Ben was a darn sight more fit and hale than Nathan had credited him with being.

Now, Tommy was staring at the rising and falling bar.

Nathan was waiting silently.

There was a tremble in Tommy's wrists, but he wasn't going to let it get the better of him. Suddenly, Nathan felt consumed with the idea that, in his attempt not to lose face and make the first move, Tommy might actually do himself an injury rather than acknowledge Nathan. Someone had to make the first decision to be the grown-up.

Okay.

"Okay, Tommy, I'll speak first. You can stop lifting now."

Tommy, now soaked through with so much sweat that his tee-shirt was completely black, let the bar drop back into the safety position, and reached down by his side where there was a towel and a large glass of water.

Tommy curled up and swung his legs together. Turning to face Nathan, he took a long guzzle from the glass before swiping the back of his hand over his mouth. "Okay, I'm listening."

"It seems there's been some bad blood."

Tommy said nothing to even confirm or deny the statement. He was going to make this hard work, Nathan realized, but now that he'd started the boulder at the top of the hill, Nathan was determined to let it run.

"If we fight among ourselves, we won't be able to defend ourselves from the people who would want to do us harm."

Tommy shrugged. "If you've just come to give me the team talk, coach…"

"No. That's not why I'm here. I just came to talk."

Tommy scoffed. "Have you checked with Lieutenant Lucy if that's an *appropriate* course of action to be taking?"

Nathan shook his head. "I came to hear your side of things."

"My side? I ain't got no side, Nate. It's me against the lot of them. Crazy amateurs with stars in their eyes. Have they told you about the shelter?"

Nathan nodded.

Tommy continued, hands expressive, his eyes alive. "The Big Winter is hard on our heels, Nate. Even if we started tomorrow—and we can't without an excavator—then it would take what? Three or four months to build. But that's time when we could be trying to survive up here in the brunt of another season of ice storms."

Nathan was impressed with the passion in Tommy and how it had begun bubbling to the surface. Tommy was a practical, pragmatic man who Nathan knew he hadn't taken enough time to get to know. He'd met them some weeks before Cyndi's death, and survival had been tough both before and after that terrible moment. Nathan knew that he'd personally been, possibly understandably, wrapped up and preoccupied with his own stuff—too much so to probe too deeply into the makeup of Tommy Ben.

Tommy gripped Nathan's shoulders. "Do you want to expose your kids to that? Because, man, they're not even my kids, and I don't think we should."

Nathan recoiled at the idea. "No, of course I don't want that for my kids. I'm not a fool."

Tommy let his hands drop. "But your friend Free is…"

It sounded odd to hear that, like Tommy was suddenly distancing himself from the group. By singling out Free as 'Nathan's friend' and not his own, perhaps Tommy had made the decision already to separate himself from the group. Perhaps all this was… a slow tearing of the collective. Tommy getting ready to leave on his own and make his own way south. The thought made sense to Nathan, and he voiced it.

"You're gonna go, whatever happens?"

Tommy stopped short of giving a firm 'yes' to Nathan's question, but the shrug of his shoulders and the breaking of eye contact told Nathan it was the most likely outcome.

And Nathan knew there was no way he could even countenance the idea of splitting from the group himself and taking his kids with Tommy, but he was also getting the distinct impression that he was closer to Tommy's way of thinking on this than Free or Lucy would ever want to acknowledge.

Their minds were already made up.

The Colorado wind farm was going to be their punch back at the Big Winter and everything it had taken from them. Nathan could see where they were coming from, too—the nomadic life wasn't one that he had any affinity for. If he could have been back home in Glens Falls, with the first buds appearing on the cherry trees in his yard, with his sons and… well, his sons, then he would have given almost anything to make that happen. But Nathan knew that wasn't a possibility. Not even a distant one. He agreed with the notion that a permanent place would be for the best, but they shouldn't settle for the first seemingly stable place they came across. The wind farm had power, yes, and a bar and chickens, but it was a long way from anywhere, and it was exposed. Once the turbines stopped working, as they would, if not this year than the next, they would have to move on anyway. Not least of all because the water was drawn up from a deep bore by electric pumps. Once the pumps were fritzed…

Nathan sighed and left Tommy to his exercise, and wandered slowly back through the facility to the main entrance. Taking up a spare parka hanging on a hook by the door, he went outside.

The eight turbines snaked in a row along the top of the ridge. They were heeled into the thrumming wind and were *whhhaaaping* around with beautiful precision. Nathan got a true sense of the awe Tony had tried to convey to him when he'd told him of his trip up into the nacelle. Now, Nathan craned his neck up and shielded his eyes against the sun, which had found a rare hole in the volcanic dust-filled atmosphere to shine through almost uninterrupted. The clouds were long streamers of white and purple. There was a chill in the air that the sun couldn't shift, though, even as Nathan moved fully out of the shadow of the building.

In the valley below, snow lay on the ground from a moderate fall that had come down two days before. It hadn't thawed any, and although it hadn't been near as bad as some weather events Nathan had experienced in the last few years, the snow was still thickly laid and showing no signs of dissipating. The all too brief respite from the bite of winter, afforded over the trip into Wyoming and then down into Colorado, was definitely over now. The air cut into Nathan's cheeks as he stuffed his hands into the pockets of the parka.

It was clear that the world was still changing, and that the Arctic Circle was either expanding or shifting both downward and westward. Maybe in a few years, if the crustal displacement continued, the area of the Earth that had once been the North Pole would be tropical seas, and where once the equator had been would be only frozen desolation.

There was no way of knowing if the fate of the planet would continue this slow apocalypse for all time. Maybe they'd never find a place to rest; maybe they would need to keep moving ahead of the cold zone for the rest of their lives.

What a world for the young to be born into.

The sky was a thin blue, and the clouds in the ragged tangles were speeding west fast. Nathan hadn't seen a bird in the sky since they'd left Glens Falls. Those that could leave had flown south and stayed there, and the others perhaps had died when their food chain had been interrupted by the lack of seasonal advance. The world was a huge screw-up now, and Nathan wondered if there would ever be any balance or equilibrium to be found for any of them.

For the first time, he felt a pang of envy that it had been Cyndi who'd taken Stryker's bullet and not him.

It shocked him to the core, even thinking it momentarily, and it dragged his mood down, which—since getting on the road to recovery—had been a lot better than it had been before the earthquake. Now, it felt like a yawning pit of cold opening up in his gut for the black dogs of depression to howl up at him from.

It didn't matter that the sun was shining and he could see for miles in unusually clean air. It didn't matter one little bit. All that mattered in this moment to Nathan was that he wished he'd gone with Cyndi —away from this never-ending winter.

The rage overtook him then, and he stood there trying to make his trembling legs move, and his useless hands into fists. He didn't need this now. He hadn't needed it ever. He didn't want to be the leader of a bunch of adults acting like kids and fighting each other like cats in a sack as soon as he wasn't around to bang their heads together.

He just wanted to be with his sons, and damn the rest of them.

Damn them all to…

The bullet sang out from many yards away and smacked into the wall behind him, blasting up chips of brick before he heard the retort of the shot.

Nathan ate dirt and began crawling backward toward the open doorway. Two more shots *tchannnged* off the metal doorframe, and another shattered Caleb's neon sign, turning it into a spray of ice-glass. Nathan felt the sleet of shards peppering his hair as he pushed his face further into the snow.

Geez.

Was this going to be never-ending? Who the hell was firing at him now?

Running footsteps, more shots, and the crunch of boots across the crust of snow approaching fast.

Nathan was unarmed and exposed, so if those boots belonged to whoever was shooting at him, then he was going to be dead in seconds. There was nothing for it; he was going to have to get to cover, either in the building or somewhere else. He just hoped that whoever had been firing would be less accurate with their shooting if they were running, and with that thought in his mind, Nathan leaped to his feet and began to run toward the door.

The entrance hall to the maintenance building exploded with gunfire, shards of brick, and pieces of torn metal and shattering glass, sending Nathan spinning to the corner of the building. He spun around the brickwork and sprinted blindly. His chest wasn't ready for this kind of exertion. It was still silted up with old phlegm and pneumonia scarring, but if he stayed where he was, he'd be dead in seconds.

The closest piece of cover on the exposed ridge was the base of the nearest turbine. The access hatch at the bottom was open, and Nathan made for that, keeping his head down and hoping against hope that the corner of the maintenance building would give him enough respite to make it to the turbine housing before whoever was firing rounded the corner.

Nathan crashed through the access hatch at full speed. The floor inside the circular turbine tower was made of aluminum, though, and the metal was covered in ice.

Nathan careened four feet across the space and smashed into the aluminum ladder which led up to the next floor some fifty feet above. Nathan threw himself out of the line of sight through the hatch as soon as he was able, crashing now into the red based step-up-transformer. The transformer took the energy created by the turbine and turned it into usable electricity for the facility—and beyond, back when it had been part of the power grid.

The crunch of the footsteps was still approaching and the sound of gunfire seemed to be increasing. Thankfully, it didn't seem that anyone was firing at the turbine. There was a chance that whoever was hunting Nathan was waiting until they got a clear shot before shooting at him.

Perhaps the plan of the attackers had been to take over the turbines for their power-generating capacity, and it would be a stupid thing to shoot them up and destroy them in the process.

Nathan's hand brushed against a wrench that had been left leaning against the step-up-transformer. It was thirty inches long and made of steel. It was also the nearest thing he had to a weapon, so he picked it up and a held it like a baseball bat.

The running footsteps were almost upon the access hatch now. Nathan got ready, trying to keep his ragged breathing steady and his feet firm on the slippery metal floor.

If the gun arm came in first, he was ready to break it, and if a head appeared, he was ready to brain it. In the end, what came in was neither.

It was a whole girl, all at once.

She'd been running as fast as Nathan, if not faster, and as she came through the door and slid past, Nathan scythed the wrench into empty air because she was already through and crashing into the ladder in the same way he had. He swung the wrench at her form and it bounced off the rungs of the ladder. The impact jarred his arms all the way to his shoulders as the tool thudded down into the place where her head had just been.

"It's me!" the girl shouted. "Nathan, it's me!"

Nathan dropped the wrench—he recognized the voice. As the girl came up from her panicked duck, she held her small black Beretta Cheetah in her fist toward the ceiling and pulled down the scarf that was covering her face.

"Syd? Syd? My god. Is it you?"

"Yah. Now get back. I've got people to kill."

It was Syd B4, the teen who Nathan had left behind in Detroit with the man who had eventually shot Cyndi in the back, Stryker Wilson. Her hair was still black and spiky, and her skin white like the snow on the ground, albeit with two red doll spots of color from running after Nathan.

The *B4* part of her name, she'd taken from the address of the apartment she'd shared with her now deceased mother. She'd gotten on the wrong side of a vicious gang in New York, who'd followed her to Glens Falls, where she'd met Nathan, and then traveled with them on to Detroit. The city where, in a desperate ski-doo chase, Nathan had almost left her to be taken by the gang leader Danny—before Syd had gotten the better of him and strangled him in the snow.

Syd was a force of nature who had loved Tony and had formed an uneasy alliance with Nathan. To see her here was the very last thing he might have expected.

Now, she pushed Nathan back away from the door and fired three shots from the Beretta out at two figures who were approaching, each of them holding Heckler & Koch MP4s and wearing arctic camouflage uniforms.

They dived for cover and returned fire.

Syd danced backward as bullets crashed into the confined space, embedding themselves in the walls and tinging off the metal.

The step-up-transformer took a shattering hit right in the center of its kilowatt gauge and spat glass in every direction. Nathan pressed his back against the metal wall of the tube. "What the hell is going on?"

"Umm," Syd said, snapping a new mag into the Beretta and loosing off four indiscriminate shots through the access hatch without looking, "they're alive and they want me dead."

"Why?"

"Because I'm here trying to warn you that they're coming." She fired off another couple rounds through the door. "Sorry, we kinda all got here at the same time. Bit of a mix-up, to be honest. Next time, I'll try to be ahead of the bad guys."

Nathan's head was swimming and his chest was a hot lump of molten iron. There were plenty of questions he wanted answered, but this wasn't the time to ask them. "How many of them are there? More than just these two you've got pinned down?"

"I dunno—seven, maybe eight. I ran into them on the road below the ridge. Tried to make it up here before they cottoned on, but I guess I wasn't lucky enough."

The news of the enemy numbers sent an icicle of fear between the molten infernos of his lungs, right into his heart.

"Tony. Brandon. The rest of them. The other attackers will be in the building right now."

Bullets zinged back from outside, dinging the turbine walls and ricocheting in. Syd emptied her mag and snapped in another.

"Yeah. It seems likely."

"You got a weapon for me?"

"Backpack. Middle pocket."

Nathan waited for the next barrage of shots to end before he leaped across the space of the open hatch, landing behind Syd. Her North Face pack was Special Ops Black and was a mess of damp snow and mud. He pulled the zipper on the middle pocket and pulled out a SIG Sauer P226 and a bunch of mags held together with rubber bands.

He loaded the weapon and pointed it over Syd's head, through the door. If he had to fight his way out of here to get to his sons, then that's what he'd have to do.

But before he could even pull the trigger to send the first bullets out through the access door, the room exploded.

10

"I don't necessarily *want* to shoot you. However, if I have to, I will. Now I come to think about it… there's several of you I would thoroughly enjoy shooting, I have to say. You, for instance, Miss B4. I would very much enjoy putting a bullet right between your eyes."

Lieutenant Price placed the business end of his Colt Government M1911 semi-automatic pistol, with its chunky wooden grip and gunmetal blue barrel, against Syd's forehead.

She didn't blink.

Syd looked hard at Price from her kneeling position and asked, "Do you think you could speak up? The thunderflash your boys threw into the turbine housing has left me with an awful ringing in my ears."

Price tapped the muzzle hard against the girl's head. "A smart mouth is a dead mouth today… I'm *sure* you heard that."

The ringing in Nathan's ears was subsiding enough now for him to pick out most of what the thick-set lieutenant was saying. There was blood drying stickily on Nathan's face, and one ear—the one that had been nearest to the stun grenade Price's men had lobbed through the access hatch—was nearly deaf, but even that was an improvement over an hour ago, when it had been completely deaf.

They were on their knees in Caleb's Bar, spread in a long line across the floor. Caleb's crew, even Rosa, looked like they had all taken a severe beating. Caleb's nose was busted, for sure. A thick double-line of blood had streamed from his nostrils over his lips and chin, and was drying now on his bow tie and shirt.

Lucy and Free were next to each other. Free's head was bowed, and the one eye that Nathan could see was growing a pulpy bruise. Lucy had a red handprint still stinging one cheek from where someone, probably Price, had slapped her.

Donie, on her knees, had tears bulbing on the end of her nose, and Dave's arm had been cut from the sling to make sure he wasn't concealing any weapons—he was cradling the injured arm and metal tube like a baby.

Tony was the only one not on his knees. Price had allowed him to sit on one of the benches holding Brandon. Nathan ached because neither of his sons were within arm's reach, but at least he could see them.

That left Tommy Ben.

Tommy Ben was not in the room, which meant one of two things. Price's men hadn't found him yet, or he was dead. The way the attackers had loosed rounds off toward Syd, in particular, and the building in general, it was a miracle that none of the people on their knees in the bar had gunshot wounds.

It was entirely possible that Tommy was lying in a pool of his own brains, right there in the gym where Nathan had last seen him.

"So, Mr. Tolley," Price began, "this is how it is going to be. There is a storm coming in. My men and I are going to hunker down here with you all tonight, and then we will head out tomorrow morning."

"Where to?" Nathan asked, not making eye contact with Price. Price was the kind of man he didn't want to give any reason to feel antagonized, especially with all those guns and his children in the same room.

"Detroit, of course, Mr. Tolley. You have an appointment with Mayor Brant in the Greenhouse, which he is very keen you should keep."

Nathan and his people had lit out of Detroit after assisting in a mini-revolution that had overthrown the elite 'Greenhousers' in their hermetically-sealed, glass-covered streets, where they lived a comfortable existence by exploiting the general population of the city. When Nathan and the others had headed west, they'd left a city with a new government and the bad guys captured. When they'd been attacked by a stealth helicopter on the road in Wyoming, by Stryker Wilson and others of Mayor Brant's people, it had led to the death of his wife. Mayor Brant was obviously back in charge, and it would seem that Brant was in no mood to give up his ideas of revenge. What Nathan couldn't work out was how the helicopter, and now Price, had found them in the wilds of Wyoming and Colorado. But that was a mystery which didn't need solving right now. There were more pressing matters.

"You caused Mayor Brant a hell'a lot a trouble, boy, and he charged us with tracking you down and bringing you home. He is, shall we say, more than a little upset by the way you repaid his generosity with insurrection, and he's definitely... *miffed*... to have lost his helicopter. In these days of extreme shortages, people can be replaced, but a highly-modified MH-60 Black Hawk stealth helicopter is a little harder to come by. And by destroying it, you added insult to injury. Which, if I'm reading Mayor Brant correctly, are the two things he is going to visit upon you at the moment we get back home."

"It seems an awful lot of trouble to go to, just to settle a score," Lucy said, looking up.

"Mayor Brant doesn't like loose ends, my dear, and you people are the loosest of ends."

Price stalked the line, looking at the group of kneeling captives. "One of the things I recognize in the vanquished is that you may all seem to be cooperating, and doing as you're told, but right now, I bet you're seething inside with plans and schemes. Especially you, Miss B4, hmm?"

Syd didn't respond, but Nathan could see the set of her jaw tightening. Syd was showing creditable restraint.

"I admire you. I *do*. That might come as a surprise to a scrawny waif and stray like you, Miss B4, but I do. I surely do. To get away from Brant's men, and get here just enough ahead of us to raise the alarm, makes you something special. It would be a shame to end all that potential now, but I need to counteract the scheming and planning that's going on in all your heads at the moment."

Price waved his arm expansively. "Right now, you've all got hope. You might be on your knees, and you might be giving the impression of being a bunch of good little captives. But I know... I *know* what is going on in your heads."

"We won't give you any trouble," Nathan whispered. "You have my word."

Price threw his head back and laughed long and generously. "I can see why people follow you, Mr. Tolley. You got a sense o' humor. People love a sense of humor."

Price scratched the side of his temple with the muzzle of his pistol as he thought for a moment. "I myself do *not* have one. I am a cold-blooded killer, who has come into his own in this changed world. Men like me don't need a sense of humor when we have enough bullets."

Nathan looked directly at Price now. He could see where this was headed. The thought of what was coming curled in his guts like a shivery shoal of cold fish.

"So, it's time for some instruction. I want to put an end to any plotting or scheming you might be considering in your rebellious little heads."

"You don't need to. Please..." Nathan's voice cracked with fear. He knew that he was safe. Brant wanted him back in Detroit. But that left everyone else at terrible risk. "I'm begging you, Lieutenant Price. There will be no plots, no schemes. Nothing. We'll stay here with you tonight without any trouble at all, and tomorrow we can begin the journey back to Detroit with you. Once the storm has passed."

As if to underline the mention of the storm, the roof of the maintenance building rattled in the increasing wind. The promised storm was about to roll over the ridge and complicate the outburst that was already erupting inside the building.

"You sound so reasonable, Mr. Tolley. So reasonable, in fact, that I almost believe you. Almost, but not quite."

Price's stroll along the line had brought him to Miriam, who was kneeling next to Larry. Sweat was standing out on the engineer's forehead, but Miriam's face was stoic.

"Look at this one, for instance," Price said, indicating the nurse. "She's not going to give me the satisfaction of showing me how scared she is. This is a woman who would go to her death rather than break down and beg for mercy. Is that right?"

Price was ratcheting up the sadism, and enjoying it judging by the smile on his grizzled face. His seven men in the room, their weapons at the ready, stood by at the same time—to a man, not showing distaste or disgust on their faces. Their expressions only showed that this was Price's thing, that it was a speech they'd all heard before and, in the final analysis, they were okay with it.

How far we have sunk, Nathan thought.

"But killing you doesn't help my cause, Ms. Nursy-Nurse. For my message to reach peak effectiveness, the *calm* ones need to be broken. The *smart mouths* need to silenced, and the *plotters* need to have all their hope extinguished, and by doing so, I can be assured of maximum cooperation and a minimum of fuss on our journey—on our long journey back to Detroit."

Price sighed like a professor at a lectern who had finished an often trotted-out lecture on his favorite theory. The very picture of a man resting on his laurels.

The storm was building, and the roof space had begun rattling as the wind increased in strength. Nathan wondered if the turbines were ready for the onslaught—ready for the rush. It seemed weird, giving over part of his thinking to bits of machinery at this point in the proceedings, but it was strangely comforting. Nathan trusted machines; he could predict their behavior in a way that, when it came to someone as mercurial as Price, he could not. And right now, he needed comfort, because he knew what was coming.

"I hope, in explaining my motivations, and why one of you needs to die a most heinous and terrifying, yet instructive, death, that I have in some way transmitted to you that there's nothing personal in my actions. They are entirely logical, and dare I say, necessary, to keep the rest of you alive. In fact, this killing I am about to carry out is more of a mercy than you realize. Perhaps there is some small part of you that will thank me for this, when you have managed to process it over the coming weeks."

Price pointed the gun at Larry's sweating, tearful face. Larry began to sob gently.

"Oh Jesus Lord, please... please... don't..." Larry said through trembling lips.

The roof rattled and boomed in the wind, and Nathan felt his guts tightening. Free's shoulders were shaking, and across from him on the bench, Tony buried his face in Brandon's hair, determined not to look at what was to about to happen.

But it didn't happen.

What did happen was that the roof space above Price's men, over the space where they had been loitering for the last twenty minutes, gave way as a single shot was fired through the ceiling, and it collapsed under the mass of iron gym weights Tommy had been placing there.

The iron rained down on the unsuspecting soldiers, cracking skulls and breaking collar bones. Behind it, Tommy jumped down firing an MP4 as he fell in a burst of wood, steel, and dust.

Miriam was already up and had head-butted Price in the guts. Nathan took the cue to scream to Tony, "Get under the table!" as the boy had looked up wildly.

Price had doubled over now, the Colt Government held limply in his hand. Nathan reached him before he had a chance to raise his head, so he kicked him in it. Price's head snapped backward—teeth flew out to clatter onto a nearby metal-topped table.

Price's men were either brained or shot, and Free joined Tommy, picking up one of the soldier's guns. Between them, they made sure that none of them would be getting up ever again.

Price was on his hands and knees now, moving groggily as Nathan grabbed him by the collar and yanked him up onto his knees. "How did you find us? How did you find us!?"

"I don't care," Larry said, and the Colt Government in his had fired twice, and Price's forehead caved in under the onslaught of the bullets. Larry dropped the gun he'd scooped up back to the floor.

"I never shot anyone before," he said as he sank to his knees.

It hadn't been just the storm rattling the roof space above the bar. It had been Tommy setting his trap. "I was sure they were going to figure out I was up there," the Texan said, shaking his head with disbelief. "I had to make a dozen trips to get the weights up there, and that roof creaks like a be-atch."

Miriam was going from person to person on the benches, giving them first aid where they needed it, some of Caleb's people having taken a terrific beating from Price's men.

Nathan was huddled on one of the plush benches hugging his sons while Tommy told him what he'd been up to since Price's team had stormed the facility.

"I heard the gunfire and came out to look, but there was nothing I could do when I saw them dragging you all in here. I kept my head down, and out of their way. First thing you learn when there's trouble is, don't come out looking for it. If I was going to be any help at all, I had to keep out of the way."

"Tommy, you were outstanding, man—I can't…" Nathan trailed off and just hugged his boys, and Tommy nodded like he understood. But at the same time as he felt relief, Nathan was frustrated by Larry's killing of Price, and Larry himself seemed to have been deeply affected by the notion of killing. He was sitting alone in the far corner of the room, sobbing. Caleb had tried twice to get near enough to comfort him, but Miriam had told the bow-tied engineer to hang back and give the man some space.

"He's got some reconciling to do," she'd said.

Free and Lucy had returned from a trip down the ridge to make sure that there were no more of Price's men, and they were now drinking coffee with Rosa, Tyrone, and Michael. Donie and Dave, his arm back in a sling, were resting their heads on each other's shoulders, not saying much. Just listening.

"So, I got the weights up there as quietly as I could, but there was no way I could be totally silent. All it would have taken was for Price's men to move, and all I'd have had was a distraction to dive down through. Much better that the sky fell in on them."

Nathan nodded. Tommy's eyes were alight with his own success. It had indeed been an audacious and risky plan, but to know that Tommy could have left them to Price, and just gotten himself away, but hadn't, made Nathan feel all the more connected to him.

"They've got two Toyota Land Cruisers, with trailers, and a ton of ammo, plus plenty of fuel and provisions for many days, weeks even," Free said, joining them. "They got radios, satellite phones, and night vision gear, too. It's a regular treasure trove."

"It'll really help us defend this place," Lucy commented, getting in early with her agenda. "Anyone comes for us again and we'll be ready."

Tommy said nothing, but Nathan caught the imperceptible shake of his head as he drained his coffee.

"Oh, they'll come again," Syd said. "Brant is insane, and he's got the power he needs to keep hunting you. I know what it's like to be hunted, and Danny had nothing on Brant."

Danny had been the gang leader Syd had all but castrated when he'd tried to rape her before leaving New York. His revenge had been personal, and vicious—but in many ways, crude and unfocused as well, reactive more than proactive. As Syd obviously understood, Brant was another kettle of fish altogether.

"We took these guys out. We'll take anyone else out, too," Lucy insisted.

Nathan kissed Brandon, who was sleeping quietly, and tucked him back into Tony's arms. "I reckon he needs changing, Tony—you reckon you can handle that for me?"

Tony nodded seriously, picking up his brother and going off to find diapers and wipes.

With him gone, Nathan turned to the others. "Lucy, you're not thinking."

Free's eyes flashed at Nathan, and he held up his hand to his friend. "Hear me out before you jump down my throat, okay?"

Free nodded, but his face was dark with thunder.

"We've been idiots. *I've* been an idiot. In all this time, since the helicopter in Wyoming, and now Price and his men here, we haven't asked ourselves one simple question."

Free looked at Lucy, but she shrugged. "What question?"

"How did they find you?" Syd offered.

Nathan nodded. "Yup, how did they find us? It's not like we left a trail of breadcrumbs for them to follow, is it?"

"They must have made an educated guess," Lucy said, but with an expression on her face that couldn't have been less convinced if she'd tried. "They knew the general direction we were traveling. They must have known Casper was a possibility."

"I might have bought that, but here, Lucy? How did they know we were here?"

Lucy was stumped, and Free was the guppy of no idea.

"Do you know, Syd?" Nathan asked.

Syd nodded. "Yes. I think so. I just tracked Price and his men where I could. It wasn't hard; I stayed about three miles behind in my truck. They left a trail of garbage and campfires and tire tracks. I didn't need to try hard. I knew they were coming for you, and my plan was to follow them, and get ahead of them when I could and come and warn you. My truck fritzed out two days ago and I had no choice but to stow away in one of their equipment trailers."

"Stow away?" Nathan whistled softly. This girl had cajones like grapefruit.

"Yeah. It was cold, but they were complacent. Well, complacent up until they found me as they were parking down trail. That's why they were already shooting when I came up the drive."

Nathan didn't know whether to hit Syd or salute her, but the more pressing issue broke the surface of his admiration. "So, you tracked them. Okay, but how did they find *us*?"

Syd shook her head and answered, "It's easier if I show you."

Syd got up and approached Dave and Donie. Nathan couldn't hear what she said to them, but they both nodded. Donie got up and jogged out of the bar.

Dave's face was a mask of shock, as if he'd just been told something that had completely blindsided him.

Free had found his voice now—the guppy had swum away from his face. "Nathan, it doesn't change anything. We should stay here; build the shelter and dig in. So what if Brant knows where we are?"

"It matters to me, Free, and if you thought hard enough about how I don't want to risk the lives of my friends, or the lives of my children any more than I have to, it might matter to you. We have to find a place where no one knows who we are, or where we're from."

Free's anger was about to bubble over, his knuckles whitened and his face drained of color. "No, Nathan. No!"

But before Nathan had a chance to answer, the decision was taken away from all of them.

11

The second earthquake Nathan Tolley experienced made the first he had felt pale almost into insignificance.

The room rocked, floor tiles splitting and popping up as the ground beneath the ridge bumped and bucked. Lights exploded as cracks snaked down walls. Meanwhile, the bar and the kitchen crashed and twisted as equipment slew from side to side like deck chairs on the Titanic.

Nathan was thrown headlong into Lucy and they sprawled to the floor as, from above, just like what Tommy had brought on before, the ceiling tore open further and a constant stream of debris and insulating materials, wood, and aluminum burst out of the roof—a hole appearing that showed right up to the sky.

"Get out! Everyone, get out!" Caleb began shouting as he and his people ran toward the door. Free picked up Lucy. The floor was still rumbling, and the building was in danger of falling down around their ears.

Nathan got to his feet. *Tony. Brandon.* "I've got to find my sons!"

Nathan sprinted for what was left of the door, stumbling left and then right as the floor rocked and plunged. The noise grumbling up from the earth beneath him was savage and primal, and complemented by the crashing destruction as the facility was taken by the throat by the tectonic giant and shaken to its very foundations.

The corridor outside the bar had already been plunged into near darkness. Only one light in the ceiling was illuminated, and it was flickering like he was on a carnival ride. Electrics buzzed with live wires snaking down from the ceiling, sparking in pools of water that were evidence of broken plumbing.

Sidestepping the growing puddles as best he could, Nathan just got past a bulging wall as a grinding crash bowed it out like a pregnant belly, plaster falling around him like dandruff and then collapsing it under its own weight. The crash brought down a huge supporting lintel, and the resulting billow of dust and grit washed over Nathan in a harsh cloud. Already damaged by the pneumonia, Nathan felt his throat closing and his lungs burning as he ran on, dodging raft after raft of falling wreckage.

"Tony!" he screamed, the dust clogging his mouth, his eyes going dry and unfocused.

Somewhere behind him, there was the *whump* of an explosion, and for just a couple of moments, Nathan's vision was lit orange by flames. The corridor returned to semi-darkness soon after, but the warmth of the explosion followed him.

The room he shared with Tony and Brandon branched off a corridor to the left. As Nathan reached the point of bifurcation, another explosion—this one much larger than the first—outdid the grumbling of the tortured earth and Nathan was blown off his feet.

He crashed into a wall that seemed to be standing defiantly against the onslaught; he could feel the shaking, and now he could feel the heat. The building wasn't just falling apart—it was burning down.

"Tony!" he called hollowly, trying to get up on one elbow, but something was holding him down. He tried to shift his shoulders, but they were held fast. Had the wall fallen on him? Was he trapped and about to be crushed or burned?

And where were his sons? Where were Tony and Brandon? Had he sent them to their deaths just before the earthquake hit?

And now he was being held down and could do nothing but wait for the fall or the flames.

"Don't just lay there, Nathan! Get up!"

Free. He must have followed him into the corridor instead of exiting the building with the others. Now, it was Free pulling at his shoulders that had, in his panic, felt like he'd been trapped and was unable to move. They had both been pulling in opposing directions.

Nathan got up and tried to walk forward, but the corridor that led to his room collapsed completely on a gust of dust, cold air from the outside, and a rumbling grind from below.

Suddenly, he and Free were outside. The defiant wall they both leaned against was the last thing standing in the vicinity. They were surrounded on all sides by the collapsed building, and the room where he'd sent his children was no more. It had gone down like a row of dominos. And as he looked up, he could see the eight turbines yawing like the tossed masts of a sailing ship floundering on rocks. The nearest, some thirty yards away, rocked and jounced, propeller sails rattling and shaking. As Nathan watched, the one where he and Syd had been captured after the stun grenades had been thrown in became unsteady. Nathan felt Free pulling him backward across rubble, away from the wobbling structure.

With the turbine continuing to wave, there was a rending of metal as the torque of the nacelle moving too far off its intended anchor had the effect of tearing the whole three-hundred-foot structure from the ground. Like Gulliver lifting his body after he'd been tied down by the Lilliputians, the entire tower began to twist and pop. Wings made of fiberglass over wooden frames dropped like fall petals, and the tower came crashing down like a redwood falling with majestic slowness.

If Nathan hadn't been so concerned about his children, he might have mourned its passing, as first one, and then all seven of the other turbines, fell lazily down with tearing crashes and rippling metal. When the last of the giants had reached their final resting places, then and only then did the earthquake cease shaking the landscape. As if it had waited until its destruction was complete before allowing itself to rest with the knowledge of a job well done.

Smoke rose from the rubble around them as small fires burned between the bricks and concrete. The debris field was total.

There was nothing standing of the wind farm, its generators, or its buildings.

And of Nathan's sons, there was no sign at all.

Nathan tottered like the next in line of the turbines to collapse. His legs were uprooted and his guts were rent, twisted like the collapsing tubes of steel. He fell like a marionette that had had its strings cut, and it was only Free's solid form standing fast at his back that kept him sitting in an upright position.

Nathan was in a world without words.

There was no language to cover this, and his thinking had completely shut down. Even the cold wind scything across the devastation was just a numb bluntness without chill. He was cocooned in sadness and desperation. There was a black ax hacking up from his heart now, and the tectonics of his body were shaking, crumbling, and bursting him apart.

He took a huge breath, the taste of the dead building all over his tongue and in his throat, cloying and dry.

"Nathan…" Free was saying, "come on, we've got to get away from here… these fires are spreading and we don't know what's going to catch fire next…"

But Nathan was rooted in spot; the base of his spine had been bolted to the earth so tight that he might have become part of the bedrock. His arms were stiff with their own internal granite, and the slopes of his shoulders were ready to accept the snow of sadness that was littering down around them.

"Give me a hand here!" Free shouted.

Feet were coming across the rubble, causing trickles of broken material to shift and seesaw. Nathan heard the voices around him, but there were no words in there that he could recognize anymore. There was only one language now, and that was the language of horror.

Hands lifted him under his arms and Tyrone's huge hands encircled Nathan's ankles, lifting him off the earth. The earth that had robbed him of his children, to add to the utter terror of losing his wife.

Flashes of Tony's face blipped across his thinking. That serious nod, taking Brandon in his arms and taking him away to be changed. Tony walking to the door of Caleb's Bar and turning...

Turning...

Turning right. Not left.

Tony hadn't gone to the room. He'd gone to the car!

"Daddy! Daddy!" Tony was shouting as Free, Tommy, and Tyrone lay Nathan on the ground away from the collapsed building.

Tony was there, throwing himself at Nathan, putting his arms around his neck and crying into his shoulder. Through his own tears, Nathan could see Brandon in Donie's arms. Next to her, sitting on the ground with her hair full of dust, was Lucy, and then Dave beside her. Everyone was okay. Everyone was alive.

Nathan cried into his son's hair, smelling his warm skin and the aroma of fresh sweat coming up through Tony's clothes. Both their sets of tears were mixing with salty clarity in Nathan's mouth. It was the most precious thing Nathan had ever tasted in his life. The tears of his boy crying with relief.

"I'm sorry, Daddy! I'm sorry! I should have said I was going to the car and then you wouldn't have thought that I was going back to the room! There were no more diapers in the room, so I had to go and get them from outside—I'm sorry, Daddy! I'm really sorry."

"It's okay, son, it's okay. I was so scared you'd both been hurt. I'm just glad you're okay. Truly, I am. Don't apologize. It's all okay. It's gonna be okay. I promise. I promise."

The feeling was returning to Nathan's body as the waves of immobilizing shock dissipated, and now his body began to get moving and his frozen blood started to circulate.

Although Nathan's party was only shaken and relieved, though, the wind farm crew had not been anywhere near as lucky. Michael, as attested to by Miriam, was dead, crushed beneath a falling wall. Rosa's neck had been broken when the ceiling in the bar area had fallen on her. Larry had broken his ankle in the rush to get out of the building. Tyrone, Bill, and Miriam were basically unscathed, but Crane could not be found. Buried somewhere under the rubble, they'd guessed.

When they eventually found him, he had already bled out from a jagged tear in his thin neck.

Which just left Caleb, and Caleb was alive, but he was also dying.

Miriam sat with his head in her lap, soothing his brow. He was crushed across the belly by a concrete block that, even if all those who were able strained at it, would not be moved. There was no point anyway, as Miriam explained to the others out of earshot of Caleb while Tyrone sat with him. "Even if we could get him out, his internal injuries are too great. The only thing keeping him alive this long is that the block is stopping the toxins from the lower, dead half of his body from coming up and flooding his system—the shock of that would kill him pretty much instantly. The best thing we can do is keep him comfortable. He won't last more than an hour more."

In the end, Caleb lasted two hours. "Raise... a drink... for me, the next bar... you get to, eh? Nate?"

It was Nate's turn to sit with the engineer's head in his lap, soothing away the sweat and the thin trickle of blood that now constantly came from the side of his mouth. "You bet, Caleb. I might even raise two."

Caleb smiled and coughed, wincing at the pain that was spreading up through his body. Caleb placed his hand on Nathan's then; it was as cold as the Big Winter, and heavy as old iron. "You look after these people for me, Nathan. They deserve someone... like you... you're a good man... *amirite*?"

"I don't feel so good right now, Caleb. In fact, I'm a hot mess."

"It just proves you... feel. And that's no... no bad thing. Promise me you'll look after them like I tried to. Please."

"You have my word."

Caleb smiled thinly and closed his eyes. For a few moments, Nathan thought the remarkable man had slipped away, but as he looked closely, he saw that there was a thready pulse still throbbing in his neck, and his chest was rising and falling gently.

Miriam took over then, and stayed with Caleb right to the end.

None of them heard what Caleb said last, or what Miriam whispered into his ear, but as he finally left his beloved wind farm, and the people he'd called his friends and colleagues, Miriam bent down and kissed him on the lips and gave him one last squeeze.

A real storm was approaching now, and as they had no shelter to speak of, they would have to get into the cars. The military-green Land Cruisers had been driven up to the rubble field by Free and Lucy. Miriam, Tyrone, Bill, and Larry—with his ankle now splinted by Miriam, with help from Tommy—made their place to ride out the storm in one of the Toyotas. Lucy, Dave, Donie, Syd, and Tommy took the other. Free joined Nathan, the boys, and Rapier in the F-350. He hadn't said anything of note to Nathan since chasing him down the corridor in the collapsing building, knowing that the boys were already safe outside and that their father was almost certainly running to his death.

"I guess I owe you an apology," Free said eventually, sitting in the cab next to Nathan with the boys and the dog in the crew cab just behind them. Nathan hadn't wanted to waste fuel running the heaters, so they were all wrapped in blankets and deep in their coats. Tony sat behind Nathan with Brandon in one arm, and his other, in thick woolen gloves, resting on his daddy's shoulder, as if he couldn't bear to not be touching him.

Nathan didn't really know what to say to Free at this point. There had been so much to deal with in the last few hours, he really couldn't organize his own thoughts, let alone guess at his friend's.

"I'm lost, Free. What's on your mind? Spit it out…"

"You've always done right by us, Nathan. If you hadn't listened to us, you might still be back in Glens Falls, and Cyndi might still be alive."

Free and Cyndi had been adamant about getting out of their hometown, though Nathan hadn't wanted to give up his business and had been resistant for a good while. But, in the end, when news came from Stryker Wilson and the supposed paradise in Detroit he promised (which never materialized), he had relented. In many ways, Free was right, but of course, Cyndi had been keen to get out, as well.

"That isn't just on your head, Free. Cyndi wanted to go, too. Just as hard, and I gave in. And who knows what might have happened if we'd stayed behind? Gangs, no gas, complete breakdown… At least we had a chance out on the road."

"Maybe. Maybe not. But all along the way, you've stuck by me. You've pulled me out of the fire on more occasions than I can say…." Free's voice trailed off.

"Spit it out, Free, come on."

If Free was about to tell Nathan that, after all they had been through together, that he and Lucy were splitting away because they didn't want to share the team with Tommy, or just because they'd had enough of traveling—and now that Nathan was a clear target in Brant's sights from afar, they felt it was just too dangerous to carry on being around him—then he just wanted Free to get it out of the way and say it.

"Free, I get it. Staying with me is too dangerous, and you've got your own life to think of with Lucy. I get it. Really, I do. You can take the Ford or the Taurus if you want one of them, and we'll share out the guns, ammo, and provisions…."

Free held up a sudden hand. "Whoa there! Whoa!" There was high color in Free's cheeks that wasn't just about the chill in the weather. "Don't go saying…"

"It's obvious, Free. You've wanted to break away since we got here. I get it. I understand."

"Nathan, sometimes you can be the biggest damn fool on the planet!" Free thumped the dash in exasperation, and then let loose a heavy sigh. "Man, I was going to apologize for letting you down by even *suggesting* we should have stayed here. Lucy and I have been talking, Nathan, and we feel like real slimeballs. You've given up almost everything for us, and at the first sign of something better, we were ready to cut you loose if you didn't agree to stay with us. That's what I want to apologize for, man. We're not leaving you. We want to stay with you and see this through. All the way. No doubt."

Nathan let that sink in for a few seconds and had to look away because of the prickling he felt at the back of his eyes. Free was basically good people, and for all her affectations and artifice, Lucy was, too. He'd said that he understood why they might have wanted to go, and he'd meant it, but it didn't stop his heart welling over with pride and friendship for Free being able to do the decent thing and come through like this.

As Nathan looked out into the falling night, the first snowflakes from the new storm began to whip around the Ford and the other cars parked next to the destroyed power station. He saw in the nearest Land Cruiser that Lucy was looking pensively through the window, toward the Ford. When Nathan caught her eye, she looked straight at him and mouthed a silent 'Sorry' in his direction.

And that was that.

The steady snowfall became a blizzard, with buffeting winds and drifting snow. Soon, the windows on the Ford had silted up with a white crust, and Free decided it was better he stayed in the cab with them until the storm had passed. There was very little sleep to be had in the gnashing teeth of the storm, and several times, debris blown up from the demolished buildings crashed against the side of the truck, shaking their teeth and startling them awake if they'd been on the edge of sleep.

Tony, Brandon, and Rapier remained curled up together, warm and snug under the dog's fur and the blankets in the crew cab. There had even been baby food that Tony had fed to Brandon, cold, but the baby, who never seemed to complain or cry without reason, had accepted the food gratefully.

Hunger gnawed at Nathan as much as the idea of what they might do when the storm eventually passed. He still hadn't heard from Syd how it was that Brant, Stryker, and Price had tracked them. In the aftermath of the earthquake, and the deaths of their friends, it seemed like a question that could wait until they fully had time to consider her idea—and the implications.

But it *was* a worry. How could they travel anywhere if they were so easy to find? Should they travel now under assumed names or find a place just for them that was as far from any roads or people as they could? And if it didn't matter where they went because Brant's all-seeing-eye would find them, perhaps the best form of defense was attack… Should they travel back north to Detroit, and have a final showdown with Brant and end this one way or the other?

No.

That didn't bear thinking about. These ideas were all running free in Nathan's head, and what he needed, first of all, was a sense that he could understand how Brant was getting his information, and then they could respond accordingly.

When eventually the storm passed, and the dawn came brightly under the covering dust clouds, Nathan awoke, realizing that he had slept well enough after all. His dreams had been free of horror and strife, with no surprise Strykers or sign of Cyndi to make his heart hurt. Just a presence—a woman who was calm, stoic, and reliable. He hadn't been able to see her face in the dream, but weirdly, Nathan had recognized her hands. The same hands that had been soothing Caleb as he'd died.

Miriam's hands.

There was something very comforting about the woman. Her confidence, and her warmth and her skills. Nathan felt that she would definitely become a strong asset to the party, someone with the smarts and the knowledge to add real value. Nathan resolved to go to her first of all as he pushed hard at the frozen door of the F-350, breaking the ice seal and letting in the chill air. Rapier barked and leaped out over his shoulder. The dog was well Ford-trained by now and must have been bursting to relieve himself.

Nathan got out into the strong sunlight, shielding his eyes against the low, harshly glowing orb beating down from the Colorado sky.

And it was because his eyes were temporarily blinded by the brightness, once he'd gotten out of the snow-covered Ford, that he realized with a thump to his heart that the Land Cruiser containing Miriam and the surviving crew from the wind farm had driven away in the night.

12

"We didn't hear them go," Lucy said as they met up next to the second Land Cruiser.

Miriam and the others must have left during the worst part of the storm if the lack of tracks or any evidence of their passage down from the ridge back to the road was anything to go by. Nathan was convinced, although he kept the notion to himself for now, that Miriam or perhaps Larry had forced the hand of the others. Nathan and his people were bad medicine. Anyone in their vicinity would get caught in Brant's crossfire. Larry's face, trembling with fear, begging for his life, was front and center in Nathan's thinking.

How could anyone want to risk going through anything like that again?

He could imagine there had been a discussion, perhaps a heated one, that had reasoned out their best bet for getting away with at least one of Lieutenant Price's trucks, its trailer, and half the provisions, guns, and ammo—and that that would be for them to make a break for it when Nathan and the others would be least likely to attempt to follow. It had taken real guts and not a little bravado to drive away under white-out conditions. It was still something that Nathan felt was too risky to attempt, but when you needed to get away from impending danger—more danger in the shape of men like Lieutenant Price—then he knew that could make you dismiss the risks and just go.

And the blizzard had completely covered over the demolished building. Ghostly humps in the snow where the wrecked turbines lay were now the only obvious reminder of what had been there before. The surrounding landscape was a blindingly complete blanket of snow. Only the largest of trees dotting the landscape were sticking up through the cue ball-smooth whiteness.

Nathan hadn't experienced snow like this since before they'd made it across the state line into Wyoming. It reminded him of the weeks they'd spent on the road from New York State to Michigan. A constant, endless conveyor belt of nothingness, bleak and threatening. Nothing like the snows when he'd been a kid, when he would have snowball fights with friends, build snowmen, or go sledding down the slopes of the valley with his daddy. This snow wasn't so much kissing the land as choking it. And as the Big Winter established itself this far south, they could expect a whole lot more of it.

God knew what conditions were like back in Detroit or Chicago now, but he could imagine that they weren't getting any better. The people in the Greenhouses of Detroit would be okay with their utilities and their hydroponics, but the people outside the elite space—their hellish life may have taken a terrible turn for the worse.

The snow was thigh-deep in places, so Tommy and Free set about digging the vehicles out of the drifts and making a space between them where at least enough ground could be cleared for people to stand without risking frostbite. There were no longer fires burning in the wreckage of the building, but some small clearing away of the snow revealed enough spars of wood from the roof to build a fire in the clearing. They used the fire to cook a few dead chickens Rapier retrieved from Rosa's coop. Where they found bodies that they could move—and the aforementioned Rosa, Crane, Price, and his men were located quickly—they laid them to rest as best they could under bricks and broken concrete.

They couldn't move Caleb, and so they covered his body where he'd died and Lucy said a few words, which were solemn yet warm. She'd quite taken to the dapper engineer, and to see him die in such a senseless way had affected her. Free pulled her close as they moved back to the clearing.

"So, Syd," Nathan said, when the last offices for the dead were complete, "how did they find us, and how do we stop them finding us again?"

Syd threw a look at Donie. "Over to you."

Donie nodded and reached into a backpack, pulling out the cop satellite laptop they'd been using to plan routes and keep in touch with whatever was left of the internet running across the nation.

"Syd thinks Stryker put some kind of spyware onto it when we weren't looking."

Syd cut in. "A couple of times after you left, I saw him looking at maps on his computer, that he closed down pretty quickly when I walked into the room. I think every time you turned the laptop on to plan where you were heading, and what homesteads and buildings off the beaten track you could spend the night in while traveling to Casper, it sent a signal to Stryker. I guess he used that information when the time was right to get himself back in with Brant, and maybe that was why he was sent out in the helo to bring you back."

Nathan's spirits, such as they'd been, sank even lower. Every move they'd made had been available—first to Stryker and then to Brant. As soon as his pneumonia had kicked in and Brant had seen they were stationary and there was a chance they might be caught, Price and his men, with Syd in pursuit, had been dispatched.

Nathan looked up at the blazingly blue morning sky. Up there, in geostationary orbit, hung the GPS satellites they had been using for months to plot their course, while at the same time allowing the mouth of the net around them to be drawn ever more closed.

"So, what do we do?" he asked.

Donie flipped open the laptop. "Dave and I think we can find the spyware payload and either disable it or get it to send bad data back to Detroit. But we reckon just turning it on further down the trail will tell Brant wherever we are."

"And that's problematic," said Dave.

Nathan grimaced. "You think?"

Donie carried on. "If we can wait here another twenty-four hours, say, and have a good chance to investigate the laptop, then when we move on, we think we can go dark."

Nathan considered it, but then asked, "Why not just dump the laptop here and leave now?"

Dave shook his head. "We considered that last night, but wouldn't it be better if they thought they still had us in their sights? I reckon, if we can work on it, we can make Brant at least think the laptop is traveling back toward Detroit. That might keep him out of our hair for longer."

"That's a high-risk strategy."

"Isn't *everything* we're doing high-risk?" chipped in Tommy, and around the circle, heads were nodding.

"Amen to that," Lucy said with a sigh.

Nathan surveyed the snowfield around them. "Okay, while you guys work on the laptop, we'll get everything else we need ready. The Taurus was okay while there wasn't this level of snow, but we're going to have to leave it here and carry on with the F-350 and the Land Cruiser. Lucy and Free, you consolidate the supplies and the trailers; Tommy and Syd, you and I are gonna go through the wreckage of Caleb's place and see what we can salvage. Let's find the kitchen under that mess first and see what we can dig out."

They faced hard, backbreaking work for the next four hours as Nathan, Tommy, and Syd uncovered the snow and levered up chunks of brickwork and collapsed metal structures, all to see what they could find beneath. It didn't take them long to find where the kitchen had been behind the bar. There were plenty of cans of soup, corned beef, and dried milk that had survived the earthquake. Plus sacks of rice, dried fruits, and packets of beef jerky which would last until the next ice age if kept right. In the end, they found more food than they could comfortably take along and still leave places in the vehicles for them to sit.

"We'll leave some of the guns behind," Nathan said as the pile of provisions grew—testament to Caleb's sound, if eccentrically applied, management skills.

"Leave some weapons behind?" Tommy asked incredulously.

"We've got more than enough for one each, plus some spares. I don't think Brandon's ready to learn to shoot yet." Nathan smiled. "We're not an army. We can take the ammo for the weapons we're keeping, but I'd rather have food than a gun I don't have enough hands to use. Make sense?"

"I suppose so," Tommy answered as he reluctantly put an M240 machine gun into the snow to make room for tins of chicken soup.

Next, they searched for where in the infirmary Miriam might have kept her drugs and first responder equipment. And there they discovered that Miriam and the others had been through the wreckage already during the night, before the snowfall had become too treacherous.

The crushed cupboards and metal cabinets Nathan had seen Miriam go to for various drugs and medicaments were near empty, apart from a few packs of aspirin and indigestion relief liquid.

"They cleared this out in a blizzard?" Tommy whistled. "They musta really wanted to get away from us."

Nathan nodded sadly. He picked up the damp packets, the three remaining bottles, and the thin, black rubber snake of a stethoscope they'd found, and put these meager things together with Elm's ledger and the bags of Native American remedies in the back of the F-350. Elm's recorded knowledge and Cyndi's application of it had kept them alive and well pretty much this long—not exactly curing Tony's asthma, but certainly keeping it at bay—so they would continue to use and learn. Aspirin and bottles of indigestion liquid were great as they were, but they were processed, made in factories and distributed by a system that was no longer operational. Yet again, it was brought home to Nathan how important it was to disseminate the information contained in Elm's ledger to as many people as possible. Lives would depend on it in the years to come.

Nathan felt some regret that part of their mission had become somewhat sidetracked, and then derailed with the death of his wife and the issues they'd come across in Casper, but perhaps the further south they got, they may well be able to spread some of this knowledge around again.

It would be a fitting monument to his wife.

"Yes!" Donie's shout was dulled by the surrounding snow, but as the morning ground on toward afternoon and the threat of a cold night spent in the trucks impacted everyone's mood, the sound of it offered a bright spark in an otherwise bleak day.

Dave and Donie had set up their small, wind-powered trickle chargers and satellite uplink station on top of the remaining Land Cruiser. They were sitting in the back seats, the chunky black cop laptop with its thick rubber corners and one of their own Windows machines linked by cables, USB port to USB port.

Dave's metal tube arm made two-handed operation of his machine difficult, even with his arm out of the sling, so he worked one-handed but was making progress anyway. As Nathan looked in through the window Donie had wound down to shout their triumph to the world at large, he saw that her fingers were flying over the keyboard of the cop laptop with incredible speed.

This was where Dave and Donie's expertise with computers, alternative energy sources, and tech in general came to the fore. Their use of the cop internet—which was still operating, if in a hugely reduced capacity—had given them up-to-date tracking and mapping abilities, allowing them to stay off the main highways when they'd needed to avoid gangs on the way to Detroit. It had also given Nathan a number of options of places to search when Cyndi, Free, Lucy, Syd, and Tony had been kidnapped by members of a gang. Dave and Donie's equipment had provided enough of a distraction for Nathan to rescue everyone and neutralize many of the bad guys in Marty's Diner.

Not being able to use the cop laptop any more would be a serious blow, so Nathan was coming around to the idea of the machine being used to fight back, rather than just have it be dumped and them be done with it.

Donie's face was alive now, though, eyes dancing across the screen.

"You found it?" Nathan asked.

"Yeah." Donie nodded without looking up. "It's a sneaky one. Military grade, by the look of it. Russian, possibly, but it could be one of ours just made to look like one of theirs. The payload of the spyware has been hidden in an always-on portion of the RAM. From what we can see, it turns itself on at random intervals to see if we're using the uplink. But it comes into its own when the uplink is operational. It bursts data quicker than you can turn the machine off, and it had a portion of code that makes you believe the machine is off, but it actually stays on for another thirty seconds and sends the data at a more leisurely pace. It's witchcraft, Nate. Pure witchcraft."

"If I had any idea what you were talking about, I'm sure I'd be impressed. I can just about turn a computer on and use a search engine. Cyndi was the whiz."

"All you need to know," Dave said, as he tapped one-handed at his laptop, "is that it knows exactly where we are, and it's talking to Detroit right now."

Dave pointed at lines of letters and numbers moving across his screen. Nathan was surprised how innocuous it all looked. Just a scroll of text. No blinking Skull-and-Crossbones or flashing danger signs. Just numbers and text, in no discernable pattern, telling Brant where they were right down to the square yard.

"And can you fix it?"

"Yes," Dave and Donie said together, emphatically.

So, Nathan left them to it.

It made him seriously antsy to know that even in this new world, where almost nothing was how it had been before, that a computer could be the thing that would lead the enemy to them surer than a trail of blood particles leading a great white to an injured fish.

The world was decidedly low-tech now. It was survive or die, and with the laptop screaming, *"Here we are!"* all the way back to Michigan, they were ever more vulnerable.

Nathan found himself scanning the horizons for a second Black Hawk coming through the air. Price had given the impression that the one they'd destroyed had been the only one Brant had had access to, but that didn't mean that, in the intervening time, Brant hadn't managed to locate another.

Nathan shivered at the thought and went back to warm himself by the fire.

As the night locked down on them, dropping an iron frost over the land, they let the fire die out and moved back into the vehicles. Tommy joined Nathan and his boys in the F-350. Both the Ford and the Land Cruiser had been repacked and stuffed with as much food, fuel, and equipment as they and the trailers could take. Tommy and Lucy had made an extra trip into the wrecked maintenance building to see what they could salvage from Caleb's Bar, as well. Lucy had scored two unbroken bottles of vodka, and Tommy three bottles of Laphroaig, along with two shot glasses.

"I'd have preferred Kentucky bourbon, but this is a close second," Tommy said as he poured generous slugs of fire water into the glasses he'd placed carefully on the dash of the Ford. When he'd recorked the bottle, he passed one to Nathan.

"Shouldn't we save the alcohol to use as antiseptic?" Nathan asked half-seriously.

"I'd rather you sawed off my leg, compadre," Tommy said, and drained his glass with a loud smack of his lips.

Nathan was more circumspect with the whiskey, and sipped at the peaty, smoky liquid, letting the alcohol burn off on his tongue before sending it down to bring a welcome warmth to his belly.

Tommy was ready to pour them both another, but Nathan shook his head. "I'm good."

Tommy shrugged and poured himself one. This one, he sipped at while they talked.

"Did I get the impression that Free and Lucy are going to stick around? Come south?"

"Yup. They both apologized. Knowing Free as I do, I know that didn't come easy."

"I guess my apology is in the post."

"Give them time, Tommy. Like you, they're assets to the party. It would be all the poorer without any one of you."

Tommy shrugged again, his eyes squinting off into the darkness. Nathan couldn't see what he was looking at. Maybe he wasn't looking out at all; maybe he was just focusing on the reflection of himself in the windshield. "They're not gonna follow me, and I'm not gonna follow them. Which is why, I guess, you've taken the reins again."

Nathan hadn't thought of it like that, but yes, he had taken charge again. He hadn't made the conscious decision to put himself forward to tell the others what they should do, and how they should do it, but an unconscious process had led him once again to be the fulcrum over which the group pivoted. At least for now.

"Just me spouting a bit of common sense, Tommy. Anyone can do that."

"Yeah, but they look to you, compadre. That's a good position to be in."

"They? What about you, Tommy?"

Tommy thought for a long time. Time enough to pour himself another slug of Laphroaig.

"Don't ask me to take sides, Nate. If you do, we might have a problem, but right now I'm happy to follow you. If that changes, and that woman starts calling the shots again, then I may have to reconsider."

Nathan knew he shouldn't have been shocked to hear such pushback from Tommy. He wasn't a natural follower, and being told what to do by Lucy must have screwed with his sensibilities big-time. "Lucy's heart is in the right place. She's not the easiest person to get on with, but she, like you, has been good for all of us."

"May be, Nathan, but I have a sense for these things, and she is trouble. One hundred percent, twenty-four carat trouble. You can listen to me or not, but when she and her boyfriend make us all dead, don't come running to me."

13

"Trouble up ahead," Tommy said, looking through the windshield as he drove the F-350 ahead of the Land Cruiser.

There hadn't been any more fresh snow in the three days since they'd left the ridge and the wrecked wind farm, so that had been a plus, but there had been a whole raft of negatives.

The snows that had swept over this part of Colorado, north of Denver, had been so deep, and the night frosts so severe, that they were having to drive at speeds somewhat less than fifteen miles an hour to stay safe—and that was when they could actually find the highway. In some places, where there were no road signs to tell them there was blacktop somewhere beneath the frigid white, they had to resort to the trick Nathan had implemented on the road from Glens Falls. Someone would take turns walking ahead of the vehicles with a pole, testing the drifts for hidden obstacles before allowing the trucks through. These were cold, hard yards to make progress over, and the days were shortening again after what had proved to be only the briefest of respites from the Big Winter.

It was far too dangerous, Nathan had decided, for them to travel at night now, which allowed them just about six hours of daylight to get anywhere. But even during the day, the landscape through which they moved was a dim twilight, the sky bruised with dust. Dave surmised that there had been more volcanic activity along the Pacific coast, which had itself pumped more pyroclastic debris into the upper atmosphere—perhaps it had all been linked to the two earthquakes they had experienced.

They'd made camps where they could but had stayed out of towns even where they'd looked safe and deserted. Being in a building when the earth was trying to shake it to pieces had made them wary of even looking into them for supplies to augment what they already had. And the constant near-twilight was affecting everyone's moods, too. Conversations were sparse and perfunctory, camaraderie at a premium, and their hope for a settled future, while it still seemed to signal what everyone wanted, had never seemed so far away.

"What's the point of finding somewhere to live if it could fall over and crush you in the middle of the night?" Lucy had asked one evening as they'd made camp. No one had argued with her, not even Nathan. It had seemed like she was just saying what everyone else was thinking.

"What is it?" Nathan asked now, picking up the sense of dread in Tommy's voice.

Tommy was acutely aware and focused the majority of the time. Even when driving, he constantly scanned the bleak, open landscape ahead of them for threats and hazards. Today, they had made better progress than yesterday. The road was clear enough to see and traverse without anyone needing to walk ahead. Still not allowing them to go faster than twenty, but it felt like they were zooming around the Indianapolis Speedway compared to how things had gone the day before.

Tommy brought the truck to a slow stop to give the Land Cruiser behind them enough warning to stop, too.

"Military, by the look of it."

Nathan's breathing quickened, and he picked up the field glasses from between his legs and brought them up to meet his eyes.

Maybe a thousand yards ahead of them was a highway roadblock and checkpoint. Across both lanes, in very much a repeat of what they'd seen on the outskirts of Casper, five ultra-light DAGOR A1 all-terrain vehicles were parked nose-to-tail across the snow-covered highway. The vehicles, tubular in construction, fast and ornery, were painted in military browns. Each one was topped with a large and ugly M2 .50 caliber machine gun and manned by soldiers in full winter tactical gear. Behind the A1s, perhaps fifteen soldiers were waiting, their weapons ready.

Nathan took the glasses from his eyes. "We can't turn off now; they're bound to have seen us."

"What's the betting that they're Brant's men?"

Nathan shook his head. "I don't know. Dave and Donie say they're sending signals back to Detroit that make us look like we're traveling back east instead of south. I mean, I could be wrong… but this might be something else altogether. Well, I hope so, at least."

"What we gonna do, boss?" Free had jumped down out of the Land Cruiser and joined the F-350 on Nathan's side, and he'd wound down the window as Free had approached.

"We're gonna have to front it out. Make sure everyone back in your truck hides anything that might immediately identify us, and for God's sake make sure the cop laptop is out of sight."

Free nodded his assent and jogged back to the Cruiser.

Four soldiers and a lieutenant came out from behind the A1 roadblock to stop them as they approached. The lieutenant—a broad woman in her forties, with a lined face and a name tape that declared her as 'Toothill'—walked forward with a couple of men and waved them to the side of the road.

"Engines off, please," she said.

"How can we assist you, ma'am?" Tommy asked, winding down his window and flashing a smile that could have illuminated a dark room.

"We're stopping all vehicles along here. There's been a spate of gang-related murders and thefts in the Denver metropolitan area. We're warning people to stay off the road as much as they can, and secondly, we'd like to make sure those we do stop are not involved. Would you mind clearing the vehicle, sir, so my boys can take a look inside?"

"Of course," Tommy said, opening the door and climbing out. Nathan exited out of his door. "Lieutenant Toothill?"

"Roger."

"My boy and my baby son and our dog are in the back here. Is it okay if they stay inside out of the cold?"

Toothill peered through the glass into the crew cab. "I don't see why not."

She waved at Tony, and like the good boy he was, he waved right back.

Free and the others got out of the Cruiser as two more soldiers came forward to look inside.

Nathan's heart had begun fluttering. What would they make of the weaponry, and the provisions? What would they want to know? And would any of this information get back to Brant?

"Do any of you have any identification?"

"Not me," Tommy said, and Nathan shook his head, too.

"We lost pretty much all that stuff over the last few months. Sometimes *we* forgot who we are." Tommy was trying to make light of the situation, but Toothill seemed like a woman who didn't have much of a sense of humor. She took out a small tablet computer from her thigh pocket and fired up the software.

"Names?"

Nathan threw a look to Tommy, which Tommy caught. "Now, I don't mean to be a P.I.T.A. here, Lieutenant, and we're all for cooperation, but roadblocks, taking names, and searching vehicles doesn't seem very American to me."

Toothill stared squarely at Tommy, and a grunt behind her stiffened. "Name?"

Nathan spoke up. "Callum Grieves. But everyone calls me Cal," he added, not really sure where the name came from that he'd just pulled out of thin air, but if there was any chance of this getting back to Brant, it was better to go with a lie than with the truth.

"Sonny Monk," Tommy said as Toothill tapped at her screen.

The soldiers finished rummaging in the back of the Ford and came back to the lieutenant. "Guns, food, ammo. Usual things. Nothing that we're looking for."

Toothill noted this down on her screen, too. "Okay, Zimmerman, go help Ventura and Blake with the Toyota."

Zimmerman saluted and turned.

He only got four yards before his head blew apart in a cloud of blood, skull, and brains. A high-velocity round had taken him in the ear and nearly blown his head all the way off of his neck. The body spun and crashed against the back of the F-350.

"Sniper!" Toothill screamed as she hit the snow. "Covering fire!"

The .50 calibers on top of the A1s lit up, firing in any direction the operators thought might hide a sniper. There was a thicket of blue spruce to the side of the highway, covered in snow, which began shaking as if a giant was shouldering his way through as the bullets from the .50 caliber machine guns burst into their midst.

To the other side of the highway, there was a raised, manmade hill with an exit ramp that started throwing up detonations of earth as rounds from the A1s clattered in.

Nathan opened the crew cab door and reached in, grabbing both Tony and Brandon by the back of their coats and yanking them out of the vehicle next to Rapier. He dragged the kids down, putting their backs against the front wheel and covering them with his body. Rapier lay alert on the seat, head on his paws, ears pricked.

"Stay down, you hear. Stay down!" Nathan said to Tony.

Tony nodded with terrified eyes, and Brandon, shocked to be out in the cold and in the noise, began to wail. Toothill had crawled to the back of the F-350 to see if there was anything she could do for Zimmerman. Nathan saw her reach out and try his wrist for a pulse, but it was a fruitless task, seeing as most of his head was six feet from his shoulders. At least she was trying, he guessed.

The .50 calibers stormed to a hush, and the spruce stopped waving.

One of the soldiers at the machine gun had slumped forward, blood spurting up from his neck and pumping across his uniform. The soldiers had taken up the best defensive positions they could, but it was clear they had no idea where the shots were coming from.

"Stay down! Stay down!" Toothill yelled to her men.

Tommy had a Glock in his hand and was looking around wildly, down on one knee. Nathan could see into the Land Cruiser, but the occupants were so low in the seats that he couldn't see any of them. All that stuck out of the open door was one of Free's legs. Nathan guessed he was laying across Lucy in the passenger seat.

"Samuels!" Toothill yelled. "You take the trees with your squad. I'll take the ramp!"

The soldier who she'd called to got up and ran with seven men into the trees as the .50 calibers fired above their heads, chopping into the trees, blowing branches apart, and exploding the trunks open into thick yellow, brown-tinged cracks.

Toothill got up, drawing her own pistol, and sprinted forward, head down, to the other side of the highway, where she was joined by six soldiers. They vaulted the collision fencing and began wading through the deep snow on the other side to get to the exit ramp.

A soldier just behind Toothill went down in a spray of blood and screaming agony.

"They're getting massacred!" Tommy spat bitterly. "We need to get the hell out of here."

"If we move the trucks, we'll become prime targets."

"I'm not going to sit here and wait to have my brains introduced to the outside of my body!"

With that said, Tommy got up and dived inside the Ford.

Nathan had only moments to consider what to do—to stay outside the Ford and run to the Land Cruiser to use it as cover or get back into the truck. There was a yell as another of Toothill's squad went down, his thigh opened up as if by a can opener.

This told Nathan that the sniper was most likely either around or inside the thicket of spruce, which was on the other side of the vehicle as he knelt beside the Ford.

"Dammit, Tommy! Damn you to hell!"

Nathan picked the boys up, rolled into the crew cab, and placed his body between the boys and the sniper side of the vehicle.

"Drive, Tommy! Drive!"

Tommy didn't need second bidding and, gunning the engine, he bumped the Ford forward, hissing and crunching through the snow toward the A1s.

Nathan couldn't see where they were at once the crew cab door he'd climbed in slammed shut under the forward momentum of the truck. He put his arms across the boys and Rapier, pushing them down as hard as he dared, bracing them for the impact he knew was going to come.

Except it didn't.

"Move! Damn you, move!" Tommy began screaming at the windshield, and Nathan could hear the rustle of Tommy's Parka as he gesticulated to the remaining soldiers in their A1s.

At least one of them must have heeded his call, as the Ford ground on through the snow with its underside scraping at the surface, the tires sizzling through the crystals. The ear-shattering rat-tat-TAT of the .50 calibers still thumping on the air.

Nathan kept his head down and his eyes screwed up, expecting a high-caliber sniper round to smash through the door of the Ford and take him in the skull or the spine, ending him where he lay. Every thump or crack as the Ford slithered along the highway made Nathan wince and tense—was the sound just being created by the conditions, or was it a piece of hot, steel-jacketed death with his name on it?

I'm a mechanic from Glens Falls. I've got kids. I've got a job. I've got a wife... had a wife... who was beautiful and smart. Why am I here? What am I doing here, about to die on a road in Colorado, nearly two thousand miles and seven states away from my home, covering the most precious things in my life from a maniac with a gun?

Nathan's thoughts became a mantra. A prayer. A plea. *Please get my kids away from here. Please.*

Tommy kept the truck moving for a good five minutes, and Nathan continued to swaddle the boys with his body the whole way. Brandon snuggled into him and Tony looked up at him again, eyes fearful but grateful all at once. Nathan pulled them closer and whispered that they would all be okay. But, in honesty, he knew that could well be a lie.

A lie that he was telling them, but also telling himself.

As the Ford slew to a halt, Nathan finally got up on the seat, trying to get a view through one of the windows at the side mirror.

Thankfully, Free and those in the Land Cruiser had taken their cue from Tommy and followed through and far beyond the roadblock. The military-green Toyota pulled up alongside them. Syd, Free, and Lucy jumped out.

Tommy and Nathan joined them. Nathan's nerves were thrumming with energy, his breathing ragged in his throat below a dry mouth that was tight with anxiety. "What the hell was that about?" he asked.

"Who cares about law and order anymore?" Lucy asked, looking back down the road. "It's everyone for themselves. Who's going to stop you hunting soldiers?"

Nathan banged his gloved hand against the side of the Ford. There was little in the way of any kind of civil system left in the country as it was. And what little remained was apparently coming under attack like this? "If you're setting up something to take the best advantage of a situation, the last thing you want is what's left of the government telling you what to do. Perhaps someone was out today sending a message," Nathan said. "God, this is depressing as hell."

Tommy was pulling an MP4 from the back of the Ford and slamming a full magazine into it. "We should travel weapons-hot from now on. We can't be complacent. And today we were."

Nathan pulled an MP4 out for himself and checked the gun over. It wasn't ever his wish to be a gung ho cowboy, but sometimes the times demanded it. "Agreed. Everyone make sure you have sidearms and quick access to better firepower if we need it. We learned a valuable lesson today. Going south isn't going to make us any safer."

Only three A1s had made it away from the roadblock.

Thirty minutes later, while Nathan and the others were planning their next move, what was left of the military presence in the area scythed up through arcs of snow and came to a stop nearby. The vehicles were built for nine soldiers each, but both had a wounded tenth laying on the cargo plate over its rear axle. Both injured men were in a bad way, blood seeping from gunshot damage beneath battlefield wound packs.

Toothill herself had been winged in the top of her arm; luckily, it was just a deep scrape, but one that had made a bloody mess of her ragged uniform. As she climbed out of the A1, a medic was trying to run a bandage around the wound.

"We don't have the capacity to escort you, as we have to get these injured men to Denver stat, but I strongly recommend you follow us at your own pace. There's a FEMA camp there where you'll be safe and sheltered."

The thought that flashed across Nathan's mind just then was that hanging out with the government anywhere right now was a recipe for getting yourself shot. "Thanks for the advice, but we're heading much further south than Denver."

"Suit yourself," Toothill answered as the medic finished her bandage, "but this is not the first time we've come under sniper fire, or attack. There are people out there who don't want a return to a lawful country."

"We know. We saw it in the north. It's why we're keeping away from cities where we can. Robber barons taking over, running cities like mafia gangs and cartels. Little men thinking they're Bond villains." Nathan stopped himself from going further, remembering that he'd used an alias for a reason with Toothill, and it wouldn't do to be giving her any ancillary information that might link the party to Detroit and Brant.

She nodded, and replied, "There are people out there who have had a taste of power, and they're not going to let it go easily. What's left of the structure of the government and the military is doing what it can to help in Denver, but there's few of us, and as you can see from today, there are people out there who want there to be fewer still. Be wary, Mr. Grieves. Be very wary, indeed."

The lieutenant shook Nathan's hand, then turned to her men.

"Okay, move out!"

Toothill got back into the lead A1 and the unit *shhhhhsed* and bumped away along the highway.

When the military vehicles had finished clearing the Toyota and the Ford, Nathan could see there were thick splashes of soldiers' blood in the snow surrounding them.

14

Three days later, they stopped at what had been a picnic area among a thick plantation of spruce.

There was a view across the plain to what the cop maps told them was Carpenter Peak, one of the white-topped, dark blue thrusts of the Front Range of the Southern Rockies. In warmer, better times, it would have been an area alive with families cooking out, the squeals of happy children, and the barks of companion dogs. Now it was a desolate, empty place where the evening was closing like a lid, and there was no dry wood to be found for fires. So, they hacked branches from the spruce and let them burn with thick, piney smoke that smarted the eyes and caught in the throat until the moisture was gone.

They'd stayed away from Boulder and bypassed Denver. There had been a little traffic on the roads as they'd moved down the state, between the two cities, but they hadn't encountered any more military or, better still, snipers. The vehicles that they had come across had either sped past or turned around and gone on their way at a rate of speed commensurate with the occupants being scared that the unknown trucks bearing down on them might have been bandits or gangsters. But these cars and small trucks hadn't given the impression that the drivers were heading south like Nathan and his party. If anything, they'd signified local traffic coming in and out of Denver. Perhaps suggesting foraging or hunting trips to supplement supplies. Whatever the reason for them to be out of the suburbs of the cities, these people hadn't been interested in stopping to shoot the breeze with people they didn't know.

These grim twilit days spread a heavy, unhappy mood around the people in the two trucks, though. Only Tony, happy to have Syd back with them, seemed more settled and less on edge. They would sit in the crew cab as either Tommy or Nathan drove, reading comics, making stupid jokes, or singing ridiculous songs. Nathan liked to hear his son coming back to something like his normal self as they drove. He couldn't have asked for anything more right now, and maybe it was only the first green shoots of a recovery, but he embraced it happily.

Syd for her part was very much like she had been when Nathan had first met her on the icy road outside Glens Falls—not giving anything away, her shields up and ready to repel boarders. Nathan knew that he might have to work hard at building bridges with the girl again, and from past experience, he knew that there was no point forcing the issue. Let her enjoy her time getting to know Tony and his dog, and the deeper stuff could come later.

The fuel situation was not yet critical, but Nathan had decided they'd take any opportunity they could use to barter their guns or provisions for gas, should one present itself. South of Centennial, on the 105, they'd already bartered guns and ammo for two tents, groundsheets, and a brazier and oil lamps. They'd also passed at least three open gas stations on the way, but all had displayed signs saying 'NO FUEL – ONLY FOOD' that looked to have been officially issued. Perhaps FEMA forces in Denver were at least getting supplies out to the outlying areas around Denver. The Coloradans manning the No-Gas Stations were wary and standoffish when it came to strangers, and hadn't wanted Nathan's party to camp anywhere nearby.

Trust, understandably, was in short supply around these parts.

Apart from a few brief snow flurries, the weather had been windy but not harsh. Nights were as cold as any Nathan had experienced, and huddling up in furs with his boys was the only way to make it through the night without their chattering teeth keeping them awake. There had been no more tremors to contend with, though, and Nathan at least was sleeping better because of it.

Now, while Nathan, Tommy, and Donie set up camp near the picnic site, Free and Lucy took their rifles and went hunting. Rapier hung about the camp with Tony while Syd took a turn with Brandon.

The baby was growing, and healthier than he'd ever been. The nomadic lifestyle suited him more than any of the others, it seemed. When left to his own chaperoned devices, the eight-month-old had begun working out not only how to crawl, but would pull himself up almost to standing before dumping himself on his backside with a happy squeal. The baby clothes they had for him would soon no longer be adequate for his burgeoning frame, and Nathan reminded himself again to make it a priority to see what they could find in nearby small towns when they moved off tomorrow.

Although there were people on the road occasionally, it seemed the vast majority of the population in the area had moved into Denver. Houses had been abandoned along the route—presumably because there was no electricity coming out to them—and at least twice they'd seen evidence of places that had been overrun violently. In one roadside property, they'd discovered three bodies, shot down where they lay. Reminiscent of their travels between Glens Falls and Detroit, Nathan had been saddened to see such wanton murder victims left untouched by the side of the road.

The evidence of the near complete breakdown in social order was taking its toll on all of them, but on Lucy most of all. Where she had risen to the challenge of becoming a de facto leader of the group when Nathan had been ill, the two earthquakes, the attack by Price's men, the deaths witnessed at the wind farm, and the sniper fire at Toothill's squad had left her quiet and withdrawn.

"I don't know what to say to her," Free had confided in Nathan the night before while Lucy had sat alone in the Land Cruiser with her thoughts, her face set and her eyes a thousand miles away.

Nathan had taken Brandon to her in an attempt to get her to come out of herself, but she'd looked at him askance, and told Nathan in no uncertain terms, "Brandon is yours, Nathan. I'm not your surrogate Cyndi. You're not going to make me feel better by dumping your problems on me."

That had hurt, cutting him deep well below the heart, but he'd tabled his rage and gone back to Free as Brandon had gurgled happily in his ear.

"She was so happy at Caleb's place," Free had said, shaking his head. "We had plans and ideas. She was alive with possibilities— that's how she described it to me, man, and now, it's like all the life has been sucked out of her."

In many respects, Nathan could understand the change in her mood. All of them were feeling it now. All of them had taken hit after hit after hit, with little in the way of respite. Although Lucy had grown up hunting and shooting with her family, she had eased into a life of privilege, marrying well into more and more money. Since Nathan and the others had found her on the highway, draped in jewels in a limousine, sitting with her dead chauffeur, her transition from the good life to whatever this was had been total.

After all, reserves of strength were finite, Nathan thought, and maybe, for now, Lucy's were all dried up. "Why don't you take her out hunting tomorrow when we next make camp?" Nathan had suggested. "You know how good she is with a gun, and we've just not needed to do any hunting for a while because we've been okay for food, but maybe having something positive to do will help. Something that isn't looking after a baby—I mean, I can't imagine babies were much of a presence in her life before...." Stopping, Nathan had thought out loud, "You know... I don't think I've ever asked her, did she ever have children?"

Free had shaken his head. "She didn't. And never mentioned having them to me."

Nathan had felt a little guilty as he'd commented, "She'd probably not thank us for considering her lack of children as having any effect on her mood."

"That's bad-man-talk, right?"

"Oh yes. If Cyndi were here, she'd be whupping my hide good for it."

"To be fair, Nate, I love you like a brother, but I'd rather not hear about your sex life."

Free and Lucy came back with a young whitetail doe they'd stalked and shot in the forest beyond the picnic area. Lucy didn't look any happier, but she did come up to Nathan to apologize for the night before.

"It's okay, Lucy, I get it. This isn't a world for any of us right now."

"Thanks. I'm just… *gahd,* Nate, how long is this going to go on before we find some peace, some place to settle? If it's not Brant, it's the very earth trying to kill us. I'm tired, Nate. So tired. I'm tired of washing in cold water and I'm tired of cutting my own hair. I've lost all my jewels and gold in trade. I have nothing left of the *me* I was before. You have Tony and Brandon… what do I have?"

Nathan couldn't answer. It was true that Lucy had lost everything of her previous life. Yes, she was building something with Free, but he wasn't from her world. He was a good man, but in another world, he'd have been the man fixing her limousine, not riding in it alongside her.

Nathan had never seen Lucy look more vulnerable than she did now, either. Hair tied back severely. Hollow-cheeked, gray around the eyes. For a woman who, even in this horror show of a world, had often managed to keep her external self appearing as she would have wanted, right now she looked like she'd aged fifteen years. Nathan wanted to do nothing more than hug her where she stood.

But she beat him to it, throwing her arms around him and burying her face in his shoulder. Her tears were hot on his neck, and her shoulders shook. Over the top of her head, he could see Free watching them, his face set but calm.

Freeson had never been someone who Nathan would have called in touch with his emotions—Nathan had always been the more open of the two of them. He put that down to Cyndi's influence again, and how in almost every respect, over the years, she'd made him a better, stronger, and more approachable person, and it seemed it was that which Lucy had eventually succumbed to under the harsh yoke of their situation. Her grief and loss at the changes of her life bubbling out through her eyes as tears and mouth as deeply felt sobs.

"Hey, come on, Lucy. We got this far."

"Yes," she said, not lifting her head from his shoulder, "but how much further do we have to go, Nathan? How *far*?"

Nathan couldn't answer the question other than with platitudes or diversions, so he said nothing and held her until she stopped crying.

Free just got on with butchering the deer. Meanwhile, Tommy took Tony and Rapier off into the woods to collect water from the river they'd seen beyond the picnic area as they'd come driving down into it. They took guns, too, and Tommy said he'd continue '*Tony's education in the art of shooting.*' Nathan was fine with that. He was just an interested amateur where that was concerned, and Tommy knew way more than he did.

Nathan looked around and saw that the youngsters were sitting in the Land Cruiser, working at the laptops and keeping Brandon occupied, but Syd... Syd was *nowhere* to be seen.

When Lucy finally unhooked herself from Nathan, wiping her wet cheeks on the heels of her hands, she went back to join Free, grabbing him by the cheeks and kissing his forehead when she reached him. Nathan heard her saying, "God, I needed that cry," and he was pleased to see the ghost of a smile playing across both their faces. It wasn't just Lucy, he thought, grinning sardonically—they could probably all do with a good cry right now. So much was being pushed down inside and left unspoken.

Which brought him back to Syd.

Syd had dropped back into the group well enough after the battle and earthquake at Caleb's wind farm, almost as if she hadn't been away. Tony had been pleased to reacquaint himself with her; they'd been firm friends before, bonding over her malamute, Saber, and because they were the nearest in age in the group—although Syd, due to the circumstances in which she had found herself and the things that had happened to her, had had to do a lot more growing up in the last few months than even Tony, who himself was nothing like the boy who'd started out from Glens Falls.

Since leaving the wind farm, though, she and Tony had been pretty much inseparable when in and around the campsites they'd made.

Syd had never hooked up with Saber again, she'd told them, not once she'd lost contact with him in Detroit. She was pleased now to be forging a strong bond with Rapier, who was a slightly smaller malamute than Saber had been. However, being smaller made him faster and able to travel longer distances without getting tired. Syd and Tony could often be found playing catch and fetch with the dog around the cars and now the tents. But even before he'd gotten caught up with Free and Lucy, Nathan couldn't remember seeing Syd before Tony and the dog had eventually gone off with Tommy.

Dave and Donie shook their heads when Nathan asked where Syd had said she was going and told him that she hadn't said a thing. They'd just assumed she was going off into the trees for necessary privacy to attend to a call of nature.

Donie looked at her watch and bit her plump red lip. "But that was over an hour ago."

Syd was a hardheaded kid, with a clear sense of what she wanted and where she wanted to be, but she was also a mess of emotions when things got on top of her. Back in Detroit, when she'd found out the gang leader Danny had fetched up in the city, Nathan had eventually found her on top of the grand Masonic Temple where they'd made their home with Stryker, contemplating whether or not to throw herself off into the night. He'd talked her down and that had pushed them together with the same closeness she'd shared with Tony, but now Nathan was kicking himself. Realizing that, in his attempts to keep the bigger picture together, he'd let a few of the smaller details slip through his fingers—and Syd was one of those details.

There were three lines of tracks in the deep snow, leading away from the campsite and into the woods, and one which was from Free and Lucy returning with the deer. Tommy, Tony, and Rapier's tracks were easy to distinguish from the lone trail heading northwest through a break in the trees at a rise in the land pointing toward the razorback of the Front Range.

Telling Free he was going to see where Syd had gotten to, Nathan took an MP4 and a night-sight from the Cruiser and took up Syd's trail.

There were probably only thirty or so minutes of twilight left in the sky, and as he headed up the incline through the trees, he heard Tony laughing as Rapier barked excitedly, letting him know that they'd returned and giving Nathan the necessary focus he needed to get after Syd.

Syd was the kind of person who, if you didn't make the effort to connect with her, would disappear from your life like smoke in the wind. This was evidenced by the fact that no one except Nathan had thought it was unusual that she'd been gone more than an hour. Nathan had expressly told everyone, in these now dangerous badlands of central Colorado, where gangs were operating with near impunity, that no one should go off alone. It was the only sensible course of action to take, but Syd was not someone who always took the sensible option.

And although it was great to have her back in the fold, it was easy to forget she was just a sixteen-year-old kid who was trying to make her way in the middle of a world gone insane. Lucy had begun showing the effect it was having on her, and Nathan had sure felt some of his lowest points on the trip to and away from Casper. Syd had been through the mangler, too, and unlike the grown-ups around her, she might still not be fully emotionally set up to cope.

Nathan shook his head at the situation as he walked—not only was he having to make decisions and keep the group together, but on the side, he was both social worker and med-psych. Yet again, he thanked whatever powers of fate that had brought Cyndi and her father to Nathan's daddy's auto shop all those years ago and had smitten him on the spot. Without that input into his life, he reckoned he'd have been in the funny farm a good few months ago.

The air was cold, and his breathing still wasn't how it had been before the pneumonia, so he found it hard going to follow Syd's prints. They were wide and deep. She'd fair marched up the rise with a determined stride. She might even have been running at some points, or at least jogging. There were handprints on the trunks of some of the trees where she'd pulled herself forward, and sights of her presence in snapped branches where she'd tugged herself up out of a ditch.

A frozen streambed cracked its ice beneath Nathan's foot, but there was hardly a trickle of water beneath. His chest was hot now, and his breath left a trail of white behind him as the rise flattened out and led to an even steeper one.

The tracks continued unabated.

What had made Syd so determined to get this far away from the camp, and at such speed? Had she seen something that was too important to even tell the others about before she left? Something passing or ephemeral that, unless she got to it immediately, would be lost to the night?

Nathan couldn't guess at where she was heading. The darkness was almost nailed down over the surrounding hills at this point. He took the Armasight Nyx-7 Pro GEN Alpha Night Vision Goggles from his backpack and slid the elastic webbing across his forehead, clipping on the chin strap as he went. He turned the mechanism on, and as the world became a ghostly green, he picked up Syd's tracks again, deep black against the eerie *Herman-Munster-green* tinged snow, and carried on.

He only got another ten strides before something hard smashed into the back of his skull and sent him sprawling unconscious into the snow.

15

On the plus side, Nathan woke warm and on a soft mattress. On the downside, his hands and ankles were tied, and the back of his skull was resting on a painful bruise the size of a duck egg.

The room lay in semi-darkness, but there was enough light from a dim oil lamp in the corner to show him rough, ancient clapboard wooden walls, stained with both age and tobacco. The room smelled dry, and of a hundred years of working men coming into the space to rest before working themselves hard again.

Nathan hadn't picked up all that information from the smell, though, in all honesty. There was a brass plaque on one of the walls marking this room as one of those which had been used as a bunkroom in a modest flophouse, where gold miners and prospectors, tired from their exertions, would come after an honest day's toil.

And there was an 1850s miner standing in the corner of the room, too. Handlebar mustache, shirt off, britches held up over his naked torso with suspenders, boots thick with dust and caked mud. A pick and a gold-panning dish leaned against the wall. His sightless eyes stared through Nathan and his frozen hands were held out in front of him, draped in a towel.

He was a waxwork.

Not the best construction Nathan had ever seen, like those in the museums of the big city, but this particular miner was a creditable stab at representing a hardworking man after his back-breaking day, just aching for a hot bath and a beer.

A stove in another corner of the room, black iron pipe thrusting up through the ceiling, was putting out some much-needed warmth into the room, but looking through the grate, Nathan could see that whatever wood was inside was burning down rapidly. Someone would need to come in soon and put some fuel on the fire, or Nathan would soon start to feel the cold. There was a quartered window behind the waxwork, and through it into the blue-black night, Nathan could see the myriad flakes of a swirling blizzard. Wherever he had woken up was gripped already in the teeth of a storm.

Nathan tried to sit up and shift position, but along with the ropes around his ankles, there was a chain threaded through the cord, which was shackled tightly to the bed frame. Nathan was going nowhere.

The last thing he remembered was putting on the night vision goggles, picking up Syd's trail, and then being bushwhacked from behind. Whoever had done that had come out from the shadows or from behind a tree with such stealth and speed that Nathan had known nothing about it.

It was all very well, telling everyone to be extra vigilant. It would have been a good idea to have followed his own advice.

But of all the places he could have imagined he'd be waking up after being poleaxed, a Colorado Gold-Mining Museum would not have been high on the list of possibilities.

Nathan heard a creak outside the door and strained his hearing to see if he could pick up any voices that might give him a clue as to what had been going on, where he was, and why he'd been tied to the bed. The wooden-slatted door opened on mechanisms that sounded like a cross between a Halloween sound effect and a hinge that hadn't been used for over a hundred and fifty years.

The figure who came in was wearing a long, stained leather duster with a black Stetson on his head that had seen better days. His jaw was square, grizzled with peppery stubble, and his blue eyes darted across his face, quick and bright. There were crystals of snow layered on his shoulders and on the brim of his hat. He'd just come in from outside.

And so had the guy in the parka, standing behind him.

"Yeah, that's him," Free said, pausing to blow on his cold hands. "That's Nathan Tolley."

The soup was chunky, with fresh vegetables and generous cubes of chicken. It had been seasoned to near perfection, and Nathan ate it greedily while Free, sitting across from him at the rough-hewn wooden table, made a stab at some explanations.

"Greg Larson, the guy who came in with me, he's head guy around here. He and a couple of his men took you down in the woods."

Nathan's duck egg bruise throbbed like he was living next door to a nightclub breaking all local public nuisance ordinances. He touched the hard mass and winced. It was warm and painful. There was dried blood in his hair, too. "Couldn't they have just said hello?"

Free grinned. "Larson asked me to convey his apologies. They thought you were the sniper."

"Me?"

"Yup. Whoever's shooting up the locals around here isn't just taking out the military. He, or she—they really don't know—has been picking off their animals, as well as taking out two of their guys who they'd put in place to guard the barns. They heard you crashing about and took no chances."

Nathan shook his head at the news. These were dangerous times indeed. He turned his gaze to Syd.

"And what about you—what was all that about? Leaving the camp on your own without telling anyone? Did they take you down, too?"

"Hardly," Syd said with all seriousness. "You'd have to get up pretty early in the morning to sneak up on me. No, I saw they'd knocked you out and were dragging you over to the museum, so I went back to get Free and the others. Donie found the road leading here on the laptop and we came up."

"Where is *here*?"

"Drymouth," Free said. "Well, technically, we're a couple of miles outside Drymouth, in their old gold-mining town. Before the Big Winter, it was a tourist attraction. *'Come pan for fake gold!'*, *'Go down the mine and see how things were done during the gold rush!' 'Sweat like a miner!'* You know the kinda thing I mean."

"Yeah. I met one of the waxwork miners. He was a little stiff and not at all talkative."

Free and Syd laughed.

The room they were eating in was lit with more of the oil lamps, and there was a roaring fire in a grate. There were furs on the floor and hanging from the walls, and there were plaques all around the place, giving information on exhibits that were no longer there; the place reeked of history. As the latest storm raged outside, though, there was a warmth and a safety to the place that felt more than comforting.

Tony, Brandon, Lucy, and the others had met up with Nathan after he'd been released by Larson. The big man, taking off his Stetson to reveal close-cropped blonde hair that didn't at all match the graying stubble on his chin, had led them here to where they could rest and eat. He'd left them in the room and said he would be back later, with all the information they might need.

The kids and Rapier were already asleep on furs near the fire. Lucy had laid down with them and been asleep in moments.

Dave and Donie were on the far side of the room with their soup, discussing whatever was on their laptop, and Tommy was at the end of the table where Nathan and the others ate, keeping his own counsel.

"So, come on," Nathan said as he pointed his spoon at Syd. "Why did you leave the camp?"

Syd set a defiant angle to her chin. "Saving everyone's hide."

Nathan raised an eyebrow.

"Yes, *all* of you. Everyone was so busy bellyaching about the situation, going off to hunt, or wasting their time on their 'puters, no one was paying attention."

"Go on."

"The camp was being watched from above the ridge. I saw a figure moving through the trees. I made an executive decision."

"Oh, you did, did you?"

"Yes. I found where whoever it was had dug in and hid myself, waiting for him to return. If you hadn't come blundering after me, making all that noise, he might not have been spooked and stayed away. Larson and his boys heard you crashing about, too, and came out to get you!"

"I still don't know why you didn't come and tell me first."

"Because you move like a baby elephant, old man. If I was gonna get shot, it was gonna be because I made the mistake, not you."

Free's expression grew priceless—he obviously thought Syd was hilarious. Nathan only felt his cheeks reddening. "Okay, point taken. But you shouldn't be putting yourself in danger like that."

"Yes, I should. I might have caught the sniper, and that would have made us all a whole lot safer. As it is, you galumphing up there after me and sending him away means we've lost him. The fresh snow will have covered all his tracks."

Nathan knew there was no point arguing with Syd when she was in this kind of mood, and so he let it drop, finishing his soup and coffee instead of arguing.

He drained his mug just as Larson returned. The tall man had fresh snow on his shoulders. He untangled himself from the duster, then warmed himself by the fire before joining Nathan and the others at the table.

Tommy still hadn't said anything, and Nathan, while not concerned about it right now, at least felt it was unusual enough to remark to the Texan that he was being extra quiet.

Tommy shrugged. "Got nothing to add right now, so I'll just listen. Scourge of the age, people opening their mouths before they've thought about what they say."

And that was that.

"So, let me apologize again for the bump on the head," Larson spoke up. "I'm sure you realize that with things the way they are, we're not going to be taking any chances."

"Yes," Nathan replied with a nod, "I suppose I should be grateful you didn't shoot first and ask questions later."

"It did cross my mind, believe me. We lost two good men in the last month, just so that S.O.B. could take a couple of goats."

Larson's voice was almost accentless, and Nathan couldn't for the life of him pin down where the big man might hail from. He could be American, European or Martian—there was nothing in it to hook him into a location. "So, what's the setup here?"

Prompted by the question, Larson explained that the *Drymouth Gold Rush Museum and Heritage Center* had been a thriving tourist business before the Big Winter. When people had stopped visiting, the staff, reenactors, and curators had either followed the hoards south or made their way to the FEMA-controlled facilities in Denver.

Larson told them that he himself had been the principal of a progressive school in Boulder, and he and a few friends had taken over the museum buildings a little over eighteen months before. There were thirty souls there now, all told. Besides him, there were nine men, eight women, and twelve children under the age of eighteen. The buildings were sound, they had a couple of well-entrenched hydroponic systems in large, barnlike equipment sheds, and they kept goats and chickens in two other sheds. The main pithead building and bunkhouse contained the sleeping quarters and main living areas of the group. There was water running deep in the mine that they could bring up with hand pumps. "It has to be boiled and filtered to remove the impurities leeching from the rocks, but it's okay after processing."

Larson went on to explain that they also used one of the nearer surface mine galleries for storage. The hydroponics setup in the barn grew enough food for the human and animal inhabitants of

Drymouth, and they supplemented their produce by bartering every few weeks on trips to the city.

That had all been fine until the change in the weather, with the Big Winter on the move south, and now with the sniper threatening their precarious livelihood. The mine itself had been worked out many years ago, but it was a good, solid, dry, and warm place to shelter below that they could retreat to if conditions worsened considerably, or it would serve as an excellent safety cell if the sniper or other attackers descended on the museum.

"As you can see, we're pretty well entrenched here," Larson said as he got to the end of his thumbnail of their facilities. "You're welcome to stay if you like the look of the place. We could do with a few more strong hands."

Nathan and Free exchanged looks. Beside them, Syd shrugged, and yet again, Tommy said nothing.

The next day dawned gray with the threat of more chilling flurries.

Through the window, the sky appeared swollen and solid. The group had slept well in the furs and blankets in the room. In the morning, one of Drymouth's women—a thin, wiry, blue-eyed ash-blonde who introduced herself as Sally—showed them how they could get to the bathhouse without leaving the main building and having to go through the snow. She also told them how to access the kitchen so they could fix themselves breakfast.

They ran into a few of the residents as they moved between washing up and making toast and eggs. The residents they did meet were friendly and welcoming. They showed them where the stores were and didn't put any limits on what they could take for themselves to cook. There was some fresh goat's cheese which tasted like heaven on the toast, and it was the best-tasting meal Nathan had had in a while.

Lucy made stupendous omelets for everyone on a wood-burning range, and while they ate, the residents of Drymouth went quietly about their business, nodding hello but not hanging around to pass the day or get news of the outside world. That in itself felt strange, but kind of understandable. "I guess they don't want to seem like they're pressurizing us to stay," Nathan commented to the others at the breakfast table in the kitchen.

"And I guess not all of us are going out of our way to be friendly, either," Lucy said, flicking her eyes back in the direction of the room where they'd slept. Dave, Donie, and Tommy had all declined breakfast and gone back to the room where they'd slept.

"We've all had a few tough days. If some of us want to use the time for a bit of R&R, then I'm cool with that," Nathan said, trying to pour oil on Lucy's tetchiness. "Let's keep a cool head, yeah?"

Lucy shrugged, and Free squeezed her hand.

By now, Tony and Syd were using each other's plates as pucks in a game of table hockey and laughing and joshing, thick as thieves. A deeper contrast to Lucy's grim face, Nathan couldn't hope to see, and it gave him something warm to carry with him.

Once everyone was washed and breakfasted, Larson came to take Nathan and Free for a tour of the mine. A heavy sheet of fresh snow made the wooden clapboard, pine buildings of the Drymouth Museum buildings look like broken yellow teeth thrusting up from a bleached jawbone. Nathan, Larson, and Free made their way to look at the hydroponics setup in one of the old two-story equipment sheds.

Inside, there were plenty of electric lights run from roof-mounted turbines, and water in vats which they pumped up from the mine workings, supplemented it with snow when it fell. Two of Larson's men were pushing a mine car along a haulageway track, from the mine-head's entrance through a set of double doors leading into the shed. The mine car had been packed with snow, and as they brought it into the building, they shut the double doors behind them and began to shovel the snow into a water vat.

"Easier than pumping it up by hand. When we do get some snowfall, we like to take advantage."

"Organize finding a few wind turbines, and I'm pretty sure Free and I could set you up an electric pump. You could run that all the hours you wanted," Nathan said, noting the red faces and the harsh breathing of the men shoveling the snow.

Larson grinned and clapped Nathan on the shoulder. "That's exactly the thinking we need. Of course, our guys are smart and they're good thinkers, but everything we've set up here has come from book learning and hand-me-down ideas. What we lack here is the truly… earthy… practicalities of men like you, Nathan."

Nathan couldn't work out if he was being complimented or patronized within an inch of his life. He didn't feel he had anywhere the full measure of Larson yet—and wouldn't for a few days, he knew—but initial indications were that the Drymouth could easily absorb him and the others into their settlement. He was sure there was steel beneath Larson's bonhomie, but right now, the place didn't feel at all threatening. And that was a premium situation in these troubled times.

Larson left them to their own devices in the shed while he went to what he called a *meeting*, saying that he would catch up with them in an hour or so.

The two men who'd been shoveling the snow finished up and followed Larson out of the shed, loping off behind him like seagulls flying behind a trawler, waiting to see what scraps would be thrown over the side.

A steady stream of Drymouth residents, some with toddlers in arms, others with youngsters by the hands, were coming out of the various buildings and heading toward the mine entrance. They were chatting, smiling, and seemed in generally high spirits.

Seeing the entire population of Drymouth for the first time, it struck Nathan that none of the residents were wearing anything that could be described as modern clothes. The men were in ancient work boots, rough-cut plain shirts, and thick denim pants. The women wore long skirts with pinafores and white lace caps. If Nathan hadn't known any better, he'd have thought he was looking back in time.

Free whistled as he puffed out his cheeks. "Why can't we find anywhere that isn't weird?"

Nathan snorted. "Maybe they just had stockpiles of old mining clothes for the tourists or actors? Who knows?"

"Or maybe they're just weird."

Nathan headed for the door they'd come in. "Come on. Let's get back to the others." They struck out across the white expanse of the courtyard between the buildings, but didn't get more than twenty yards, before Nathan heard an engine fire into a deep rumble, and Lucy shouting, "Tommy! Tommy! Wait! Don't go! Stop! Stop!"

16

As they reached the area where the Land Cruiser and the F-350 had been parked overnight, they saw Lucy standing with her hands on her hips and watching the Toyota, now unhooked from its trailer, bumping through the snow back toward the road.

"Tommy!" Lucy called fruitlessly one more time, just as Nathan and Free reached her.

"What's going on?" Nathan asked.

"Damn Tommy and his strong silent type act!" Lucy hissed as the back of the Toyota disappeared from view into the trees.

"You want me to go after him?" Free asked, pointing at the Ford.

Nathan shook his head. "Let's find out what's going on first. When Tommy's got the bit between his teeth, there's nothing that's gonna make him come back until he's ready. Come on—let's get inside."

Back in the room where they'd spent the night, Lucy was still apoplectic. She paced and thumped the table, and if she could have worked off her tension by stamping her feet and having a tantrum, Nathan felt convinced she would have.

"He's so stubborn! Doesn't want to listen to reason or offer up his own solutions. It's just his way or the damn highway!"

"So, what went down?" Nathan sat down with a coffee that Donie put into his hand as they'd come back inside.

Lucy's eyes flicked to the door, as if to make sure no one from Drymouth was loitering or about to come in. "All I said was that this looked, like Caleb's place before, like a good place to think about staying for a while."

"And?"

"And Tommy just shook his head in that sarcastic way of his. Rolled his eyes at me and said I was, as usual, bringing up my ideas from where the sun won't have warmed them."

Nathan sighed. He'd thought that the rivalry between Tommy and Lucy had at least settled down now that he was well enough to be back leading the group. But alas, that seemed not to be the case.

"So, where has Tommy gone? Just to cool off?"

"He wouldn't tell me. Just stormed out like a child, unhooked the trailer, and drove off before I could stop him. My clothes are in the back of that truck! If he doesn't come back, I'm going to have to dress like the women here, like an extra from *The Handmaid's Tale*!"

Lucy didn't calm down for some time, and so Nathan spoke with Free, Dave, and Donie while she sat boiling in the corner.

"What do we make of this place, then?"

Dave and Donie were noncommittal, but did tell Nathan about what Tommy had asked them to do before he'd had the run-in with Lucy. Donie pointed at the laptop. "First thing this morning, while you guys were off in the bathhouse, Tommy asked us to set up the uplink and see if we could get any information on Greg Larson."

"Did he say why?"

"Nope, and we couldn't get a signal anyway. The clouds must have brought a lot of dust in with the storm. It'll settle down in a day or so, but until then we're internet blind."

Why would Tommy be so anxious to find out about Larson? Was he just applying the principles of due diligence? Tommy hadn't shown that much interest in Dave and Donie's technical expertise in the past, so why now? And why hadn't he come to Nathan with his concerns?

Syd came back in with Rapier, who she'd taken outside for exercise, and to have a look around the mine workings herself.

"Did Tommy mention anything to you last night or this morning?" Nathan asked her as she got herself a coffee and fed some breakfast scraps to the dog. Syd shook her head. "He's probably only said seven words to me since I got back with you guys. I get the impression he's not too comfortable around the fairer sex."

"Ain't that the goddamn truth!" Lucy said from the corner.

Nathan didn't want to wait for Larson to come find him, so he left the others to find him—with instructions to Donie to keep trying the uplink to find out if they could get the information Tommy was after—Nathan heading to the mine entrance himself.

The old mine had been given a touristy makeover, more signs, a barrier, a kiosk for a staff member to take tickets from, and mine cars which looked more like roller-coaster carriages than authentic nineteenth century mining gear.

Three of the cars were backed up in a small siding inside the entrance. The roof had been shored up with the thick trunks of trees, but when Nathan rapped one with his knuckles, he was greeted with the hollow ring of metal. All fake. There was also a line of dim electric lamps leading down along a tracked slope. The illuminations had been made to look like old-time Davy Lamps, and he figured they were being fed by power lines from turbines standing somewhere up on the hillside.

A man Nathan didn't recognize stepped out from the shadows further down the incline. He was dressed like the rest of the men of Drymouth, and had a grizzly gray beard which reached to his sternum. Nathan might not have known him, but he knew Nathan. "Can I help you, Mr. Tolley?"

There was no overt threat in Beard's voice, but Nathan immediately felt uneasy. Beard had taken up a position in the middle of the track that was obviously defensive, and it was one that would not allow Nathan to pass with just a "Hi" or a "Cold morning today, isn't it?"

Beard looked as if he was fixing to make sure no one went down the mine, and if they tried, he was going to stop them.

"I'd like to speak to Mr. Larson, please."

"I'm afraid that's not possible. He's in a meeting." Beard crossed his arms across his chest as if it would end the conversation and Nathan would just turn around and go away.

"Yeah, I know. But this is important."

"So is the meeting. I ask that you go back to your room and await Greg. I'm sure he'll be with you before dark."

"I really want to speak to him before then. If you could…"

"But I'm not going to." Beard dropped his arms and widened his stance.

"Hey, there's no need for you to get bent out of shape."

"Then don't give me a reason to bend you out of shape, Mr. Tolley."

And that was that.

Whatever Tommy thought he knew about Larson, Nathan wasn't going to get the opportunity to quiz him about it until whatever the *meeting* was about was done.

Nathan trudged back through the snow, through the near dead silence coming off the hills, acoustics heavily truncated by the snow. The sky was still fully pregnant and looked about to burst open at any moment. It didn't help assuage the pit of damp anxiety which was building in his gut. With Tommy taking the Land Cruiser and leaving the trailer behind, they were all effectively trapped here until he came back. There was no way they could get away from Drymouth with everyone and their gear.

Damn Tommy and his moods.

Nathan approached the main building where the F-350 was parked, one side half-buried in the snow that had come during the night. There looked to be something odd about it, though.

The snowdrift should by rights have extended all around the back of the truck, but the back end of it was mostly clear, back where the two metal doors opened above the tailgate into the steel utility box they used to transport gear and themselves when the need arose.

Nathan saw there were many footprints in the snow, too, as if a couple of guys had been at the back of the truck clearing away the snow from the doors. As he got closer, he saw one of the locks on the door had been busted open. Someone had been going through their gear, and hadn't cared at all who knew it.

Nathan reached the back of the truck and pulled at the door. It swung open easily, and he looked inside. It seemed like all of the food, camping equipment, and personal effects—like Tony's box of comics—were still there, but the guns were gone. Where once there had been two canvas bags of military hardware and ammo, there was nothing.

Nathan smashed his hand on the door, slamming it shut, and turned around and went back the way he'd just come. He didn't wait till he reached Beard before he called out and got the man's attention.

"This is not acceptable! Someone has been through our gear—without permission—and taken our weapons."

Beard was back in the center of the tunnel. "Be reasonable, Mr. Tolley. If we'd have asked your permission, would you have given up the guns? I really don't think so."

Nathan couldn't fault Beard's logic, but that didn't stop him wanting to thump the smug man of questionable parentage in the face with a balled fist. "You will go down there now, and you will get Larson, and you will bring him here."

"Not possible."

"Then you will take me to him."

"Again…"

And that's when Nathan threw the punch.

Beard was a big man who didn't move fast, but he at least had the wherewithal to move back as the punch connected with his chin, thus taking more than fifty percent of its potential sting away at once.

Nathan followed through with a harsh left, which caught Beard just below the ribs and sent him down on one knee, *'Oooofing'* as he was winded.

"I don't need my guns all the time, pal."

Nathan punched Beard hard in the side of the head and the man went over like a felled log. It had been a long time since Nathan had had a full-on fist fight—probably not since the one with Sonny Shapp in grade school when the other boy had said something he couldn't remember about Nathan's daddy. He'd sent the boy sprawling back over a chair in the classroom to the cheers of the class, who hated Sonny Shapp, and to the immense annoyance of the teacher, who'd pretty much dragged him by the ear to the principal's office. It hadn't been his finest moment at school, and punching Beard's lights out wasn't his best moment in the Big Winter, but it sure was satisfying.

Nathan made sure Beard was in the recovery position on the floor before he began to jog down the tunnel.

There wasn't much of the original excavation left from the nineteenth century. The tunnel down to the galleries had been widened at some point, and the walls reinforced. The walls themselves looked old and cracked and dangerous, but Nathan could see this was just window dressing that had been created to give the impression of an old, rackety mine's workings. Just the fact that he could stand up to his full height and still have some clearance above his head told him that a fair amount of money had been spent on the place to get it up to tourist specs.

The incline steepened about a hundred yards into the interior and was now obviously following the old route into the place. There were sections where wooden stairs had been constructed to make the going easier, and all along the incline were guardrails on both sides for people to hold on to. He passed a couple more waxwork miners in their perpetual tableaux of frozen work. Faces ruddy with sweat and streaked with dirt, picks in hands, eyes red-rimmed and vacant. They loomed up out of the dark as he descended like shipwrecked sailors whose bloated bodies were coming up from the depths.

After moving another hundred and fifty yards down into the hillside, Nathan came to a T-Junction which led both left and right into worked-out galleries. To the left, the tunnel was crammed with equipment boxes, crates, and catering pallets of tins and dry goods. The Drymouth community was well-stocked—no wonder they hadn't been concerned about how many provisions Nathan and the others took for breakfast. There were precious few lights along the walls into the storage gallery, but from what Nathan could see, apart from a narrow gangway, there wasn't an obvious route to a place where thirty or so people could hold a meeting, so he took the other spur.

Again, this gallery had been widened to allow tourists to go down into the depths of the mine to experience the claustrophobic atmosphere of the working conditions, but the ceiling here was much lower, and Nathan had to bend awkwardly to keep his head from scraping the roof.

The lights were less frequent, and Nathan found himself having to squint to see as far down the tunnel as he could. The air was becoming thick and warm also, which came as a stark contrast to the world of the Big Winter, but here it was cloying and uncomfortable for his still recovering lungs. As he moved, having to bend lower, it became easier for him to make forward progress on his hands and knees. But the gallery was curving off to the left up ahead, and Nathan could no longer see where he was heading.

Then, the lights in the tunnel flickered and went out.

Nathan prepared himself for full darkness, but the tunnel wasn't pitch black. Up ahead, around the corner, there was a dim, greenish glow. It pulsated and warped, throwing crazy shadows over the walls. It seemed other-worldly, completely unnatural, as if there was a silver edge to the glow which cut through its thin fingers of light.

Nathan could just about see his hands on the floor of the tunnel, but that was about it. The rest of the gallery shifted between deep shadows and dim illumination as he knelt there.

Should he go on?

Or should he go back to the others and wait for Larson to come and harangue him for punching out Beard?

The knot of anxiety in his gut pulsed with the light. He couldn't imagine what kind of meeting was being held that needed to be lit in this way, but it sure didn't feel right. Of all the things he'd seen since they'd left Glens Falls, this hands-down ranked as the weirdest, and it wasn't getting any more explainable with his staying here.

Back? Or go on?

He'd come this far, so maybe if he just got to the curve in the tunnel and looked around it, he might get a better idea of what was going on. Pushing the growing sense of unknowable fear back down into his stomach, Nathan crawled on.

The tunnel kept curving, and it was a good fifty yards more before he could see further than the vertical horizon of the wall. The green glow was, if anything, pulsing faster now, with the regularity of a tension headache. The enveloping darkness around it made it all the more intense, too—thumbing his eyes with its sickly shades.

The tunnel now led another thirty yards, and beyond that, it opened out into a wide, black space that pulsed with the green glow. Nathan could only guess how big the chamber beyond the tunnel was; it wasn't vast, but he estimated it might be perhaps twenty yards across to a far wall that was moving, like the tunnel he was in, between green tinged shadow and full darkness.

Then there was a sound. Not voices exactly, but a murmuring that was redolent of low voices chanting something barely above a whisper. If the voices were saying anything, then there weren't any words in there that he could pick out—he just heard a constant tone that seemed to be in concert with the lights.

The floor of the chamber must fall away sharply, though, because Nathan had no chance of seeing what was going on beyond the tunnel's mouth. He couldn't even see heads moving about. All there was for him to see was the chamber, and the pulsing lights, and all he could hear, apart from his own ragged breathing on the syrupy air, was the tone—the human generated tone—emanating from the chamber itself.

Nathan gnawed at his knuckle as he looked forward and then searched back the way he had come.

The dark, the green pulse, and the noise seemed to come together in a perfect concoction to induce and amplify a heavy sensation of dread. As if it had been created specifically to make anyone in the vicinity fearful and on edge. Like the deep rumbling bass frequencies Black Metal bands had once used to heighten emotion and engagement in their audiences, or the way horror film music had given one all the cues needed to generate the correct emotions before the shocking revelation of the monster... the atmosphere in the tunnel seemed deliberately created to make anyone nearby reach the verge of panicking and running.

Nathan began to edge backward, suddenly realizing that he was way out of his depth now, and there was no point in going on to see what Larson and his people were up to. Them making sounds and lights like this didn't make you want to stick around because, pretty soon, someone would be welcoming you into their circle with beer and cake.

He crawled back three more yards, and there he began to turn.

And then he heard the child crying.

From deep in the chamber, it was a hollow sobbing, with a keening wail rising up after that, floating down the tunnel like an accusation.

Don't leave me. Don't leave me.

Or, that was what it seemed to be saying.

Please. Please help me.

Nathan knew it was his mind creating the words, but the implication was clear. There was a terrified, unhappy child down there, and Nathan was about to leave it to its fate.

The harsh memory of Nathan almost leaving Syd to be taken across the ice by Danny in Detroit hacked up into his mind. He'd made the calculation back then that it was better for his family if he let Syd go and kept himself alive. It was a decision that he'd regretted harshly ever since that day, and now he was being placed in the same situation again.

Could he leave a child in fear, or should he do something about it?

The crushing weight of the decision pressed down on him, but in the end, it became not a hard decision at all—because now in the green light, with the accompanying tone of dread filling the space, the child's sobbing was given voice.

"Stay… stay… away from me!"

The crying child was Tony.

17

It took Nathan a few moments to make sense of what he was seeing, and even then, it wasn't something that could be easily taken in or processed.

There was a huge, silver flying saucer in the cavern.

It was fully twenty yards across, and the machine was bristling with antennae and chunky-looking tech. It was supported on four thick hydraulic legs, and there was a loading ramp that had been lowered from the belly to rest at an angle of forty-five degrees.

As Nathan watched, white smoke began to belch from vents at the back of the craft, and the greenish-silver glow filling the chamber and lighting up the eyes of the residents of the Drymouth settlement came from a pulsing ball, maybe three feet across, in the center of the craft's top side.

The twenty adults in the room were knelt down on prayer mats and were facing the saucer. In between them and the craft were the children.

Each one had been strapped into a chair facing the saucer. Their arms were behind their backs, and their legs had been taped to the legs of the chairs. Those too young and small to be sat on the chairs were in two pens just beyond the chairs. In the second pen, Nathan could clearly see Brandon, still swaddled in his blanket, and at the end of the row of chairs, tied in like the others, there was Tony.

The other children in the row were sitting quietly, mouths tightly shut of their own accord, unperturbed by the situation they were in—as if they were used to it and had experienced it many times before.

Tony was struggling in his seat, though, trying to free his arms, and he'd managed to push out whatever they had put into his mouth to silence him.

"Leave… me alone!" Tony was coughing now, and perhaps about to have another asthmatic episode. It would be the first for months if it came, and these freaks were doing this to Nathan's son, putting his life in danger by stuffing whatever that was into his mouth and giving him cause for panic.

Nathan wanted to get up and run into the chamber and gather up his children and get the hell out of there, but the presence of an MP4 and an AK-47 hanging from the shoulders of two of the men checked him.

Now, one of the women had gotten off her knees and begun attempting to put the gag back in Tony's mouth.

"No! Please!" A hacking cough burst out of his mouth as he tried to catch his breath. "I have... asthma... please! I'll stop shouting. Please! I promise!"

The woman dropped the gag, which looked like it was made from cotton wool, and then placed a pair of earphones over Tony's ears, and a close-fitting pair of dark glasses over his eyes. "No more trouble from you, you hear? No more trouble."

In the chair, Tony nodded, and Nathan felt as if his heart was boiling in seething lava.

The rest of the children were already in their headphones and dark glasses, their faces turned toward the saucer ramp. Nathan scanned them again, just in case he'd missed Syd. She was certainly young enough in actual years to be included in this mad setup, but the way she carried herself and projected her hard-won maturity might have kept her from being included in this abomination. Nathan hoped that was the case. Not that her resisting Larson had caused injury... or worse.

The clunk of feet on metal took Nathan's eyes from Tony's predicament in the chair, over Brandon in the pen with the other toddlers and babies, to the sound clanging from the saucer.

Larson's feet emerged first from inside the craft, but he was no longer dressed like the others. The material of his pants was silvery-white. His boots were white and clunky, like heavy ski boots that had been modified with metal plates in the soles. His hands were in thick white gloves, and his top half's clothing was made from the same material as his pants. There was a huge, unwieldy, space-type helmet under his arm, and as he came down the ramp, Larson pulled earbuds from the side of his head and wiped a sheen of sweat from his forehead with a gloved hand.

He stopped at the bottom of the ramp and surveyed the scene in front of him, raising a hand in greeting. "I have returned from Calisto One."

There was a ripple of spontaneous applause from the gathered congregation. "I have spent nearly a week's Earth-time with the Calistans, making preparations for our Transubstantiation. The Calistans are very pleased with our progress here. They have commended you all for your work and your resolve in re-educating the children."

Larson swept his free hand down the line of kids, ending with his finger pointing at Tony in the chair.

"And the Calistans particularity welcome the new blood to the mission. Tony, I see, will need a strong level of instruction to get inculcated into the program, but Brandon is young enough for us to take him at this delicate time, and shape all his thoughts to the correct alignment. We have done well, my people!"

The craziness of the situation began washing through Nathan with a tide of chilling energy. He couldn't understand why the Drymouth residents were believing the pure BS that was spilling out of Larson's mouth. But then, how had all the crazy, charismatic leaders of the past persuaded people to follow them? Koresh in Waco. Jones in Guyana. Manson in California. There were always people with the ability to turn minds to their fell purposes, however out of whack those ideas were.

Add Greg Larson to that list.

Whatever had led these people down here to believe Larson was in contact with alien beings inside what was half filmset-prop and half adult playhouse, Nathan just couldn't figure out. He just wasn't wired that way. But couple the Big Winter with a sense of desperation, and a need to follow someone who they believed could rescue them from the apocalypse, and there would always be people who would follow.

Many people were sad, desperate, and lonely—with holes in their lives that can only be filled, they would say, by outside influences. All you needed was the right words, the right environment, and the right props. Whether it was a cult religion or a cult alien overlord, there were people who would not question, and once you had them hooked…

All that was very well, Nathan thought, as he looked down on the insane scene before him, but understanding it was one thing, and getting his children away from it, and out of the mine without weapons, backup, or a plan was quite another.

Nathan tried to think through the situation logically. Tony, now that they weren't trying to gag him, was in no immediate danger from the situation. Brandon seemed fine in the pen, and whatever was being piped into Tony's ears wasn't causing him any distress yet.

Nathan thought back to how he'd watched the Drymouth residents going down into the mine earlier. The children had all been with them, so there was a good chance, when the *meeting* was over, that they would all be brought back up again. Larson must have known that Nathan would be murderously angry about having his children taken like this, and that was probably why the group had taken away their weapons that morning.

If Nathan was going to have any success in effecting a rescue, it made more sense to wait—however much that hurt, to leave his children in the clutches of Larson and the others—until they made their way to the surface.

Nathan screwed his fear and dread down, and began to crawl back up the tunnel, keeping his eyes toward Tony and Brandon until they were completely out of sight. The green glow in the tunnel lit his way to where the tunnel began to curve.

He took one more look down behind him, and then he struck out toward the T-Junction.

And that's when Beard kicked him in the face.

The big man had been coming the other way and had turned the corner just as Nathan had taken one last look back the way he had come.

Beard's heavy work boot connected with the side of Nathan's head and sent him sprawling onto his back, with a stinging pain in the side of his head to match the bruise on the back of his head, and a painful ringing his ears. Beard was on him before Nathan had time to focus his eyes. Burly hands encircled Nathan's neck, and the gray beard, stinking of old food and tobacco, washed its unpleasant stench into his nostrils.

The man was taller and heavier than Nathan. He had the element of surprise, and had already disorientated Nathan with the kick to the side of the head, but there were two things he didn't have.

What Beard lacked was two children in the hands of a chamber full of crazies, and the desperation of a father determined to get them back by whatever means necessary.

Nathan could feel Beard's thumbs crushing his windpipe, but that didn't deter him. He thrust up with his knee—twice—into the soft, yielding space between Beard's legs. The big man gave a gasp, and the hands at Nathan's throat relaxed momentarily. It was all Nathan needed to grab Beard's wrists and twist his fingers away from his neck, and then pull Beard forward. Nathan smashed up with his forehead, crashing into Beard's nose and popping the bone and cartilage there in one hit. Then Nathan turned Beard's wrists over, and as his feet scrabbled for purchase, he flipped the man over and wedged him against the wall, kicking out with his knees, this time into Beard's stomach.

Beard opened his mouth to call for help, but Nathan was way ahead of him. Nathan struck sideways with his elbow and cracked Beard in the side of his jaw.

Such was the desperate force Nathan had used that he felt and heard the bone fracture against the onslaught. Beard raised his hands to his mouth, forgetting Nathan in the moment of injury, and received another vicious, bone-cracking blow to his cheekbone.

Nathan rolled up onto his knees. There was no way he was going to give Beard another chance to raise the alarm. He punched Beard hard, full in the face on his already broken nose as the man's head snapped back. Then he grabbed two handfuls of wiry whiskers and struck the back of the man's head on the floor as hard as he could.

Again.

Three times.

On the fourth, he felt something give in Beard's body, as if a bowstring that had been stretched taut had suddenly been cut loose. Beard's body was limp now, and lifeless. The eyes rolled back into his sockets, blood seeping from his nose, and his chest had stopped moving.

Nathan sat back, his hands shaking.

Gathering himself, he felt for a pulse in Beard's neck. He couldn't find one. The man was dead. Skull smashed in, the life leaving him like an ejected pilot from a crashing airplane.

Nathan knew he couldn't leave the body here to raise the alarm, and so, pushing from his mind the disgust and regret that he'd ended up killing someone with his bare hands, Nathan stood up. Now in a part of the tunnel that gave him good clearance, he stooped and lifted Beard, knowing he had to focus on saving his sons, and he put the man's lifeless body over his shoulder. Because the dead body had no muscle tension, it quickly became slithery and awkward. As Nathan moved back up through the tunnel, breathing hard, focused only on getting out, he had to stop several times to reposition the body and carry on moving.

The light from outside the tunnel was streaming down from the entrance now, and it renewed Nathan's hope that he would make it out of the mine before Larson and his crazy followers came out after him.

The air got colder, cutting into Nathan's chest, but it felt good to be on the way out of the soupy atmosphere.

With his breath torn and catching, his legs under the weight of the body feeling like molten lead, and his head swimming with a mixture of remorse and elation at reaching the entrance, Nathan made it through the opening of the mine to dump the body in the deep snow, laying up against the access point. Nathan didn't have time to think, though. He fell to his knees and began shoveling snow over Beard's broken body. When Larson and the others came out of the mine, it would be better if they thought that Beard had been called away on some errand, rather than been killed and dumped.

Before Nathan covered Beard's still showing pupils with snow, he gently closed the man's eyelids. The contrast between the way Nathan had killed him and the way he touched the still warm eyes could not have been greater, and Nathan felt that gap acutely. Briefly, Nathan bowed his head, said something like a prayer to something he didn't know if he believed in, and then got up.

"Well, it was kind of you to bury Bobby in the snow, but I think we'd rather he was laid to rest in our graveyard," Larson said in Nathan's ear. "So, if you don't mind, dig him out again."

"It's a tourist attraction. Did you really not think there would be an emergency exit?"

Nathan and the others were tied to chairs in the family room. Rapier was tied by a chain through his collar to a leg of the stove. Tony and Brandon hadn't been returned from the mine, and Larson was there pacing. He was out of his spaceman gear, and back to being dressed like all the others. His face was ruddy, but his manner was calm.

"Where are my sons?"

"That's for me to know and you to find out, Nathan. And right now, I don't know if I'm minded to let you find out. I'm very unhappy that you killed Bobby. Bobby was a good man."

Nathan strained at the bonds holding his wrists. Free and the others had been tied up for some time, it seemed. They'd already been in position when Larson and the others who'd been waiting for him outside the entrance to the mine had escorted Nathan back to them—after he'd dug Bobby out of the snow.

Free had been bleeding from the nose from a blow, and Lucy had a swelling eye. Dave's metal-covered arm had been twisted behind his back and tied in place, and the sweat on his face and his bulging eyes told Nathan that he was in considerable pain. Tied up beside him, Syd held onto Rapier's chain as she and Donie stared at Larson with pure hate in their eyes.

"I'm sorry, Nate," Free said, looking up through teary eyes. "I tried to stop them, but they had guns and threatened to shoot Tony. If Tommy had been here…"

Nathan shook his head. "It's okay, Free, I've seen them. They're okay, I think. Larson needs them for the weird crazy stuff that's going on down in the mine."

Larson, who was standing between his two men from the mine with their MP4 and the AK-47, stepped forward and belted Nathan in the chops. The blow hurt like hell, turning Nathan's head almost a hundred-eighty degrees. Nathan bent forward and spat blood on the floor.

"You cannot ever understand what I'm building here, you dolt! You're the crazy ones. Living your life like it doesn't matter. Not caring about the higher powers and forces at play in the galaxy! You are fleas on the back of my world."

Lucy looked up at Larson. "If I were you, I'd get back on your antipsychotics, my friend. I think you're having an episode."

Larson struck Lucy, too, and Free yelled and screamed, trying to break his bonds and get at the Drymouth leader. "You touch her again and I'll…"

"What? Give me a hard stare? Look at me askance? Oh, you people are such inferior stock. No imagination. Nothing to help you progress. Just stuck in the *morass of ordinary*. Like so many people before you."

Nathan swallowed the blood in his mouth and looked hard at Larson. "I just want my boys, and we'll get on our way. It was a mistake coming up here, and I'm sorry about Bobby, but it was self-defense. He was trying to strangle me."

Larson smiled thinly, his eyes slivers of steel. "Well, if that was his final wish, perhaps one of us should finish the job."

MP4 and AK-47 thought this was very amusing.

Nathan shook his head. "All we're trying to do, like you, is survive."

Larson turned on his heel. "Okay, Nathan, I'm not without mercy. Let's call it quits, shall we? You and your fellows can be released now and go on your merry way. How does that sound?"

"Like there's a catch."

"Not a catch, as such, but a payment for the time you've spent here, the resources you've taken, and the death of my good friend, Bobby. I think you owe us for that, don't you?"

Nathan knew what was coming and was determined not to play along. "Just spit it out, Larson. I know what you want as payment. You want my kids."

"Not yours anymore, but potential Calistans. Now, doesn't that sound a much more inviting prospect than them eking out a desperate existence in the snows of Dead America? Once they have been educated, and are ready to be transubstantiated to Calisto One, they will have a life that you could never offer them. One a simple man like you could never conceive of. Let your sons come to me, Nathan Tolley. I'll be a better father to them than you could ever be."

Nathan pulled at the bonds on his wrists, but they were far too tight, cutting into his skin and cutting off the circulation to his fingers.

Oh, Tommy, Tommy. If there was a moment now when you could fall through the ceiling and shoot these SOBs dead, and rescue us, now is the moment to do it. Now, Tommy. Please let it be that you left here to make a plan, to find out a way to defeat Larson and his fools.

Tommy. Please. I need you now. My children need you now.

As if on cue, there came an enormous thumping at the door. It startled Larson enough to make him step back, and it made MP4 and AK-47 flinch involuntarily.

Nathan's heart swelled.

Tommy, here to help them stop this madness?

And yes, in a way, it *was* Tommy.

The door opened and the Texan was pushed bodily into the room, hands tied behind his back.

There was also the handle of a knife, sticking out between his shoulder blades and surrounded by a spreading pool of blood.

18

Tommy remained facedown on the floor, a froth of blood working its way out of his mouth in a stream of bubbles. The breath behind it was labored, cracking and clicking like popcorn cooling in a pan. The man's fingers twitched and curled in his bonds behind his back, and the side of Tommy's face that Nathan could see was scrunched up with pain. The Texan was in a world of agony, and the depth and angle of the knife told Nathan that if Tommy didn't get any medical attention soon, then he wouldn't be long for this world. Rapier whined and whimpered, eyes filled with concern for the injured human.

The two men who'd come in behind him were Drymouth residents, dressed alike. One held a rifle, the other a Glock.

"We found him up on the ridge with binoculars. There was a fight. He came off worse," Glock said, pointing at the knife in Tommy's back.

"For God's sake, get him to a doctor!" Nathan roared. "He's going to die if you leave him like that!"

"Nearest doctor is in Denver, thirty miles away at the FEMA hospital. It's just starting to snow, and anyways, I'd quite like to watch him die," Larson said, his voice shot through with all the calm of a scientist about to dissect a live rat. "What do you say? I'll light the fire and we can have marshmallows."

Larson toed Tommy with his boot, and the Texan groaned through blood-painted lips. The eye Nathan could see was unfocused and moving rapidly in the socket.

"Please, Larson. There's no need for this…"

"What is it your bible says? An eye for an eye, a tooth for a tooth? My bible says a Tommy for a Bobby. Fair exchange is no robbery, as they say." Larson pulled up a chair and put it down inches from Tommy's head. He sat on it while his men kept their weapons at the ready, even though everyone else in the room was tied up.

"Now isn't this cozy?" Larson asked, staring down with fascination at Tommy's face—slathered in blood, eye flickering, chest rising and falling but never seemingly able to take a full breath.

"Not as quick and intense as Bobby's death, I'm sure you'll agree, Nathan. A stabbing is so much cleaner in some ways than just beating someone's brains out against the concrete. I'm sure Bobby didn't know a lot about it once you'd started. Tommy, on the other hand… I get the impression that he's aware of everything that's going on around him now. I'd bet all his senses are heightened. All his faculties acutely attuned to his surroundings. He may not be able to communicate to us right now, perhaps because of shock or blood loss, or maybe just because his throat is full of fluid draining from his lungs."

Larson's words were unbearable in Nathan's ears. Coupled with watching Tommy near enough to dying in front of him, a wave of nausea and panic had begun barreling through him. There was no other hope of rescue now that Tommy was out of action. No other people in the party to come through and at least cause a distraction. For the first time since Cyndi had died, Nathan felt the last of his dwindling store of optimism drain and dissipate, like the bubbles of blood frothing out of Tommy's lips.

"Okay, okay. Whatever you want, but please don't let him die there in front of us. Please. Get him to a doctor. It wasn't Tommy who killed Bobby, it was me. Let the others go. I'll stay here with you. Do what you want with me. Just let me see my kids—after that, I don't care. Just… please… let Lucy and Free help Tommy. Let them take him back to Denver. If there's just one shred of human decency in you, Larson, do this. Do this, *please*."

Larson smiled. The expression on his face said his victory was complete.

Nathan knew he was broken. He knew there was no fight left in him. All that he wanted to do, whatever happened to his body, was to ensure his boys lived. If that had to be as part of Larson's cult, then so be it. At least they would be alive. It would have to be enough.

There was a tinkle of glass off to Nathan's right.

AK-47 sighed like a man seeing the woman he loved, and the side of his head blew out before he crashed to the ground, dropping the gun.

Glock was taken in the chest by another round tinkling through the window. He pitched forward, crashing into Larson, who was trying to get out of his way but wasn't quick enough. They crashed to the floor together, arms and legs entwined, a long streak of red like a daub from the brush of a careless painter covering Larson's face with its thick stroke.

Rifle and MP4 leaped to the wall to either side of the window and made their guns ready to return fire, but they may as well have stayed where they'd stood to begin with, for all the good it did them.

The wooden clapboard walls behind them split apart in two places, half a second apart. First MP4 and then Rifle went down, spewing blood in gouts and brains in a gray slurry across the floor, slivers of fresh white bone in the mess.

Larson was propelling himself across the room, trying to get to the door and ducking down so that he couldn't be seen through the window.

"Oh my good *gahd*!" Lucy shouted as another hole burst open in the wall, spitting splinters at her shoulders. The high-velocity round which caused it, Nathan swore, lifted strands of Lucy's hair in the rush of a generated breeze as it passed over her head.

Larson spun like a dancer trying too hard to impress an audience, his arms thrown out. The top of his head was stove in by the force of the round and, before he hit the floor, another burrowed into the top of his arm, exited through his shoulder, and slammed into his temple.

Larson lay back like a man settling gently into bed, his lips trembling on his last breath and his eyes locked on Nathan.

The room was quiet. Even Rapier had stopped whining.

The carnage had lasted all of nine seconds.

All Nathan could hear was Tommy's labored breathing and the sound of footsteps running outside the window, crunching through the snow at breakneck speed, heading for the building.

"Can anyone get free?" Nathan asked the room while pulling at his own bonds. He had no idea who was approaching the building. Was it the sniper, or one of the Drymouth residents with a gun, ready to take revenge on them for getting their leader killed?

He just didn't know.

The general consensus in the room was that everyone had been tied far too tightly for them to make any headway freeing themselves. Whoever was coming, their feet now clumping up the steps to the raised verandah outside the main building, would be able to walk into the room, if they so desired, and shoot them all in the head with ease.

Nathan and the others watched the door as they heard footsteps coming down the corridor outside. The boots were heavy, making the same sound that a Drymouth resident might make if they were approaching.

"Let me do the talking," Nathan said. The words had sounded right in his mouth, but he suddenly realized he had no idea what to say.

The footsteps stopped outside the door and, with a crash, it was kicked open. A figure in arctic camouflage came in, face covered with a black balaclava and hands snug in tight-fitting gloves. The figure—Nathan couldn't tell if it was a man or a woman—came in and went to each of the dead men, rolling them over to check that they were all confirmed kills.

There was a long rifle on the figure's back, with an attendant, chunky rubber telescopic site. Nathan didn't know the make or model of the rifle, but it looked modern and deadly. Arctic had a pistol on both sides of their utility belt, and a long bowie knife in a holster on their thigh.

"Who are you? What's going on?" Nathan asked, suddenly finding his voice.

No answer. The figure moved from body to body, silently.

"Did you kill Larson and the others?"

Arctic got up from where they'd been kneeling next to Larson and pressed his or her index finger to where their lips had to be hiding behind the balaclava. The message was clear.

Be quiet.

Arctic took out the bowie and went around the room, cutting the bonds of those in the chairs, and of Tommy on the floor, allowing his arms to thump uselessly to his sides. Re-sheathing the knife as Nathan and the others rubbed their wrists to get their circulation going, Arctic turned to Tommy. The Texan was still face-down on the floor and breathing harshly through a mouth creased in pain.

Arctic undid the studs on the front of his or her camouflage jacket and reached inside, pulling out a thin, white, paper-wrapped package, some fifteen inches square.

Nathan knelt by Tommy. "Can you help him?"

Arctic said nothing and just ripped open the paper around the pack. Inside were a tray, gauze, wound packs, medical scissors, and tape, plus a small bottle of sterile water, a stitch kit, and a tube of medical glue.

Arctic worked quickly as the others looked on, horror and concern etched onto their faces. The figure used the scissors to cut the material of Tommy's coat around the knife wound. Beneath the material, the wound was sodden with blood, and bubbles were appearing around the blade forced into the skin. Nathan could hear the wound sucking and gurgling as Tommy breathed. The blade had gone through the ribs over his lungs and had penetrated the organ. Every time Tommy tried to fill his lungs, the wound sucked and bubbles frothed.

Arctic got ready. The top was taken off the glue, the gauze was readied, and a wound pad was teased out of its two-part covering.

Donie was looking away, and Free held onto Lucy's hand so tightly that his knuckles had lost all their color.

Arctic grabbed the knife's handle and yanked it out of the wound in Tommy's back with one swift movement. The blade came free with a swell of fresh blood, and Tommy's fingers clenched in agony against the floorboards. Gauze was applied to the wound, and Arctic grabbed Nathan's wrist and pressed his hand down hard, applying all the pressure a hand could.

Arctic readied the wound pad and the glue. When Arctic was ready, they hissed one word, "Now." And Nathan lifted the gauze.

The wound was deep red and black-lipped.

Nathan could see through the layers of skin and down past the bones of Tommy's rib cage. Arctic wasted no time in applying a wound pad to soak up as much blood as possible. Two more pads were utilized in this way. When the worst of the blood was staunched, Arctic applied glue to the length of the two-inch wound and then pushed the lips of the opening together.

After a few seconds, the wound was stuck closed, and Tommy groaned gently. Arctic put another pad over the now closed wound and stuck it in place with tape.

"FEMA field hospital. Denver. Now!" Arctic hissed again, with still no chance for a guess to be made about their identity or gender.

Without another word, Arctic ran from the room, leaving only heavy footsteps retreating into the silence.

Free, Lucy, Dave, and Syd took Tommy to the back of the F-350 and headed out toward Denver. Donie had agreed to stay behind with Nathan to search for the kids and to make sure there was someone in each party with the IT smarts to nurse the laptops through contact with Brant's spyware without giving away their locations again.

The snow, falling in gentle flakes, was mostly holding off. There was a storm coming, and it wasn't going to hit for a while, but it was going to hit hard when it did.

The emergency first aid Arctic had performed on Tommy at least gave him a fighting chance. Tommy's breathing had settled quickly, and blood had stopped draining from his mouth. Before

Free had driven away, Tommy had grabbed Nathan's hand and pulled his ear close to his mouth. "Cruiser. Down the road a ways. Keys… in the tailpipe."

Nathan had squeezed Tommy's hand, and then closed the doors to the utility bed of the Ford as Free pulled the truck away.

Nathan didn't like splitting up the party like this, but he had to find his boys, and there was no time to be wasted in getting Tommy to the FEMA field hospital in Denver.

The Drymouth adults put up no resistance as Donie and Nathan searched the museum and its buildings, ready with their Glock and the MP4. With the death of Larson, all of the purpose seemed to have drained from the settlers. As if the hold Larson had had on them had immediately been dissipated as soon as he'd taken both bullets from Arctic's sniper rifle.

They found Tony and Brandon locked in the equipment shed with the other older children.

Tony ran at his daddy as he was released, hugging him tight and burying his head in his stomach. They found Brandon in a cradle, in a room with the other youngsters. Sally, the woman they'd met at breakfast a dozen lifetimes ago, was looking after them. She said from behind the door that she wouldn't "give them any trouble," and added, "Don't shoot me… please."

The boys were none the worse for their ordeal. Brandon looked like he'd slept through the whole thing. Tony cried, but insisted he was okay when Nathan quizzed him.

Within the hour, Nathan and Donie had the surviving Drymouth residents up in the main building with the children. There were only three men left alive, and they had given up without a fight.

Like Sally, left to look after the children in the equipment sheds, they didn't want no trouble."

It was astonishing to Nathan to see the change in them, now that the iron grip of their guru had been released. They looked lost, vulnerable and bereft. The children were quiet, obedient and sitting quietly as if they were in the presence of a disciplinarian teacher and dared not talk out of turn.

All ears and eyes were trained on Nathan, both the upturned faces of the children and the adults looking at him with rapt attention. The expression on their faces said the same thing with one voice—"tell us what to do."

Tell us what to do.

Nathan was shaken by the lack of agency in the room. It was as if they had all been programmed to be unable to think for themselves. He wondered if they felt the same way he once had, when he'd been brainwashed in the silo owned by Strickland Grange. Back then, the man and his people had been able to convince Nathan, by use of drugs and electroshock therapy, that Cyndi and his children were dead, and that he was giving up his life to Jesus. It had been a horrific situation—which had only been reversed by the shock of seeing that Cyndi was still alive when she and Tommy broke into the silo to rescue him.

It didn't seem that these people before him now had been brainwashed with drugs or electric shocks, though. They had been willingly led by the nose by the charismatic Larson, and now all they wanted was for someone else to fill the gap his ending had left in their lives. Nathan had prepared a speech in his head, that was going to tell them he was going to make contact with the authorities in Denver and tell them what had happened here, and that maybe the FEMA forces there might be able to help them, but the words just stuck in his throat. He didn't want to meet their mindless anticipation to be told what to do, and what they should think.

He didn't want to be their new Larson.

So, he left them to it, and walked out of the room without a word.

The Cruiser was exactly where Tommy had said it would be. There was still half a tank of gas—easily enough to get them to Denver to meet up with Free and the others.

On the driver's seat, Nathan found what he assumed Tommy had left the settlement to go find, back when Dave and Donie's satellite uplink had failed to connect to the internet. Tommy had been to the library in the town of Drymouth, the one that had given the museum its name. There were newspapers in the Cruiser, stamped with the Drymouth library mark. They were stained and damp, obviously having been taken out of a weather-compromised building. Each had a story about the arrest of "Cult Leader" Greg Larson some five years before. He'd been charged with false imprisonment of children, and of unnecessary cruelty to adults, all perpetrated in his farmstead up near Boulder.

There were lurid stories of people being forced to give up their children to Larson's weird project. And reports of how the children were 're-educated' with sensory deprivation tactics, their parents sucked dry of all their cash—this to be put into Larson's mission to build his "Transubstantiation Craft."

There were also blurry pictures of the silver saucer-shaped construction, which Nathan immediately recognized as the craft he'd seen in the mine's chamber.

A trial had taken place, but in the end, Larson had been acquitted when all of the prosecution's witnesses—the people who'd lived on the farm with him—had withdrawn all their statements and changed their stories to support him.

Larson had gone back to the farm with his 'people' to carry on waiting for their *"Transubstantiation to Calisto One."*

Nathan read over everything, realizing that Larson and his people must have moved it to Drymouth as the Big Winter had worsened, to enable him to carry out his sick and twisted rituals.

There was plenty of background about Larson. A former drug addict, thrown out of the teaching profession for taking science classes and turning them into discussions about Calisto One and the aliens who would come to save humanity one day. His mental illness—and that was what the newspapers decreed it must have been, perhaps being a psychotic condition which had been induced by drug taking—had not robbed him of his faculties to persuade or convince the gullible, the lonely, the paranoid, or the emotionally needy. It all told a story that was all too familiar, and one that, because of the privations and horrors of the Big Winter, was all too ready to suck up anyone vulnerable in its wake.

Nathan sighed, shook his head, and threw the papers into the snow.

"Let's do this. Denver, here we come."

19

Denver was an open sore.

It was a shame that the threatening weather was still holding off, Nathan thought as they rolled through the suburbs of the city, because a fresh fall of snow would have hidden much of what was making the city so hard to take in.

The first thing that had hit them was the smell.

In the crew cab, Tony, with Brandon and Rapier, had started sniffing at the baby's diaper to see if he needed to be changed. But it hadn't been Brandon making the smell, and even with the windows closed, and the air vents' plastic covers snapped shut, the F-350 had filled with a wrenching odor that made Nathan's eyes water and his guts turn over.

Donie put her hand over her mouth and nose, finding it difficult to breathe.

"What's that smell, Daddy?" Tony asked as the 85 going north from Castle Rock took them through Littleton and onto the city beyond.

"Death," Nathan said quietly, and after that, no one remarked on the stench. They just let it get on with darkening the mood and turning their stomachs.

They passed many dead bodies, some half-covered in snow which had been there a long time, at least since before the last storm. Other bodies were fresher, much rimmed with frost and flakes, but also with sprays of blood on the snow where they'd been shot.

There was a burned-out bus on an off-ramp, with the driver half in and half out of the cab. He'd been forced through the windshield by an impact, or pushed himself through in a desperate attempt to escape. His arms were held out stiffly in front of him in a frozen mockery of pleading, his Regional Transit District cap skewed on his decomposing skull.

The streets lay beneath thick blankets of snow, and the buildings that abutted the road were either burned out or burning. Plumes of smoke rose into the gray, burgeoning clouds. On the horizon, to the west, the rising slopes of the Rockies bit into the sky like teeth. It was as if the whole rotting city was being consumed in a troll's mouth like carrion.

With the heaters blowing as hard as they could, Nathan still felt the shiver of disquiet as they rolled on at ten miles per hour. The roads were clogged, not just with corpses, but with vehicles on both sides of the highway. They would occasionally see a Jeep or a 4x4 moving off into the distance, and at one point, Tony pointed up at the sky as the black dot of a military helicopter moved off into the distance.

They had to stop several times to check snow drifts on the highway, which were blocking their way, to see if there was anything more solid than just the snow beneath them—and when they did, the rat-a-tat-tat of small arms fire seemed to echo around them from all directions. There were many small, dirty battles going on in the city, it appeared. Whoever was fighting, Nathan had no idea, but a rapidly increasing feeling of dread and an encroaching sense of doom assailed his thinking like the reek of the dead city.

It looked like the buildings they could see had been deliberately torched, perhaps to discourage people from trying to live in them.

Nathan got the sense that if you were going to stay in Denver, then you were going to be herded to where you could best be controlled by whoever the ascendant authority was—whether that be FEMA or a City Baron like Brant in Detroit. The uneasy feeling within the city limits was all-pervading.

"Roadblock," Donie said as Nathan's eyes flicked from the road to nearby burned-out buildings.

Bringing his attention to what was up ahead, he saw that the road was closed by a succession of concrete blocks with red and white striped poles between them. Soldiers—well, he assumed they were soldiers, but anyone these days could get themselves a uniform and be anyone they wanted—patrolled behind the blocks on both sides of the road. Two stubby-looking APCs were parked alongside them, and there was a camouflage-painted, demountable knock-down cabin with dark windows and a porcupine of antennae on the roof.

It looked official, but appearances could be deceptive.

A soldier came forward, ducking under the central pole, and raised his hand for Nathan to slow the truck.

Nathan had vivid flashbacks to the Arctic Sniper—who he'd assumed was the same person to have taken out Toothill's men at that other roadblock, and with vicious efficiency. He was surprised to find himself wincing in anticipation as the soldier came forward, expecting a high-velocity round to smack into him at any moment.

Composing himself, and pushing the thought from his mind, Nathan wound down the window.

"Business in Denver?" the soldier asked, looking through the window at Nathan and then past him to the crew cab.

"We have a friend who was brought to the FEMA hospital. We wanted to see how he is, if that's okay?"

The soldier's face was set, his mouth thin and bloodless. "That'll be five hundred dollars."

Nathan blinked. "I'm sorry?"

"You want to go on through here, that'll be five hundred dollars, or the equivalent in gold." The soldier was completely matter of fact in what he was requesting, as if it was something that he said a dozen times a day.

"But, we want to go to the hospital—that's all. I don't have five hundred dollars."

The soldier looked past Nathan, and his eyes rested on Donie. Nathan could see her leg trembling in the periphery of his vision, as the anxiety created by the soldier's salacious expression bled out through her frame. "There are other methods of payment we might consider."

He pointed directly at Donie. "Three hours in the cabin with her. But that's the best I can offer."

Nathan stared, appalled at the level of corruption that was so baldly on display here. If the soldier's uniform, and that of his comrades, was a legitimate expression of government authority in the city, it wasn't just Denver that stank.

The soldier shrugged. "Take it or leave it. You can try and find another way into the city if you want, but right now the Clancys and the Ramirez gangs have got their sides of the city sewn up tighter than a dead nun's holy of holies. And trust me, their tolls won't be as generous and accommodating as ours. Up to you, buddy."

The vertigo in his gut almost stilled his mouth, but Nathan had to check. "We're not interested in that. But we do want to know if an F-350 came through here in the last day or so. Had an injured man."

The soldier shrugged and met Nathan with a steely gaze. "Information is extra, too."

Nathan wound up the window, a foul taste in his mouth. He turned the truck around, bumping over the central reservation and going back the way they had come. The stunned silence in the cab lasted a considerable time. Donie's knee didn't stop shaking for an age.

After all that they'd been through, Nathan hadn't thought there was anything shockworthy left that that Big Winter could throw at him.

How wrong he had been.

His horror at the soldier's suggestion mixed with anger and grief for the country and civilization Nathan had lost. He didn't think he'd ever stop grieving for it. Nathan took an off-ramp into a built-up suburb and pointed the truck east along the road. Rows and rows of houses that had once been neat and presentable stared out on them with dead, black eyes.

Like those on the highway they'd left, many of the buildings had been burned out or half demolished. Bodies littered the snow in places, and at one point they saw a small pack of perhaps half a dozen dogs pulling at a body that was mostly covered in snow. Rapier's ears pricked up and he stared through the window as if he disapproved of how far his cousins had descended into the same barbarism as the humans.

When Nathan felt they had traveled far enough east, he turned to go north again, to see if they could find a route in. The houses on the east side of Denver were low, ranch-style dwellings surrounded by trees and small parks. Before the Big Winter, this would have been a well-appointed neighborhood, with all the amenities, schools, and facilities any family could wish for. Now, the atmosphere was one of deep foreboding, chill silence, and a very real sense of unease.

There had been fewer cars traveling along these streets, and consequently, the snow here was much deeper. Nathan was forced to slow the F-350 down to a snail's pace, which only added to his sense of vulnerability.

"Keep your gun close at hand," Nathan whispered to Donie, and she nodded, lifting an MP4 from the footwell and holding it ready. Nathan had no idea why he'd whispered, really. They were grumbling through the suburb in a huge F-350, belching exhaust and crunching through three feet of compacted snow. It wasn't like he was going out of his way to conceal their presence in the truck.

Nathan paused the forward momentum of the Ford for a moment and checked the magazine in his Glock. It was full, and he knew he had three more mags in the side pockets of his pants. The last thing he wanted to do was get into a firefight with whoever the Clancy or Ramirez gangs were, but it was better to be prepared for all eventualities.

"It'll be dark soon," Donie said, craning her neck up through the windshield to scan the sky. "Those clouds aren't going to be holding onto their loads for much longer. Should we stop for the night? Get some food into us and see how things are in the morning?"

The subtext from Donie was that she'd had more than enough today. The horrific state of Denver, the soldier's unalloyed suggestion of sexual exploitation, and being separated from Dave were taking their toll. Nathan could see that she wasn't making a suggestion about what they should do—this was more of a plea than an idea.

Nathan nodded and pulled the truck into the driveway of a ranch-style property that was almost entirely enclosed in a pen of cock-spur hawthorn—the broad, flat trees were denuded of all leaves by the winter, but their bushiness and abundance in the house's yard would give the F-350, with its attendant trailer, at least some semblance of cover.

Nathan got out of the truck, Glock in hand to check over the house after telling Tony to stay where he was until told it was safe to come out. Donie sat in the truck also, just staring ahead through the windshield. Nathan got the notion she was mightily relieved to no longer be playing Russian roulette with the Denver streets.

The front door to the house was open and scraped back on broken hinges. From the street, the roof had looked intact, and a good bet to offer shelter outside the claustrophobic confines of the truck. Now, he'd see the inside. Nathan made a quick reconnoiter of the rooms. The lounge area with its broken windows was a write-off, shelter-wise. Snow had gusted through the windows over many months, and the room was as chill as a freezer store. Out back, in the kitchen and utility room, away from the street, the house had fared a little better. Although it was cold, and Nathan's breath hung in clouds around him, the kitchen was dry and the windows were intact, and it was the same with the utility room which led, through a white UPVC door, out to a yard glutted with snow and a surrounding barrier of hawthorn.

They would be able to set up the camping stove in here, and cook some warm food, and huddle together in sleeping bags on the camping mattresses they had stored in the trailer. It wouldn't be a five-star residence for the night, but it would give them the chance to stretch out, and as the house wasn't overlooked by any other properties, Nathan thought they could at least allow themselves to have a little light to go with their warm food.

Tony and Donie, now seeming more like her old self now that she'd spent some time in the truck getting her head together, helped Nathan bring the provisions and equipment they'd need into the house for the night.

Rapier had proved to be a good guard dog since he'd joined the party, and he was happy to sniff around the yard and do his business before joining the others in the house.

In relatively short order, as night fell over the city, they had the stove set up and Nathan began warming beans and sausages while Tony made coffee.

Donie had the satellite uplink running to the laptop on a wire leading through to the yard, through a cat flap in the back door. She'd had to pick the ice from it before she got it open—it hadn't seen a cat through for many a month.

"Yes!" Donie made a fist as the laptop linked to the satellite, and suddenly they could again pull information from the severely compromised but still limping along internet. There wasn't a lot of information about the FEMA operation in Denver that Donie could access, but one page told them the field hospital and refugee camp had been set up in the City Park Pavilion—the pavilion's Spanish architecture showed yellow walls, red roofs, and two towers overlooking Ferril Lake.

The City Park Pavilion was about a mile east of downtown and three miles from where they were now. Donie was able to work with the cop maps on the laptop and at least approximate a route for them to take in the morning. What the internet wasn't telling them now was what gang territories they would have to traverse in order to get to the FEMA camp. It also didn't tell them what they would be expected to offer up of their provisions or themselves to get into the camp.

"That's something we'll deal with when we get there. Maybe we can offer some of the weapons as trade. I dunno... or maybe find a way in without needing to go through whatever passes for official channels these days."

Beside Nathan, Donie typed furiously at the keyboard. Due to the atmospheric conditions, they often didn't know how long they'd be able to maintain the patency of the uplink. These sessions generally had to be intense, fast, and packed with only salient information gathering.

"Damn it, Nate, there's almost nothing here. Nothing that's going to help us find a safe route in, that's for sure. FEMA isn't bothering to update its pages with anything approaching useful."

"I guess they have a vested interest in not making sure people get through safely," Nathan replied sadly. "How will they take their tolls otherwise?"

Donie sighed, and then gave a little yelp of surprise. Her hands flew off the keyboard as if she'd been stung.

Nathan looked up from the stove. "What is it?"

"Oh my god," was all Donie said as she turned the screen of the laptop around so that Nathan could see what she'd just seen.

There in the center of the screen, blocking out everything else, was a still picture of the Mayor of Detroit, Harvey Brant. The picture had been taken when Brant had been displaying the widest of grins on his face. There was text running beneath his jowls, and the words Nathan read there almost stopped his heart in his chest.

Hello, Nathan. Thanks so much for logging back in! You think you're the only man with his own hackers? We've cracked your code, and we know where you are. Be seeing you very soon!

Nathan and Donie didn't sleep.

Nathan held Brandon in his arms, sitting up in his sleeping bag. Tony rested his head on Donie's thighs and she stroked his hair while he drifted away into a restless, broken slumber. Even Rapier was restless, picking up on the tension created by Brant's message on the laptop.

"Should we leave here now?" Donie had asked as they'd left their meal uneaten and the coffee going cold.

"I have no idea," Nathan had replied truthfully. "If he's got another helicopter like the last one, he could have men here in three or four hours. Otherwise, it's over a thousand miles of hard roads and Arctic conditions between us."

"I shouldn't have turned the laptop on. It was stupid, but I wanted to see if there were any messages from Dave. I'm sorry."

"No need to apologize. I'd have done the same in your position, and it made sense to look for routes into the city."

Donie let out a long sigh. "I guess our coding skills aren't what we thought they were."

"I don't think any of us are quite as good as we need to be," Nathan said slowly with a sad smile, squeezing her shoulder. "We just do the best we can with what we've got."

"I don't know how much I've got left, Nate. I'm all used up."

They sat in silence for nearly an hour, until Donie checked her watch. "Still five hours until dawn. I'm not going to sleep. I don't think I'm ever going to sleep again."

"I hear you."

If Nathan could have run at the wall and knocked himself unconscious, he would have. He was dog-tired and beaten, and now he was going to have to find a whole galaxy of new reserves to fight the battle that he knew would come next.

Brant was not going to let them go. This could only end in one way, with Brant ended or Nathan gone. There was no middle ground—no deal that could be made that Brant wouldn't go back on or double-cross. Brant wasn't a chess player; he was a demolition charge. He really would use a hammer to crack a nut, as he had the demeanor of a school bully given the opportunity to wield real power, and that was the most dangerous of combinations. Nathan could feel a battle preparing to be fought in his thinking. Should he stick with the others, or would he be better off running with his children? His friends would be safe from Brant and he would have the opportunity to get as far away from Denver as he could.

If Brant was on his way there, though, as the message had implied, then this city would be the ground zero of his revenge.

Nathan was so lost in the moment of his thoughts that it took Donie's tight grip on his wrist to alert him to the fact that someone was pushing open the front door to the house, and forcing their way inside.

20

Nathan woke Tony by shaking his shoulder gently. The boy was about to grumble something, but Nathan put a hand softly over the boy's mouth and pointed to his ear to make the boy listen.

Rapier was up, sniffing at the kitchen door, which Nathan was already glad they had closed before settling down for the night.

Outside in the corridor, Nathan could hear two sets of footsteps. They were being made by intruders who were trying to be stealthy. But in the acute silence in the house, with Nathan's now significantly heightened senses marbled with shots of fresh adrenaline, he heard every shuffle and creak.

Nathan put Brandon in Tony's arms and prayed to the god of infants that he wouldn't wake up and start to cry. Donie was already reaching for the MP4 and Nathan slid the Glock from beneath the spare sleep roll which he would have used for a pillow if he'd gotten any closer to sleeping.

They both pushed back the sleeping bags and stood up. Nathan went to the door and stood by the side it would open toward and readied himself to shoot. Donie hung back, the machine gun at waist height, her finger in the trigger guard.

The noise of the two people making their way stealthily toward the kitchen door continued unabated. Nathan's throbbing heart boomed in his ears and his mouth dried like a creek bed in high summer as the handle began to turn.

Nathan's eyes sweated with anxiety, his tongue traveling the brick-dry surfaces of his lips.

The door began to open, and the muzzle of a pistol pushed through the gap. The angle it was at pointed it directly at Tony.

Nathan pulled the trigger of the Glock and the round crashed out of the gun. The invader's gun dropped, there was a scream, and a body fell back.

Nathan was preparing to fire again when he heard a voice he knew—"Christ, Nathan! It's us! It's me and Dave!"

The voice belonged to Free.

The irony that, in this moment, Dave's life had been saved by Nathan weeks before, was not lost on the group. The bullet Nathan had fired had slammed into the metal tube encasing Dave's arm, still strapped across his chest in a tight sling. The bullet had then ricocheted harmlessly up into the ceiling.

Dave had been propelled backward by the force of the bullet hitting the tube, and he'd crashed into Free, sending them both sprawling.

"How many times have I told you not to lead with the gun!?" Donie yelled at Dave as she checked him over in the weak light coming from the oil lamp in the kitchen. The report from the gun had startled Brandon to almost inconsolable crying, which took Nathan many minutes to deal with—walking up and down with the child, whispering in his ear, and rubbing his back to soothe him. Tony just kept rubbing at his ears, as the gunshot in the confined space had caused a painful concussion for everyone in the room to deal with.

Nathan was glad to be holding the baby and dealing with the crying because, left to their own devices, he knew that his hands would be trembling over the notion that he had very nearly killed Dave where he'd stood. Free had picked himself up and taken the gun from Nathan's frozen hand, telling him to go and deal with the baby because Dave was going to be okay.

Donie's anger at Dave soon dissipated and she wound up taking him back to the sleeping bags and hugging him tight, resting her head on his shoulder, but she also told him, "You do that again and I'll kill you myself."

When Brandon had settled and Donie had stopped squeezing what life there was left in Dave, Nathan asked them how they'd found them.

"We were waiting for you to log on. We figured that if you spent another night on the road, Donie would try the uplink. It was us that triggered Brant's message the first time. Once we realized that he knew we were in Denver, there was no point trying to hide that fact. So, once you logged on, I managed to get a GPS reference on your signal before you cut the uplink. We got it down to about a square click in the area, and it was just a matter of searching the streets until we found the truck. But we couldn't tell you we were coming, and we had to check the house quietly in case it was a Clancy or Ramirez gang trap."

The words had tumbled from Dave's lips like he couldn't get them out fast enough—probably because he was still coming down off the rush of surviving being shot at point-blank range. Nathan still felt the electricity and relief coursing through his frame. It was going to be a good while before Nathan came down off his own plateau.

"So, where's Lucy and Syd, and how's Tommy?"

Free's face fell and, for a horrible second, Nathan thought that Free was going to tell him the worst news possible about one or all of them, but Free just shook his head and said, "They're okay…"

Nathan felt the relief flooding through him in a warm wave, even before Free finished...

"…I think," he said.

Nathan looked at him hard. "What do you mean, you think?"

It was then that Nathan noticed how red-rimmed Free's eyes were, and how his skin had lost three or four tones of color. He looked hollowed out and on the very edge.

"They're in the camp. We haven't seen them for two days. We can't get in and they can't get out. It's not a refugee camp, Nate. It's more like a prison."

This wasn't what Nathan had expected to hear, let alone what he'd wanted to hear. They needed to get out of Denver and they needed to get out of it soon—there wasn't a moment to waste.

"What? A prison?"

Free nodded sadly. "FEMA's running the place like no refugee camp I've ever seen on TV, man. They take your money, your weapons, and your gear for themselves. Call it tolls and taxes. If you want to get to the hospital, they call it your medical insurance, but it's just a massive exercise in criminality."

"We saw some ourselves on the highway coming into Denver," Nathan said. "They wouldn't let us in unless we could stump up five hundred dollars. Told us we'd have to go through gang territory if we didn't have the cash… or…"

Donie flashed Nathan a look that told him she didn't want it to be common knowledge what they'd asked for instead of money, but Dave caught the look and touched her arm. "It's okay, baby, they tried the same with Lucy and Syd. They told them where to get off, too. We made it through the Clancy quarter. Cost us most of our guns and food, but we figured we'd be okay for food when we got to the refugee camp. We couldn't have been more wrong. They let Tommy and the women in for the last of the food, spare fuel, and all but the last of our guns. If we'd have stayed any longer at the checkpoint, they'd have taken the Cruiser, too—I'm sure of it. After that, they wouldn't let us back in, and they haven't let the others out."

"Lucy and the others are trapped in there?" Nathan asked, incredulous. A feeling of dark horror had begun building in his heart.

Free nodded, his eyes raking the floor like lasers.

Nathan felt like he was being hit from all sides as the sheer awfulness of the Denver situation became clearer. "Is this what the government has become? Just another bunch of hoodlums and scum?"

"There is *no* government," Dave corrected him. "All systems have broken down, and FEMA's become just another shade of the mafia. Denver is just a place for them to generate income based on the lie of trying to help people. There's no guarantee that Tommy has gotten the medical treatment he needs now, but whoever that was who shot down Larson and his crew really did save his life. By the time we got to Denver, he was awake, eating, and feeling a whole lot better. Lucy treated him with wild opium lettuce juice from Cyndi and Elm's stock for the pain, and by the time we got to the City Park camp, he was feeling a whole lot better. How he is now… that's anyone's guess."

It was four hours until dawn now, and Nathan wasn't going to rest until they were reunited with the others, whatever it was going to take.

"We need to find a way to get into the camp. Any ideas?"

Free shook his head. "You think we didn't try? It's locked down tighter than a can of beans. They've got the whole park surrounded by a ten-foot fence covered in anti-climb paint and razor wire. There are guard towers with machine gun posts, and there's only one way in or out. We can't fight our way in. We'd be dead before we got thirty yards."

Dave's face was grim. "There's no way through the perimeter that we've found. The only way in is to buy your way through the main gate. And then when you're inside, you're put to work.

Unless you have the dough to buy your way out, you're pretty much an indentured slave."

Free made a fist and thumped it gently against the wall. "Nathan, I guess there are ways for a woman to buy her way out... but..."

"It's hopeless. I wish I had better news, but I don't," Dave finished.

Nathan rubbed his temples, trying to think. "If they aren't going to let us in without the ability to pay, I guess we're going to have to find ourselves something to pay with."

"What?" Free, Dave and Donie asked in unison.

And when Nathan told them, they thought he had finally gone completely crazy.

Dawn came with a slow but heavy sleet on the wind that splashed and spat into the snow. Nathan worked until dawn making things ready. Donie wasn't happy about being left behind in the house to look after the kids with Rapier, but it was going to be way too dangerous to bring Tony and Brandon along—especially if Nathan's plan went south.

Now, the men drove slowly through the suburb, stopping every five minutes or so to wind down the windows and listen to the city. It didn't take more than half an hour to get a fix on the sound they needed to follow. Dave had enough grip in his healing fingers to drive the Cruiser and operate the gears as long as they were driving this slowly. Any faster, or if they needed to make a quick getaway, and Dave would need to slide out of the driver's seat and give up the wheel to either Nathan or Free.

Nathan had the MP4 ready, Free had an A-15 with a bump stock, and they both had backpacks with extra ammo in case they needed it.

The sound of gunfire got nearer, and when they felt they were close enough to approach whoever was fighting on foot, they parked the Cruiser and got out into the sleeting air.

There was a block of low one-story residences, which backed onto a four-story condo with views over downtown, right up to the Rockies. The mountains were just picking themselves out of the night with weak dawn light, their white peaks becoming visible first and floating in the near black like the sails of a mighty armada.

The crackle of gunfire around the condo was sporadic, but it gave Nathan and the others enough cause for concern. They went in low, running fast through the bushes beneath the trees and on through the backyards of the derelict buildings.

Free had told Nathan there were turf wars going on all over the city. The Ramirez gang would get a toe-hold in one area, steal what they could from the Clancys, and retreat. The Clancy gang, in turn, would move in on Ramirez territory, find one of their weapons or food stores, and attack. The battles sometimes went on for days as both sides dug in and tried to outwit the other side. FEMA troops were just happy to let them get on with it. If the gangs were fighting each other, FEMA could get on with screwing the steady stream of refugees who were being told they would be safe in Denver and were making their way there, full of the hope that was going to be cruelly lifted from them in the same fashion as their money and food.

Nathan and the others hunkered down below a low garden wall. Flashes of muzzle fire were coming from a window high on the fourth floor of the condo. That fire was being returned from what had once been a hardware store on the other side of the street.

"Ready?" Nathan asked.

Dave and Free, their faces intense and their weapons gripped tight, both nodded.

"Take no chances, remember. If we don't get away with it today, there will always be tomorrow and the next. All we need to do is make sure we're not seen."

They split up then, Free and Dave going toward the condo with Nathan doubling back the way they had come through the snow, sleet dampening the outside of his jacket and getting in through his hood to sliver with an uncomfortable chill down the back of his neck. He sprinted hard in a wide semi-circle, across the street and through an alleyway, and leaped a fence into a backyard behind the hardware store.

There behind the building, in the back road between two blocks on the estate, was what Nathan was looking for. A midnight blue Lexus RX 4x4 parked behind the store. It had been used to take whoever, from whatever gang, to this location, and as those in the store were busy fighting their little battle, it stood to reason that they might not have the manpower to post a guard on their car.

Nathan's call had been a good one.

The Clancys' Lexus was parked tight against the wall on the far sidewalk. He vaulted the fence at the front of the yard and hurried across the road toward it, keeping as low as he could. If the houses in this area of east Denver were anything like the others he'd seen, then there wasn't going to be anyone left to watch his streaky attempt at espionage and thievery. That certainty, however, didn't stop him from checking underneath and around the huge metal pig of a car parked at the back of the abandoned hardware store.

Nathan was breathing hard and sweating enough for streams of it to roll down his face and into his eyes, but none of that deterred him from allowing himself a few slivers of elation because his plan had worked out—so far.

He tried the handle of the Lexus and the door came open on smooth hinges. The gang members in the store fighting their battle with those guys across the street in the condo were not expecting to get robbed like this, and hadn't taken any precautions with their security.

It took Nathan less than twenty seconds to search the glove compartments and side pods and look behind the sun visors for the Lexus' electronic door opener and ignition key. These guys might be the top dogs in this territory, but like dogs, they only thought about the moment, about how fast they could eat the latest meal that had been put in front of them, and not about looking after their supplies of food for tomorrow.

Nathan eased himself into the driver's seat and clicked the door shut with a satisfying thump. The Lexus wasn't more than five years old, and it was a solid piece of machinery. Nathan had always enjoyed working on them when they'd come into the auto shop in Glens Falls, and the idea of stealing one from the bad guys made him happier still. He waited for another burst of gunfire on the other side of the hardware store, and then he started the engine.

Back where they had parked the Cruiser, Free and Dave were already waiting. Free had scored a late model Toyota RAV4, green and a bit beat-up. There were three bullet holes in the rear fender and it didn't have a spare tire, but it was sound enough. Dave hadn't managed to come back with anything, so Dave drove the Cruiser, Nathan the Lexus, and Free the RAV4 back to the ranch house where Donie was waiting impatiently with the kids.

Her eyes were wide with admiration as the small convoy pulled up to the drive.

"It worked!"

"Yes, indeed," Nathan said with a wide grin. "So, Free, reckon this haul will get us in and out of the camp?"

Free was standing at the tailgate of the Lexus and pulled out a metal-cornered flight case on silver wheels. It thumped into the snow and Free bent to undo the two latches. The lid came up, but because of the angle at which everyone else stood, only he could see inside.

Nathan saw his friend's eyes widen with shock, though, and then recompose on his face into something like avarice tinged with genuine joy. Free reached into the box and pulled out something from within.

"Oh, I think we're going to have no problems at all getting in or getting out," he said with an edge of triumph in his voice as

Nathan and the others stared with awe at the M67 fragmentation grenade Free held in his hand.

"And there's about twenty more of these suckers in the case," Free said. "We hit paydirt, Nate. Freakin' paydirt!"

They made it through to the perimeter of City Park unmolested by FEMA or any of the Denver gangs.

The sleet had turned into a heavy, fat-flaked snowfall, which kept all but the hardiest people off the streets in even the sturdiest of SUVs. The experience Nathan and the others had gained in driving across the snowy wastes of the Midwest stood them in good stead when the conditions were like this. They took it slow but steady. Winding through the streets, avoiding FEMA checkpoints, they made it to their destination in a little under two hours.

Nathan, and Tony, with Brandon, took the Lexus. Donie and Dave had the F-350 with the trailer and Rapier in the crew cab, and Free drove the RAV4.

Once they reached the high, razor-wire-topped fence, Nathan could see how it would be impossible, under normal circumstances, to scale or break through the impenetrable barrier.

Under normal circumstances, indeed.

Before they moved around the other side of City Park to the FEMA entrance, Nathan put the other piece of this plan into action. In case of emergency, he wanted to ensure there *was* a way—in abnormal circumstances—to break through the fence.

Once that was set up, they parked the F-350 and the trailer behind a row of low houses. They were as derelict and dead-eyed as any of the others in the city but would afford cover for the vehicle from all eyes unless such eyes were already looking for them.

What was left of the provisions and weapons were removed from the Cruiser, leaving only a meager amount of fuel in jerry cans, and just a sniff of canned food. Donie would again wait here with Brandon, Tony, and Rapier, and yet again she wasn't at all happy about it.

"Both my arms work, and I'm not a damn nursemaid," she said with blazing eyes as Nathan and the others prepared to leave.

"Neither am I," Tony said with all seriousness, "but I have to look after Brandon most of the time. Donie, to be fair, I could really do with a break."

Donie's face melted into a smile at Tony playing the adult, and Dave stepped forward to hug her. "Please, this could still all turn to crap, and I'd rather you were here if we need to get us out. I'm sorry, baby. This isn't about your gender. It's about how I feel about you."

Nathan and Free hung back, giving the two lovers some space to hug and kiss. Tony, holding Brandon to his chest, looked on sagely as if he completely understood what had been said and what was happening.

Nathan ruffled the boy's hair and hunched down so he was face-to-face with his boys. "You look after Brandon and Donie, you hear? All being well, we plan to be out of there in less than twenty-four hours. I need you all to be ready to leave at a moment's notice, okay?"

"Sure, Daddy. You got it."

Nathan kissed Tony's forehead and stood up.

"Let's roll."

21

Snow, their constant companion, blatted against the windshield of the Lexus, and the wipers on full power squashed the flakes out of the way in smeary clutches of ice.

The near blizzard conditions sucked all of the color out of the city as they rolled around the perimeter of City Park, turning north from East 17th Avenue, where they'd found the edge of the park, onto York Street, and from there they approached the entrance to the Denver City Park-cum-Refugee-Camp-cum-FEMAFIOSA swindle.

The wide expanse of York Street was just layering up with more and more snow, with no vehicles moving along it save for Nathan's Lexus and Free's RAV4.

The snowfall was so intense, they could just about make out the sides of the road, and maybe twenty or thirty yards ahead of them at any given moment. At least the street had been cleared of broken-down cars at some point in the past, and so their way wasn't impeded by wreckage.

They pulled into the entranceway where eight soldiers manned the checkpoint in their oilskin capes topped with Advanced Combat Helmets and goggles. A soldier came forward, waving Nathan to bring the Lexus to a standstill and wind down the window.

"Is he one of the soldiers you saw before?" Nathan whispered through thin lips. Next to Nathan, Dave was already leaning back in his seat, groaning.

"No. Shift's changed, I guess," Dave replied, wiping at the moisture on his face. They'd poured a little water on his forehead to make him look feverish, and he'd been rubbing at his eyes with the heel of his good hand all the way from where they'd left Donie, to make them look painful and bloodshot.

"Good," Nathan hissed. "Or this might be a very short conversation."

"State your business," the soldier said as the window came down on smooth motors.

Nathan leaned forward. "My buddy here is in a lot of pain; stomach's tender and he's running a fever. Might be his appendix. We don't know. They said you guys had a field hospital here."

The soldier nodded and wiped at the silt of snowflakes building up on his goggles. "That all depends on what you got to pay for your taxes and health insurance, sir." The *sir* was said with the same sound as someone treading in a morning gift a dog might leave on the floor when he couldn't get access to the yard. It was the least respectful sounding use of the word *sir* Nathan thought he'd ever heard.

"We know. The RAV4 behind me, you can take. We have a couple of guns and a crate of tinned ham inside."

The soldier studied Nathan's face and eyes through his goggles. "This Lexus is mighty fine, sir."

"It is, but we need it for all our people. Please take the RAV4. I've got an MP4 you can have, too, if it'll help."

Dave groaned some more, looking for all the world like he was delirious with pain, the fingers of his good hand working at his thigh, then making a fist and thumping it. The soldier saw all this, but didn't look like he gave a damn. All he was interested in was what he could score in so-called taxes.

"I'll need to check with my commanding officer. Wait here."

The young soldier trudged back through the blizzard, his shoulders and helmet covered in white like the peaks of the Rockies Nathan might have been able to see if the graying snowfall hadn't been erasing all views of the city, flake by flake.

Nathan wound up the window so that, when he spoke, no one outside the car would hear him.

"Good work. You can have an Oscar when this is all over."

Dave winked surreptitiously at Nathan and whispered, "I'd like to thank the members of the Academy…"

The soldier had checked with whoever he had to and was on his way back. Nathan took the window down again. "Lexus, or you can turn around and find the other hospital in Denver that doesn't exist."

The soldier was smiling at his joke, and Nathan would gladly have reached through the open window and shaken him warmly by the throat.

"Okay, okay. He needs a doctor."

In actuality, Nathan had predicted the soldiers would want the Lexus rather than the RAV4, and that's why he'd hidden the majority of their firepower within the beat-up Toyota, gambling that the soldiers wouldn't bother to look for contraband in a vehicle given up willingly.

When Nathan, supporting the Oscar-worthy Dave, made the transfer into the smaller RAV4, Free whispered under his breath that Nathan was a goddamned genius, and that he'd made every single right call they'd needed that day.

The checkpoint barrier was raised, and the soldier, who'd taken the Lexus' key fob and ignition key, waved them through with a cursory gesture. He was more concerned with his new wheels.

The roads inside the park, although now receiving a heavy fall of snow, had at least been cleared recently, and that made traversing the tree lined avenue a lot easier than the roads approaching the park. The City Park Pavilion was easy to spot up ahead, too, even though its red tiled roof was covered in snow. It was the biggest and tallest building in the park, with two sixty-foot towers reaching skywards, the warm yellow of its brick walls showing through the white snow in plenty of places.

The approach to the pavilion, however, was like a journey through another world.

Row upon row of white, square, pitched-roofed tents ran away from the road in every possible direction, like the headstones in Arlington National Cemetery. The Denver Zoo and the local golf course were covered in the serried ranks of tents, some of them heavily bowed down under the weight of snow. Thousands of dwellings. Thousands of refugees from the Big Winter.

Tent flaps moved as the RAV4 crunched slowly by, showing children with dirty faces, mothers with hollow eyes, and broken fathers—the very corruption of the American family unit peering out with hungry stares. Meager cooking fires sputtered as the snow fell.

There was a pile of body bags at one park trail junction, which rose like an accusatory pyramid of defeat. And soldiers were unloading yet more stiff body bags from the back of a small electric truck. Their faces were grim, their work silent.

Three more bags were thrown onto the pile. The outline of the contents of one that slithered from the peak, bumping lazily back to the base, was no larger than Tony.

The sight made Nathan heartsick.

"I had… I had no idea… it would… man." He ran out of words.

They passed another truck where soldiers were handing out sodden bags of rice to a queue of silent women with blankets wrapped around their shoulders, all speckled with snow. Their feet stamping in the cold, their breath hanging over the line like a pall of despair.

Nathan scanned the faces of the women in the line, expecting at any moment to see Lucy or Syd holding out their hands, waiting for the insult of one small bag of rice to be gifted to them by the

FEMA soldiers. It was like something from a TV report on the aftermath of a war or a tsunami, not a scene from downtown America.

They rolled around a small lake as they crawled forward toward the pavilion. Fish cages held up with flotation tanks dotted the surface of the water. Men wrapped in blankets, like the women they'd seen before, were walking along jetties, pouring food into the cages for the fish beneath. Nathan saw one man reach into the bucket he was holding, take a look around, and then eat a handful of whatever was being given to the fish. His cheeks were sunken, his eyes so far back in his head that they'd need a telescope to see beyond the end of his nose. His balding head looked like the worst case of alopecia Nathan could imagine. Patches of raw skin showed next to what was left of the tufts of his hair. His thin jaw worked methodically at whatever he'd put into his mouth, and it was clearly an effort for him to swallow, but it was an effort he was prepared to make.

Nathan had to look away in the end. It hurt too much to watch.

They were stopped by a soldier outside the pavilion who told them to park on a concreted area some fifty yards away from the entrance. Dave put on his best appendicitis act again, and Nathan and Free supported him to walk toward the building. In the periphery of his vision, Nathan could see the soldier checking out the windows of the RAV4, no doubt wondering what had been left by his guys at the gate that he could 'tax' himself.

If they hadn't had a mission to complete, to find Tommy and the women, Nathan would have run headlong from this hellish vision of governmental exploitation.

He remembered back to when he and Cyndi had been considering whether or not to leave Glens Falls, and how she'd pretty much laughed in his face when he'd said with all seriousness that the government wouldn't let the population fend for themselves —that they would have a plan to deal with the Big Winter, and that everything would get back to normal.

Cyndi had been a prepper through and through. If it hadn't been for her, they wouldn't have had their initial supplies and bug-out provisions to get them on the road in his daddy's old Dodge coupled to an Airstream trailer. Cyndi had understood perfectly that the only person you could rely on when push came to shove was yourself, and maybe family and friends if you were lucky.

Denver City Park illustrated that attitude he'd originally had, writ large.

Thousands upon thousands of people had trusted the government —such as it was—and it had let them down in the most spectacular of fashions. Fleecing and robbing them blind in return for minuscule handouts, an opportunity to breakfast on fish food, and then to finally end up slithering down a snow-slick mound of body bags.

Mentally, Nathan apologized to the memory of Cyndi. Without her foresight, planning, and determination, they wouldn't have made it fifty miles from their house, and he would have died with his kids in the snow.

The pavilion had once been a wide open exhibition space and rentable venue for conventions and seminars, back before the Big Winter. It was high-roofed and thick-walled. But if the smell of Denver had been bad coming in, then the stench inside the FEMA field hospital was a dozen times worse.

Like the rows of tents outside, the space had been filled with rows of metal-framed beds that looked like they'd come from a 1930s film set.

The frames were white-painted tubular metal, topped with thin mattresses and threadbare blankets. It seemed that every bed was occupied. Many people were laying as still as death, their eyes open and looking listlessly at the ceiling; some were sitting, throwing up violently into bowls. Everywhere, people were coughing or groaning. In an area across the floor, there were cots and beds filled with children. The keening wail of youngsters in pain drifted across the space as Nathan and the others walked through, looking for some sort of doctor or authority figure.

"I'm feeling a whole lot better," Dave whispered. "This looks like the kind of place where you wipe your feet on the way out."

Free's grim face was set to avoid breaking. "Never seen anything like it, buddy. Never."

Nathan shook his head as they walked on. "We just need to find a doctor and locate Tommy and the others. We are not staying."

"Amen," Free and Dave replied.

"Yes? *What?*"

The voice was harsh and cut through the sounds of wailing and vomiting. From a tiny office, a small, bearded man with oily hair and a grubby white coat, a stethoscope around his neck, had begun marching toward them.

The doctor pointed at Dave. "Have those damn soldiers let you in through the wrong entrance again? God almighty, it doesn't matter how many times I tell them that triage is at the other end of the building! Do they listen? Do they, hell!"

"Umm…" Nathan began, but Grubby held up a finger and wagged it.

"I'm not interested. He'll have to get in line with all the others. Unless you have more taxes to offer up, of course. That's if the robbing monsters outside have left you with anything. I don't suppose you have any cigarettes, do you? I'd kill for a smoke right now."

Nathan shook his head. "We just…"

But Grubby wasn't having any of it; he shooed them along the rows of beds "Get yourselves along to triage. I don't have time for this. Other end of the building. They'll try and get you seen within the next seventy-two hours."

Nathan felt his eyes bulging with shock.

Grubby sighed. "We have a backlog. Christ, everyone has a backlog. Even our backlog has a backlog. Just go now, and get in the line. I'm expecting thirty or forty deaths today. That seems to be the average, so there will be beds becoming available. That's the best I can do. Now, go!"

The triage area—such as it was, because it bore no resemblance to anything that Nathan had experienced in the trips he had made to various emergency rooms over the years, for Tony's asthma or Cyndi's trials with preeclampsia during her pregnancy with their first son—was just a vast sea of people. There were perhaps five hundred or so, sitting on the floor, leaning against walls or rolled into balls, covered in blankets. The line to the triage point, if that's indeed what it was, was a higgledy-piggledy mess that snaked at torturous angles back and forth across the floor space. There were children in the arms of their parents who had whey-colored faces, and sweating men coughing. Women with broken limbs. There were puddles of blood on the floor between the rows, patches of vomit, and other liquids that Nathan could only guess at.

At the head of the line, three figures in white coats, a man and two women, were examining those nearest to them. When they'd finished with an exam, they wrote on a sticker and thumped it onto the shoulder of the patient, then pointed through a door into an area that Nathan couldn't see into, at the back of the pavilion. There was only natural light flooding into the triage area through the pavilion's widows, and it was as gray and lifeless as the figures standing in line.

The three of them stood back. Nathan had no intention of joining the line, but didn't want to be seen acting suspiciously, thus drawing the attention of FEMA soldiers to throw them out.

As he looked at the front of the line, however, he saw that one of the women in white coats was also writing on a clipboard, and next to her, folded neatly over a chair, was another white coat. Perhaps it was a spare—a clean coat to put on if the one she was wearing got too dirty. It occurred to Nathan that, if he had a white coat, he might be able to move freely through the field hospital without arousing suspicion, to find Tommy and the others that way.

"Free, I'm going to try and get that coat up there. You guys wait here, and when I get up there, do something to cause a distraction."

Free looked incredulously at the multitude of people moaning, crying, and groaning in the line. "What the hell could I do that's going to distract the doctors from *this*?"

Nathan didn't know, but said, "Think of something. Anything."

And then Nathan headed forward.

In some places, he had to step over people laying still on the floor, and around puddles of bodily fluids which could honestly have been anything. The floor in places was running like an open sewer. A man with a mop and a bucket, wearing a boiler suit, was making some attempt to clean it, but he was fighting an uphill battle.

None of the people in the triage area seemed to mind Nathan pushing past them. Their various maladies seemed to have robbed them of any fight, or perhaps they were used to being treated this way.

Nathan made his way almost to the head of the line, and there he began insinuating himself between two women standing silently, both of them holding babies. One of the babies was crying, but the other looked like it would never cry again.

Nathan breathed an apology, and then he pushed through. He was almost in reach of the chair and the coat. The medics looked dog-tired and were dealing with intense exams of ill refugees. All it would take was for Free to take their attention toward the back of the hall for a moment, and if he did, Nathan was sure he could whip the coat away.

"Come on, Free. Come on…"

Somewhere behind him, a woman began to scream. "My God! Look!"

Nice, Free. Good job.

But then other people were gasping and yelling, and Nathan felt himself being pushed sideways, away from the chair and the coat, by a tide of humans trying to get away from something.

Surely, Free and Dave hadn't caused *this*…

"It's coming in!" someone shouted.

"It's gonna crash!" called another.

As the press of bodies propelled Nathan some five, eight, and then accelerating past twelve yards away from the pavilion widows, he caught sight of a black shape falling from the sky.

A Black Hawk helicopter, like the one that had found them on the road to Casper, belly-flopped onto the concrete outside the pavilion, its rotors still spinning crazily. The fuselage tipped sideways and the blades bit into the ground, snapping and whirling through the air. The pavilion windows shattered as shards of metal from the crashed copter exploded into the building, scything down people like wheat at harvest.

Screams of terror ripped the air apart, and gusts of wind blew snow into the building, sending the temperature crashing down in half a second.

Nathan was pushed back further by the rush. He almost went down, the press of bodies making it impossible to see the window, the coat, or to the back of the room where he hoped

Dave and Free were also getting out of the way. Nathan planted his feet, steadied himself, and let the stream of bodies go around him like a rock in a flooded river.

Through the broken windows, he watched as the Black Hawk fuselage rolled completely onto its side, and the rotors chewed into the concrete, finally breaking apart, unable to cause more damage. As the broken hull rocked, soldiers began running toward it from all directions.

Nathan took his opportunity as the crowd of patients stopped pushing—moving to fight his way back to the chair. The doctors who had been at the head of the triage line had abandoned their posts as the helicopter came down, and the coat was available for him to take, wrap up under his arm.

The helicopter hadn't caught fire—there was black smoke venting hard from the exhaust ports, but no licking of flames. Whoever had been in the Black Hawk had been blessed because of that at least. The soldiers who had rushed to the copter had gotten the side door open and begun reaching inside, pulling at the crew and passengers.

What Nathan saw, though, with an increasing sense of dread and horror, made him wish the Black Hawk had caught fire on impact, because the first person the soldiers pulled from the wreckage to slither down to the ground, to then bend over and vomit, was Detroit Mayor Harvey Brant.

22

Nathan backed away from the windows as fast as he could, even as the still vomiting Brant was ushered away from the Black Hawk in case whatever fuel that was left in it did go up in flames.

Nathan forced his way between the members of the crowd toward the doctor's tables, trying hard not to add to their ills or injuries, but mindful that he had to get away *now*. A hand fell hard on his shoulder, and he turned with a clenched fist ready to punch whoever it was who'd laid a hand on him.

It was Free, forcing his way through the crowd from the back of the room.

"Did you see who came out of the 'copter?" Free asked, his face painted with shock.

Nathan took Freeson by the bicep and pushed him ahead. "Yes, I did. Free, we have to get Tommy and the others now. If Brant's here, he's here for us. Where's Dave?"

"We got separated in the panic, but he wasn't hit when the windows came in, I'm sure."

"Okay, so you find him, and meet me back at the entrance we came in. With Brant here, we need to speed this up. I'll find Tommy or try to find some records that might tell us what happened to him. You guys do what you can to locate Syd and Lucy."

"Roger that," Free said, and with that, he spun away into the crowd of ill refugees.

Nathan pressed himself against a wall. As the panicked bodies swarmed past, there was enough space for him to take off his jacket and put on the white coat. The pockets felt heavy, and when he reached in, he pulled out a stethoscope and a name badge that told him the coat belonged to a Dr. F. L. Smart. There was no ID picture, so that was a plus, but the initials gave no sense of whether Dr. Smart was male or female. Nathan dropped the badge into his pocket—no point raising suspicions in people who knew Dr. F.L. Smart. He put the stethoscope around his neck like he'd seen Doctor Grubby display when they'd come in. Nathan left the triage area, still carrying his North Face jacket under his arm, and found a place to stow it behind clean laundry cages that were being kept at the end of the main bed area.

As Nathan had noted when he'd first come into the pavilion, there were hundreds upon hundreds of beds… and all of them were occupied. Nurses were tending to some patients, janitors mopped at puddles, and occasionally a doctor, face grim, would flit from bed to bed like a ghost. Nathan did everything he could to avoid eye contact with the medics; he didn't need to get into a conversation about something he knew nothing about. Finding Tommy wasn't going to be a case of just zeroing in on the Texan in a matter of moments. Many of the patients—those who weren't sitting or throwing up into bowls, anyway—were hunkered down beneath the sheets, heads turned into pillows. Nathan was going to have to make a systematic search that he didn't have time for, and hope that Tommy was able to walk out of the building with him to get back to the RAV4. That in mind, he picked up a clipboard and chart from the nearest bed; its occupant, an old woman with a cloud of white hair, lay sleeping beneath the sheets.

As he walked, pretending to consult the charts, his head remained bent, trying to give the best approximation of a harried, overworked medic, and he scanned the beds as he went. When it came to those with their faces turned away, he paused momentarily to check over their heads and ascertain gender or age. Those whose hair didn't match Tommy's peppery, iron gray stubble were passed over. Nathan wondered if Tommy would still be wearing the USMC baseball cap. He'd put it into Tommy's hand before he'd been driven away from Drymouth, and as the royal-blue, gold-embossed Marine Corps cap had been a permanent fixture on the Texan's head, it seemed worth looking out for here, too.

Nathan walked on as slowly as he dared without arousing suspicion, checking beds left and right, and doubling back a couple of times to check on people who had their heads below the covers, trying to shut out the noise and stench of the hospital.

A quarter of the way down the ward, Nathan saw him. The blue cap was in place. Tommy was sitting up in bed, and there was a good color to his cheeks. His knees were drawn up under the covers, and he looked like a coiled cobra ready to strike.

It was clear Tommy wasn't happy to be here, but he looked a lot better than Nathan had been expecting. The Texan was three rows of beds away, and he had his head turned, neck craned, looking toward the triage area of the pavilion—trying to see, Nathan guessed, what had happened after the Black Hawk had come down.

Nathan quickened his pace, but even though he wanted to go in a flat run, he still didn't want to present himself as being anyone out of the ordinary. There might be a commotion, and a sense of horror rippling through the building because of the crash, but there would surely be members of the medical staff who might raise the alarm if they felt Nathan was a dangerous interloper.

Nathan and Tommy locked eyes as the Texan moved his gaze back along the ward. It took a moment for Tommy to parse out what he was seeing—Nathan in a white doctor's coat—but when the recognition blossomed on his face, Nathan returned the smile.

He was fifteen yards away when Tommy's expression changed, just as Nathan's arm was taken in an iron grip and a voice barked. "This way, Doc, you're needed. Now! The civilians can wait."

Oh hell.

Nathan's arm was being gripped and his body turned by a FEMA soldier who immediately began pulling him away from Tommy. With one last desperate look back at his friend, Nathan let himself be dragged back the way he had come. All he could do was remember a couple of significant landmarks on the wall—a poster about boiling all water, and a widow with a broken pane covered by cardboard that would lead him quickly back to Tommy when he'd finished whatever he was being taken away for.

The soldier marched Nathan double-time through the crowds of beds, through the triage area, and through the door at the back, to the immediate area where the doctors he'd stolen the coat from had sent the patients who'd been triaged. There were soldiers at the door now, pushing out people who had stickers on their shoulders and chests.

"But I've gone through already! Why are you sending me back here?" one yelled, and he was given a rifle butt to the temple for his trouble, sending him to the floor with a crash. "You need to get *that triaged* now!" the soldier said, pointing at the new gash he'd created in the man's skin.

The soldier looked at the other people who'd been pushed out of the room. "Anyone else want another reason to see a doctor? Coz I got plenty more where that came from!"

Those with stickers shook their heads and moved out in an orderly fashion. Nathan was brushed past them, and on through the door.

Inside was what might have been a further assessment unit, or a holding and overspill area to be used until beds became available in the main part of the hospital.

Doctor Grubby was there already with a medical light in his fingers, checking over Mayor Brant's eyes and getting him to follow his finger. Nathan stopped in his tracks at the sight of the old enemy.

The soldier placed a hand in the small of his back and mercifully propelled him out of Brant's eye-line, toward another bed where a woman in a pilot's uniform was laying, her arm at a crazy angle looking broke as hell. Her face was a mask of pain, her jaw tight, her lips just a slash where they were compressed. Her name tape identified her as Major Champion.

Nathan was impelled to the side of the bed, and there he looked down on Champion.

"Give me something for the pain!" she spat at him.

"Sure," Nathan answered, trying to ban from his voice any suggestion that he had no damn idea how to do that, or who to ask, or where the painkillers might be kept.

There was a tinkle of keys behind him as Doctor Grubby said, "Here. Get me some Ibuprofen while you're there."

The soldier caught the keys Grubby had tossed to the bed and put them in Nathan's hand. "Make it quick. She's in agony."

"I can see that," Nathan said, and then he walked away from the bed. It occurred to him again that he didn't know where the drugs might be kept, but he couldn't risk making it obvious he didn't, so he took three steps toward the back of the room. No one said anything, so he guessed he was at least going approximately in the right direction.

"I'm going to have you hung for this!"

Brant's voice cut across the room, and they stilled Nathan's heart. Had he been busted?

No.

Brant continued his tirade, and it clearly wasn't directed at Nathan, but Champion. "You should be able to fly that thing in all weather. That's what I pay you for, you damn imbecile!"

"I'm... not a miracle worker, sir... I said we should have... waited for the storm to pass before we attempted the flight! The Black Hawk hadn't been serviced in... an age. Pointing a gun at the pilot doesn't make an aircraft more... airworthy!"

"Don't answer back, you moron! Shut up, and hope I change my mind about lynching you in the nearest damn tree!"

Nathan's blood chilled at the threats made by Brant to Champion. He remembered how, back in Detroit, Brant's men had gone to the Masonic building and executed a number of the residents on his orders, just to make sure Nathan had nowhere safe to return to. Brant held human life in such low regard, it was a wonder he wasn't telling Grubby to give Champion a lethal injection where she lay.

Nathan had reached the back of the ward now. A series of white cupboards sat beneath worktops stacked with medical supplies, blood test tubes, bandages, empty syringes, and all manner of other first aid materials. There were no drugs to be seen.

He'd been given keys, so it followed that there would be a locked cabinet to find. None of the lower cupboards had locks on the doors, but there was a row of metal cabinets above them. Two had locks.

It had to be two, didn't it?

Which one?

Nathan made a play of working his way through the keys while he tried to work out which was the cabinet he should go to first.

Fifty-fifty.

His life might hang in the balance if he chose wrongly, if Grubby or the others, only ten yards behind, became suspicious.

"Hurry up, man!" Grubby yelled. "We don't have all damn day!"

Nathan chose.

He raised what he suspected was the most likely key to the cabinet on the right. His hand was trembling, and he shielded it from those behind him as he pushed it into the lock.

Please turn. Please turn.

The key stuck.

No.

He shifted his weight, pushed harder, and the key turned in the lock. The door swung open. Relief rushed through him as he eyed the boxes and bottles of pills. He found Ibuprofen quickly, but would that be enough of a painkiller for Champion? Ibuprofen was for headaches and general aches and pains. It wasn't going to touch the pain in her busted arm.

Think. Think.

When his daddy had been dying, the doctor had prescribed strong painkillers for him. A morphine derivative, the doctor had said. It had come in a liquid form.

Could he remember the damn name?

Nope.

It began with a *D*, he was sure. He remembered pouring it into a medicine cup for his daddy to sip through trembling lips. Lips that had trembled like Nathan's hand was shaking now.

He thought about making a dash for the door, taking his chances with the soldiers. Maybe he'd be able to push through; maybe they wouldn't open fire because of all the civilians who might get hit... *No, don't be stupid, Nathan. They won't care a damn about collateral damage.*

He turned a bottle around so that he could see the label.

D... *Demerol.*

Yes. That was it. Demerol.

Nathan took the bottle and picked up a small plastic medicine cup from the counter, turning back toward Champion and the others. Brant was moving from his bed toward the pilot, though. He was preparing to harangue her where she lay, his finger already pointing. Nathan took one step and then another. Steps that would take him ever closer to Brant. Ever closer to the moment where he would be busted and his life would be over.

"I was told by General Carter that you were the best! I was told that you're his best pilot! What a crock! You couldn't fly in an itty-bit of snow. You're a disgrace. A damn disgrace! I could have been killed! Do you realize what that might have meant? Me! The Mayor of Detroit killed because some useless fly-girl couldn't handle a bit of snow! Where did you get your pilot's license? From a damn fortune cookie?"

Nathan was at the end of the bed now, three feet between him and Brant as the man stabbed his fat little finger at Champion. For the pilot's part, she was not responding. The pain was still swimming in shoals of suffering across her face and her eyes were fixed on Brant. His finger came ever closer. Spittle flying from his mouth as he shouted.

"I'll make sure you never fly again, fly-girl! You mark my words!"

Nathan unscrewed the cap from the bottle of Demerol and poured 20mls—the same dose he had given to his daddy—into the cup.

Brant was getting more and more irate, and seemed to be doing so because he wasn't getting the reaction from Champion he wanted. Nathan winced as Brant poked his finger down on the break in Champion's arm.

She screamed hard, trying to turn away, but Brant was enjoying the reaction *now*. He stabbed at her again with his stiff little index finger, flecks of white saliva at the corners of his smiling mouth. Champion screamed again and pulled the broken arm across her body in an attempt to get it out of Brant's reach, but he just leaned further in. Poked her again.

No one else in the room moved. Not the soldier. Not Grubby.

Not Nathan.

If he intervened, he would be a dead man. But there was also no way he could stand by and watch as Brant tortured Champion for his own amusement.

"Not so confident of your abilities now, are you? Not so smart and clever now, are you, you worthless piece of scum! Not willing to risk it all now, are you? Ha! You know your place now! You know your place!"

Then Brant made a fist.

Nathan broke.

He couldn't just watch the poor woman be hammered like that by Brant. Brant, the man who had made his friend betray him. Brant, the man who had been the driving force behind the death of the love of Nathan's life. Brant, the man who had tracked them across the states, willing to put whatever resources it took to catch up with Nathan into fulfilling his sick desire for squalid revenge.

Brant raised his fist above his head, ready to bring it down on Champion where she cowered, desperately trying to protect herself from the mayor's imminent onslaught. And Nathan dropped the bottle on the bed, took a step forward and, in his mind, kissing both his sons goodbye, grabbed Brant's wrist.

23

Brant roared and ripped his hand smartly from Nathan's grip.

"How dare you touch me...!" Brant began, but that was just before the mayor's eyes seemed to spin in his head like cherries in a slot machine, and the jackpot of recognition paid out in his head. His mouth opened slightly. His gasp was audible. He was summoning up the words, and the fist he was about to bring down on Champion became an accusatory point.

Nathan hit Brant.

Hard, fast, and with unstoppable force. His fist connected with the point of Brant's chin and the man's head snapped back on his neck. Brant fell like a cartoon.

He crashed back onto the floor, his toes turned up, his arms outstretched, and a near comical grin of unconsciousness on his face.

"Stay where you are! Do not move!" the soldier was screaming at Nathan, his M-16 pointing directly at his head. "Raise your hands. Now!"

Nathan did as he was told.

"Doctor!" the soldier yelled at Grubby. "Get out there, and tell my guys to get in here now."

Grubby, face slick with sweat, nodded and headed for the door.

"Belay that order!" came a voice from an unexpected direction. It was Champion on the bed, cradling her broken arm and struggling to sit up. Grubby stopped in a half-turn, unsure what he was supposed to be doing now.

"Ma'am?" the soldier asked, a look of confusion on his face. "I need to secure the room and get this man into custody."

"No, you don't," Champion said.

"Ma'am?"

"What's your rank, soldier?"

"Private first class, ma'am, and I…"

"Be quiet, soldier. I outrank you by about thirty-seven stripes. Are you going to argue with a superior officer?"

"No ma'am, but…"

"But me no buts, soldier!" Champion was sitting up now, struggling with the pain, but she had a steely look of determination on her face. She turned her attention to Nathan. "Get out of here while you can."

Nathan lowered his hands. "I…"

"Ma'am!" complained the soldier. "You can't just…"

Champion screwed up her eyes, and then flicked them open at the soldier. "You stood by while that man tortured me in front of you and the doctor. *Tortured* me. How about we make a deal? You let the only guy in the room who tried to stop him go, and I won't have you court martialed where you stand!"

The soldier licked his lips, flicking his eyes from Nathan to Champion and back again.

"Lower your weapon and stand down, soldier. That is a direct order!"

The muzzle of the M-16 wobbled, wavered, and then came down to point at the floor.

Champion returned her gaze to Nathan. "Now, get out of here. Run and don't stop running. And, sir…?"

Nathan looked back at her even as he began turning.

"Thank you," Champion said. "There's not enough people like you."

And then Nathan ran.

Tommy's bed was empty. *Of course*, it was empty.

Nathan had jogged between the beds, white coat flapping behind him—looking, he hoped for all the world, like a doctor on his way to an emergency, not away from one. For all the reasons he had to get out of the pavilion as fast as he could, he wasn't going to leave Tommy behind.

He'd staggered to a halt by Tommy's bed. The covers were drawn back, the pillows askew.

Nathan cursed under his breath and looked around wildly. He couldn't see Tommy anywhere, and there was no time to search. Champion might be able to hold off the soldier and Doctor Grubby by pulling rank, temporarily anyway, but pretty soon Brant was going to be awake—and he outranked everyone in the building.

There was nothing else for it; he was going to have to get out now and formulate a plan later to come back and find Tommy and the others. No point in being dead right now. The current plan had worked out okay as it stood, but now he had only minutes to get out of the City Park Pavilion and away from Brant's impending ire.

Nathan broke for the main entrance, nodding to a duo of soldiers as he went and ignoring the calls of several patients on their beds who thought he was the real thing. He made it through the door and onto the snow-covered forecourt, and dashed toward the RAV4—which, thankfully, had not taken any damage from the downed Black Hawk still steaming and cooling in the increasing intensity of the blizzard.

He was mere yards from the RAV4 when two things happened. First, his heart leaped upon seeing through the blizzarding snow that not only were Free and Dave waiting for him in the car, but sitting on the back seat, gesturing to Nathan to get a move-on, was Tommy. But, second, all around the camp, alarm sirens started up, cutting through the air like wailing animals.

Perhaps Brant was already awake.

Nathan climbed into the RAV4 beside Tommy. "You took your time," the Texan said.

"No time for explanations, we've got to get out of here."

Free, in the driver's seat, turned his head. "Not without Lucy and Syd."

"Brant has seen me. The sirens are going off now, and that might be for me. We cannot stay—we'll have to come back for them."

Tommy shook his head. "We can pick them up on the way out. I know exactly where they'll be right now."

Stymied, Nathan said, "Okay. But if they're not in this truck in five minutes, we'll have to come back."

Nathan could tell, from his hunched shoulders and ever-tighter hands on the wheel as Free slew the RAV4 around, heading in the direction Tommy had indicated, that his friend was not at all on board with Nathan's 'five minutes' pronouncement. But that was something Nathan would have to deal with if they didn't find the women immediately.

Two minutes later, Nathan's relief was total. They found Syd and Lucy in a wooden kiosk on the south side of the park. They were doling out thin soup to a group of mainly male laborers who were working to clear more areas for tents and dig sewage lines.

They didn't need to be told twice to abandon their posts and squeeze into the RAV4. One of the laborers called to Lucy as she sprinted toward the car. "What about our soup?"

"We've downsized. It's now a self-service restaurant!"

Snow flecked their hair and skin. And while their lips were blue with cold and their teeth were chattering, they were glad to see Nathan and the others.

"It was either the soup kitchen or the FEMA brothel," Lucy said pragmatically. "We both chose soup."

Nathan filled everyone in on what had happened with Champion and Brant as Free pointed the truck toward the entrance to the City Park. Although the sirens were still going off all around them, there didn't seem to be much activity in the park itself to suggest that a manhunt was underway.

"Could be just a drill," Tommy suggested.

If it was only a drill, the soldiers at the checkpoint onto York Street were treating it with extreme seriousness. Free brought the RAV4 to a halt seventy yards away, surrounded on both sides by row after row of sad refugee tents.

The air fizzed with flakes, making everything gray and indistinct. In happier times, this would have been a day for warming your toes in front of a good fire, waxing the runners on your toboggan, and waiting for the snow to stop so that you could take the kids outside for a crazy afternoon of sledding. But not today.

Through the snow, Nathan could see that two APCs had been placed nose to nose beyond the checkpoint, and there were at least double the number of soldiers there than before, all of them looking like they were waiting for trouble.

"We're not getting out that way," Free said grimly. "It's a lockdown."

Nathan nodded. "Plan B, then."

Free reversed the RAV4, turning it around as innocuously as he could without wanting to raise suspicion, and they trundled back toward the pavilion.

"Keep it steady," Nathan said as they sailed past the building and the crashed Black Hawk. There were now sentries at the door, and other soldiers were manning the broken windows shattered by the crash, but it still didn't seem that the FEMA forces were going crazy trying to find them.

Yet.

Please be a drill.

Perhaps they were so confident that the new, high metal fences around City Park, and the closed-off main checkpoint, would keep anyone inside, and it would just be a case of systematically searching the camp tent-by-tent to find interlopers. There was no panic, so the sirens must be to put everyone on alert. They certainly weren't checking any of the vehicles moving around the inner roads, and it was that kind of sloppy complacency that might get Nathan and the others out of the City Park camp in the next five minutes.

When they reached the southern tip of Ferril Lake, Free turned the truck off the road and began bumping across the snowy grass and between the trees, toward the razor wire-topped metal fence.

Refugee tents hadn't been set up in this area yet, but if the influx of desperate people continued, it wouldn't be long before they were. It was fifty yards across the rough ground to the wall, and Free pulled to a halt twenty yards from it.

The snowfall was heavier now, if anything, making the air more dense and difficult to see through. It might not cover their activity completely, but a FEMA patrol would need to be pretty close before they'd be seen. Nathan jogged to the tightly grilled fence while the others hunkered down behind the truck.

He'd explained briefly to Lucy, Syd, and Tommy what was about to happen, and now he was looking for the lines he'd set earlier, which were going to make what he'd explained happen.

He found the wires poking through the view grill in the fence after a minute of anxious searching. He looked desperately over his shoulder to see if he was being observed from the road or the distant machine gun tower, itself almost lost in the blizzard. The sirens had cut out as they'd traveled around Ferril Lake, so maybe they weren't about them and were just a drill.

Maybe.

Nathan gathered the five wires in his hand, counted to three, and pulled them hard.

He had seven seconds to sprint back to the RAV4 for cover before the grenades he'd laid as his Plan B would explode against the fence on the other side.

The crump of the explosion was loud, but possibly deadened enough by the snowfall not to echo all the way across the camp.

But there was no point taking any chances. Nathan looked over the hood of the RAV4. As the smoke cleared, he could see that there was a hole in the fence big enough for a man to crawl through—just—but not to get the car through.

"Grab what you can and go!" Nathan ordered everyone as he reached into the truck to get an MP4 and a spare couple of grenades. Around him, the others also gathered what they could and headed toward the hole in the wall.

Tommy was moving awkwardly after what he'd told them on the drive had been *'Civil War level sawbones surgery,'* but at least he *could* move.

Nathan pushed Syd and Lucy through first, and then he waited until the others had gone through before throwing the gun to the snow beyond and crawling through himself.

Donie, who had heard the explosion from the house behind which they'd parked the F-350, was waving from the other side of the street as they ran across the snowfield to her.

"We need to get on the road, now!" Nathan shouted.

It was jam-packed in the F-350.

Dave and Donie traveled in the utility shell with Tommy after they'd dumped some equipment, while Lucy and Syd crammed into the Crew Cab with Tony, Brandon, and Rapier. Free rode up front while Nathan drove.

The fresh snow was making the roads treacherous, but that would be the same for any FEMA soldiers who might already have investigated the hole in the fence and called for reinforcements. And though a ten mile an hour getaway wasn't the most exciting of escapes, the tension in Nathan's gut was absolute. They had to get out of the city, and fast.

Tommy was in pain, but he was coping, and Lucy and Syd were warming up in the cramped space with the dog and the kids.

"We've got about seventy miles of gas," Free said, checking the gauge. "After that, we're screwed."

Seventy miles wasn't going to be enough of a space between Brant and the party for Nathan. Seventy-thousand was more acceptable.

They headed south through the Denver suburbs, the storm building and becoming dirtier. At least the falling flakes would be covering their tracks and making it more difficult for them to be followed, but it was slowing them down even more. The weight of the F-350 gave it good traction, but progress was still hard going.

The wind was also becoming more brutal, whipping snow into whorls and gusting sheets. Snow blew down off the roofs around them, sometimes dumping buckets' worth of the stuff with a thud on the hood, or thickly on the windshield. Several times, Nathan or Free had to get out and clear the windshield by hand because the wipers couldn't cope. It was a war of attrition, so that if the storm didn't abate soon, they would surely lose.

It seemed like the entire North Pole had been lifted into the sky, glaciers and all, and was being dumped, dumpsterful by dumpsterful, onto Denver in general and the F-350 specifically.

Visibility was so difficult now that the nose of the truck almost clanged into the roadblock before they saw it.

"Whoa! That was close!" Nathan shouted as he slammed on the brakes. If they'd have been traveling at more than the pace of a crippled snail, they wouldn't have been able to avoid a collision.

Nathan squinted through the windshield to see what was what. A green Lexus NX 300h and a white Jaguar F-Pace SUV were nose to nose across the street, making forward progress impossible.

Nathan put the F-350 into reverse and thought about backing up, but Free put a hand on his arm. "No, wait. Look."

Nathan followed his finger.

Through the swirling flakes, Nathan could just make out the outline of a body laying facedown in the snow. A spreading pool of blood seeping out around the head. As he looked closer, he also saw there were two bullet holes in the door of the Lexus, and behind the door was a slumped figure. Behind the Jaguar, there were two more bodies, and then, resolving out of the whirling snow, balaclava in place and sniper rifle up, and rested on one hip, was a figure who looked to be Arctic. The person who had saved their backsides in Drymouth.

Nathan jumped down from the truck and approached the figure who was standing stock-still, seemingly waiting for him. "Are you following us?"

Arctic shrugged. "I was here first. Perhaps you were following me."

The voice was still little more than a hiss, but Nathan had at last convinced himself of what he only could have suspected before. Arctic was a woman.

"What are you doing?"

"Killing bad guys. Why aren't you killing bad guys? The less bad guys there are, the better for everyone, no?"

"I'm no executioner."

"Then you will die. You will be executed." Arctic turned and began to walk away.

"Wait! Please. The man you helped, the one who was stabbed. He's in the car. I'm sure he'd want to shake your hand."

Arctic paused, and then turned back. "I don't want thanks. I'm just doing what I should do. I have a gift. I'm using it."

"Please…"

Arctic shook her head, sighed loudly with a tinge of frustration, and moved back to the F-350 and looked inside. Nathan followed and spoke up first.

"Tommy… this is the woman who saved you at Drymouth."

Tommy's eyes widened.

Arctic pulled back her hood, tore off her balaclava, and shook her brunette hair free. She was perhaps thirty-five, with a face that was thin, dark eyes, and a nose that had been broken several times in the past. Her chin was scarred with thick red chunks of flesh.

"I saw your fight, mister. You would have beaten them if they hadn't stabbed you in the back."

Arctic held out her hand and Tommy took it.

"You can have the cars if you want. I can get another easy enough. The gangs here are very stupid," she said.

Nathan didn't know where it came from, but he said it anyway. "Come with us."

Arctic looked at him as if he were talking in Swahili. "Why?"

"We have some bad guys on our tail. We could do with the help. We can offer food, and some shelter and company."

"What makes you think I want them?"

"I don't. But I'm offering anyway."

Before Arctic could answer, Lucy made a sound, retched, and scrambled out of the truck into the snow. There, she bent forward, putting a gloved hand on the side of the truck, and began vomiting copiously.

Nathan's heart sank.

Here he was trying to get Arctic to join the group, and he hadn't been paying attention to the members of the party he already had. He was transported back in his mind to the patients in the pavilion hospital, retching just as Lucy was now and throwing up into bowls. The smell of illness and death in the place came rushing back to his nostrils, and he felt his guts turning over at just the memory of it.

"Lucy... my god, I didn't think. Could you have come into contact with whatever was making the refugees sick in the FEMA hospital? Are you ill like them?"

"Oh, now you wish you'd left us behind?" Lucy asked, bringing her head up for a moment and fixing Nathan with a tear-smeared stare before bending over to vomit again.

"No, of course not. I just... we should have been more careful, is all." Nathan caught sight of Brandon and Tony through the open door, through the flurrying snow. Had he failed to protect his kids, and keep them away from a potential plague?

Family first, son.

"Careful is a luxury these days," said Arctic, as if nothing else needed to be said on the subject.

Nathan felt like a heel. He sketched an apologetic expression on his face as Lucy uncurled and stood up, wiping her hand across her lips. "The only physically infectious thing I've come into contact with is Freeson, and I've caught his disease, Nate. I'm pregnant, you doofus."

24

"Carmel Mackintosh," Arctic said once she'd gotten into the Jaguar with Nathan, Tony, Brandon, and Rapier, and once they'd rolled off into the snow. The Lexus had been full of bullet holes and blood, so they hadn't taken that. The Jag's occupant gang members had been killed outside the vehicle, though, and it had just been a case of dragging their bodies to the sidewalk while Free, stunned to find out he was going to be a father, had siphoned the gas from the Lexus to complement what was already in the Ford's tank, all the while breathing curses and blowing out his cheeks and shaking his head as Lucy's news sank in.

Nathan led the F-350 through the storm, south down the spine of the city, sticking to suburban roads where he could but, when they became impassable, doubling back onto the highway. The storm was keeping the FEMA APCs and A1s off the streets for now, and they hoped to make it out of the city as soon as they could.

Carmel had agreed to come along *'for the time being'*—but didn't think it would be a *'permanent thing.'*

"Why not?"

"I guess you guys are looking for a place to settle down, right?"

"That's the plan, yes, if we can keep out of Brant's way and stop him tracking us down."

Carmel shook her head. "Settling down's not for me. This world —this Big Winter world—has afforded me an opportunity I never thought I'd be presented with when I got back from Iraq."

"I figured you'd be ex-forces. No one shoots like that for a hobby."

"Special forces, yes. Five tours, zeroing bad guys doing bad things. Cold, clean kills."

Nathan couldn't imagine what it was like to have that kind of job description. "Give me a hot, dirty engine every time."

Carmel shrugged. "I don't ask you to like what I do, Nathan, just to understand it. If I hadn't been around back at Drymouth, neither would you."

Nathan knew she was right, but it didn't make him feel any better. Maybe he wasn't built for this world. It had been an odyssey, that's for sure, and he'd defended himself when he needed to, and he was pretty sure he would always step up to the plate when his children or his friends were threatened, but Carmel's life seemed so removed from his own.

Even now.

"I came across that gang last night. They'd stopped a woman and her teenage boy at their roadblock. They didn't give them the opportunity to just walk away and leave their gear for the gang. Nope. They raped the woman on the back seat of the car in front of her son. I couldn't get a clear shot without hitting the woman or her boy. The gang had a laugh, a smoke and a drink, and waited for the next car to come along. I could only make the shot after the gang had killed the woman and her boy in the car. I wish I'd had it sooner. God. This place."

"You make a compelling argument."

"I'm just looking at the facts, Nathan. The gangs are bad, FEMA's bad, and the guy chasing you down, Brant, is bad. Who's good anymore? I'm not good in the classic sense, but someone has to take a stand."

They drove on in silence for a while, the houses rolling by on either side, the Jag buffeted by the wind. A street blocked with a burned-out, overturned Mack semi sent them back the way they had driven, looking for a cross-street that would get them back up onto the highway.

The route and the progress were torturous.

At every turn, Nathan scanned the road ahead for FEMA vehicles, but there were none… which made Nathan a little suspicious. Sure, the storm was raging, and no one in their right mind would be traveling right now unless they had to, but to see no FEMA vehicles or checkpoints was more than a little odd, compared to what he'd seen in the city already.

"Don't say it," said Carmel unexpectedly.

"Don't say what?"

"Don't say it's too quiet. You know what a screw-up that can be, tempting fate."

Nathan decided that he liked Carmel.

He may not like her making herself Colorado's self-appointed executioner, but her demeanor was comfortable, and she seemed unaffected and genuine, not someone who would screw you over at the first opportunity they got. Like Stryker Wilson had. Like Harvey Brant had. Carmel was a bitter pill to swallow, but she was an antidote to some of the horrors the Big Winter had thrown up.

Like Free and Tommy and Lucy and Syd, and more recently Donie and Dave, he felt she would be a good person to have around when the ordure hit the rotating prop.

The suburbs gave way to the plain between Denver and the first risings of the Rockies. Nathan only got occasional glimpses of the distant mountains as the 36, designated Daniel's Park road, passed through the suburb of Shadowbrook and left the city behind. They weren't traveling any faster, as the snow had put paid to that, but there was a definite freeing of Nathan's concerns about still being in the city. A journey that should have taken twenty minutes or so had, with detours and double-backs, taken nearly three hours.

There was about an hour of daylight left, but Nathan had already turned on the headlights of the Jag to try to make the I-36. Out here, that road was no more than un-metaled farm track carved into the flat land, stuffed with fresh fluffy snow getting deeper all the time. If the storm continued like this for much longer, forward progression would be almost impossible.

Nathan stopped the Jag and jumped out into the knee-deep powder. The F-350 pulled up behind them, and Nathan, wind-blown snow stinging his eyes and scouring his face, trudged back to the window as Free pressed for it to go down.

"Nearly dark," Nathan said. "I'm not happy with the idea of carrying on during the night, but I don't think we have any choice."

Free considered his friend's words, and then flashed a concerned look at Lucy beside him. Lucy's eye blazed. "Don't start that, Freeson Mac! I'm pregnant, not made of glass. You don't need to make decisions based on my passenger, and if you don't want a punch in the nose, you won't start now."

Nathan smiled inwardly. Cyndi had said much the same thing to him when they'd left Glens Falls—*"Pregnancy isn't an illness, Nate. For thousands of years, babies were plopped out in the field, in between the mother scything the wheat and then grinding it into flour."*

Nathan felt good about having the ghost of Cyndi's words in his head. It was the first time in a while that he'd felt comfortable with her memory. Perhaps Lucy's pregnancy would do more than cement her relationship with Free. Maybe it would have a positive effect on Nathan, too.

New life from old.

Free began to argue with Lucy, but she waved a finger in his face. "No. Nathan, we're good. We're not making more than ten miles an hour anyway; I'm in more danger of breaking my fist on Free's face than I am of having a miscarriage because of the conditions. I vote we go on."

And so they did go on, into the dark.

"Wait," Carmel said, peering through the Jag's side window at the mirror. She wiped condensation from the glass and peered closer.

Nathan brought the SUV to a halt and pulled on the parking brake. They were pulling up a slight incline in the plain, another fifteen miles from Denver. The snow was pattering and blattering against the bodywork. It was endless.

Even though it could only be seen in the cones of their headlights, the sense of having it all around the car made it feel like they were being held in the grip of the Big Winter, and like it was letting them know that they would never escape.

"What is it?"

"I don't know."

Dave appeared out of the gloom and Nathan lowered the window. A gust of flakes washed into the car, peppering his skin and twanging his spine at the base of his neck.

"You saw it, too?" Dave asked. Nathan was nonplussed.

"Yeah," Carmel said. "We're high enough here to see back along the plain. Headlights. One, possibly two cars."

Nathan looked into the mirrors—he could see nothing.

"Maybe they've turned off the road," Dave said, shielding his eyes against the snow and looking back down the trail.

"Or they've seen us stop and turned off their lights," Tommy said, appearing at Dave's shoulder.

"We're miles from anywhere out here. Who would be traveling at night, in this filthy weather, unless they had to?" Tommy continued, checking the magazine in the MP4 he was carrying.

"I told you not to say it," Carmel told Nathan.

"I didn't."

"Yeah, but I bet you thought it."

Nathan got out of the Jag and hiked up the incline at the side of the road, Tommy and Dave following. Nathan had pulled the binoculars out of the door caddy, and now he used them to scan the snow-flickering darkness as best he could.

There was nothing to see. No cars, no lights, no houses suggesting a dwelling where whoever was following them could be heading. The dark landscape was, to all intents and purposes, a desolate wasteland of snow.

He turned his attention toward the direction in which they'd been traveling, south. They were near enough at the top of the rise, and there was a gentle slope ahead—as far as he could tell from the Jag's headlamps down into a valley, anyway. A light twinkled through the mess of snowflakes. He couldn't make out if it was a building or a vehicle heading toward them. The one thing Nathan did know was that they were stuck on the road. Going cross-country over unknown, snow-covered terrain was suicide.

"We can't go back, and we can't go sideways. We have to go on," Nathan said. "That might be a farmstead down there. There's a light and it's not moving. We might be able to get the vehicles off the road there; get some cover and see what turns up. And if we're dug in already, we might at least have a chance of fighting them off if they want to engage in gunplay, whoever's coming."

The others agreed. Tommy moved up to the Jag with his MP4, getting Tony and Brandon to hunker down into the footwell behind Carmel's seat. Rapier lay down next to Tommy, nose on his paws.

Carmel had two Colt semi-automatics in holsters on her belt. She checked them over, put a round in each chamber, and held them on her lap as Nathan drove forward through the effervescing flakes swirling down from the night clouds up above.

The storm was a constant presence around them, its wind rushing over the SUV and the trucks, snaky and buffeting, wearing down their resolve and making the bodywork rattle and the chassis vibrate.

They didn't see a light behind them again, but that didn't mean they were not being followed.

The twinkling light ahead grew and stayed steady. It had the warmth and glow of an oil lamp rather than one produced by electricity. Nathan thought that it being a farmstead had perhaps been a good call, and as they got closer, the road began to run along a low, chain-link fence on the same side as the light up ahead. It was a definitely a farm fence, the kind used to keep stock in the correct area. There were no signs of cattle, but he saw his hunch had been right when a sign came up for *'The Lazy Q Ranch and Bison Tour.'* Nathan pulled the Jag through an open gate, and the F-350 followed.

The oil lamp was burning in a window of the ranch house, but there was no other light coming from the building, and certainly not from the windows on this side that Nathan could see. Nathan got out of the Jag, followed by Carmel and Tommy, guns ready.

"Don't say it," Carmel said, repeating her mantra.

The front door to the property was up on a short veranda behind a rusted screen. Snow had drifted up against all of the walls three or four feet high, and the wind was still cutting across the plain as sharp as tomahawks.

Tommy and Carmel covered Nathan as he pulled at the screen, kicking away a pile of snow that had gathered at its base. The screen door squealed open on protesting hinges, and he saw that the mahogany door beyond it looked rotted at the base with damp and age. This was not a building which had been used in a long time.

And yet, there was an oil lamp burning in the window.

Nathan touched the door handle with his gloved fingers and paused.

"No. I don't like it. Let's get back in the cars and go on. If we're being followed, let them do their worst. This place doesn't feel right at all."

"Agreed," Tommy said.

"Yup," Carmel added.

"Daddy!" screamed Tony.

Floodlights came on all around them. Five FEMA soldiers were pointing their M16s at the occupants of the F-350. Lucy, Free,

Dave, and Donie got out of their vehicles with their hands raised. Syd got out of the car last, keeping one hand raised while shushing and placating Rapier. She closed the door on the dog's wet black nose and raised her other hand.

The Jag was surrounded by several soldiers, and standing with them was Harvey Brant.

Brant was holding Tony in front of him, pulling the boy's hand up behind his back with cruel intensity. Another soldier was pulling Brandon from the back of the Jag and cradling the baby in his arms.

"Hello again, Nathan," Brant said. "Nice of you to drop in."

"Once we cracked your ineffectual little hack on our system, and found you, we thought we'd be able to get you back to Detroit with minimum fuss. Lieutenant Price always was an overachiever, but I'm a man who likes to see himself as an enabler, Nathan. So, I gave him a shot. Mea culpa. My bad."

There was a laptop open in front of him, with a wire running away under the rotting door to a satellite uplink outside. Brant turned the screen around. The screen showed an infrared picture of the Jag, the F-350, two APCs, and the farmhouse. The picture was fuzzy, but the hot engines of the vehicles showed up fine.

"Once my boys got in touch with FEMA here in Denver, and they let us have access to their live keyhole satellite imagery, we just followed you out of the city. We saw which way you were heading and got here before you. It's not rocket science, but it sure feels like it."

Nathan sat across the table from Brant. Apart from three soldiers, they were the only ones in the room inside the old farmhouse. There was still only one oil lamp, and it was making black hoods of Brant's eyes.

Brant had pushed Tony into the arms of a soldier and marched up to Nathan. Nathan had thought he was going to pay him back for the punch in the pavilion hospital right there, but Brant had just smiled. "Shall we go in?" he'd asked, and then he'd motioned Nathan inside, to be followed by the soldiers.

"Your problem, Nathan, is that you really didn't know what you were up against. You thought too small. You thought I was just a small-time hoodlum who'd got lucky and taken over a city. But, I have to tell you, Nathan, that my skillset is something more... useful. Not only am I an enabler, but I am also a facilitator. And what I'm starting to facilitate is the Reunited States of America. Can you imagine it, Nathan? Little old me, a Kissinger? A Washington? A founding father of a new nation? I really like the sound of that. What do you think?"

Nathan said nothing. The wind was battering the house, howling around the roof and walls with a banshee wail that could have chilled hearts to a standstill, if Brant hadn't already had that covered.

"Well, okay, you don't want to play, so, Sergeant Perry?"

The nearest soldier to the table, pointing his M-16 at Nathan's face, answered, "Sir?"

"Mr. Tolley doesn't want to play. Go outside and kick the baby to death."

"Sir," Perry said without question, and he headed for the door.

"Stop!" Nathan screamed.

Perry kept marching—and he reached out, putting his hand on the door handle.

Brant smiled. "Sergeant Perry, stand down. I think we have an understanding now."

Perry came back to where he had stood before, lifted his gun, and aimed it squarely at Nathan's forehead.

"So, Nathan, as I was saying. What do you think?"

"I think you're going to kill me, whatever I say."

"I think you're right."

Brant put his hands down flat on the table, turned them inwards, and interlocked his fingers.

"This is what I'm doing to America, Nathan. Putting it back together. Detroit has already linked up with Chicago and Casper—sharing resources, expertise, and weaponry. Did you think I was coming to Denver just to catch up with you and explore my options for revenge? Of course not. You were just the cherry on top. Tomorrow, I go to a meeting with leaders from Boulder, Salt Lake City, Omaha, and the head of FEMA forces back up the road a'ways, General Carter. We're at the start of something *big*, Nathan, something really big. You, you're just small fry. But I *am* going to enjoy frying you."

Brant laughed at his own lame joke, and Nathan swallowed. There were three rifles on him, weapons-hot. His friends and his family were outside surrounded by soldiers. If he wasn't going to die in this room, he was going to die very close to it.

And, Nathan was hot. Hotter than he'd been in an age. The sweat of that heat standing out on his forehead, running down his cheeks... his knee was moving involuntarily, and he could feel his heart beating so loud that it could have crawled up his neck and moved into his brain between his ears.

"It's me you want, Brant. I was the one who screwed things up for you in Detroit. Though, judging by how you've recovered, not screwed you up nearly as much as I might have hoped."

"Well, no. There has been a recovery, and a strong one, at that."

"You don't have to hurt my children, or the women."

Brant guffawed. "Equal rights now, my friend, especially for women. Everyone gets hurt now. It's a better world all around. No one gets left out."

Nathan thumped the table.

"Temper, temper, Nathan."

"The kids then. Please. Let them live. I don't care what you do to me..."

Brant cocked his head to one side, regarding Nathan like a man might regard a steak he was about to greedily tuck into.

"You know, Nathan, if you knew what I have planned for you, I think you really would care. In fact, I know you would. It's very, very nasty."

There were no options left.

No one to come to the rescue.

Carmel was outside with Tommy under arrest with the others. His children were in the firing line, and he was locked in a room with a madman who was going to take his time killing him, and enjoy every damn second of it.

The room was sucked down to a dried husk. Nathan felt at once tiny and powerless, as well as strong and invincible. A man with nothing to lose really has nothing to lose. But a man who has no way out still has at least one way out, his daddy had told him. When you're in that position, it just comes down to how many you can take with you.

Nathan was alone with the soldiers and Brant. He was a man with no way out.

Brant pulled a .44 Magnum from inside his jacket, cocking it before pointing it at him. The gun looked ludicrous in Brant's pudgy little hand. It looked almost too heavy for him to lift.

No way out. Except the *only* way out.

Nathan knew then, in that moment, after all he'd been through, that his story was probably over.

But that didn't mean he wouldn't go out fighting.

"Okay, Brant," Nathan said, opening his palms. "You win."

25

"Prepping... *being* a prepper... isn't just about digging a hole in the ground and filling it with cans of corned beef, bags of lentils, and a chemical toilet," Cyndi said.

Nathan eyed the two new, ten-pound sacks of rice Cyndi was moving into the garage, to put with her racks of bulk dried goods like beans and pasta, plus tubs of dried fruit, and cans of ham, chicken, and tuna, and seeds and piles of shelf-stable prepared meals. Alongside those, gravity-fall water purification equipment, and purification tablets, stoves, kerosene, tents, and a dozen other things that looked like a prop list for the apocalypse.

"True," Nathan said. "All you're missing is a hole in the ground. Good thing I have a place for my tools at work. There's no room for them here in my garage, among the tent-pegs and fire-starters."

Cyndi swiped the top of his arm and then, almost as an afterthought, nuzzled his neck. "Trust me, one day we'll need all this. I hope we don't, but the way things are going with the weather, it might be the best decision I ever made. But that's not the point I'm trying to make. You're a prepper, Nate."

"I am not."

"You just don't realize it."

"Well, I know my backside from a hole in the ground, so I suppose that's a start."

Cyndi smiled and put an arm through his. "I still think the jury is out on that, buddy."

"Ha!"

"Look, I'll prove it to you, right?" She walked him across to the other side of the garage and pointed. "What's that?"

"A can of oil."

"Why do you have a can of oil?"

"Is there a prize at the end of this?"

"If you're lucky, I might road-test my latest acquisition from Victoria's Secret."

"Oh my."

"Back to the oil."

"Kinky."

She swiped him again. "Answer the question."

"Okay! It's spare engine oil, in case the engine of the Dodge needs it."

"So, you're prepared...?"

"I guess."

Cyndi undid the zipper on Nathan's jacket and put her hands inside around his stomach. "And when you're driving on the highway, and there's a lot of traffic, and there are mad dudes around swapping lanes, and taking risks, what do you do?"

"I spot escape routes. I taught you to do that. Highway driving is like chess. You have to know your strategy three or four moves ahead, so you say... where am I gonna go if the dipstick ahead slams on the anchors? Am I going to go left, or right? Can I brake hard, or will that send the doofus behind me up my tailpipe?"

"Exactly, you're prepared. You're a prepper. You have a strategy; you have a plan. It's one for the moment, but it's a plan. That's all I'm doing. I have a plan. I have a strategy. That's all." Cyndi smiled.

"Okay, I get it. I do. If it makes you happy..."

"One day, it might make us *all* happy. Thinking like *this*. It's the oil for the engine of our survival; it's the space on the highway we'll steer into if there's an accident up ahead."

"I love you, Cyndi Tolley."

"And I love you, Nathan Tolley," Cyndi said, reaching under the front of his shirt with her quick, cold hands. "But there is one plan you haven't made."

"Oh?"

Nathan's pants fell down as Cyndi giggled.

"One that stops me undoing your belt. Nathan, prepping is all about making sure you don't get caught with your pants down, showing your whole backside to the valley!"

Nathan's opened palms flipped over and he gripped the edges of the table. Pushing up with his knees and emitting a guttural roar that came from the very depths of his chest, he lifted the thick oak table off of the floor and prepared to be shot.

Sergeant Perry reacted first, and two bullets embedded themselves in the wood close to where the soldier might have expected Nathan's head to be. But Nathan was already ducking, so that even if the bullets had made it through the wood, they would have missed him completely.

The Magnum boomed, but such was the speed and attack and power that Nathan had put into lifting the table, Brant's shot went wildly wide.

Preparation.

That's all it was.

Nathan had tensed his legs like heavy duty springs on a hair trigger. He'd prepared for where on the edges of the table to grip to get the best leverage to lift it rapidly and make a barrier between himself and the armed men in the room. He'd *prepared* for exactly when he would need to throw the table up, so that he could dive underneath it, drawing the fire of the other soldiers.

He fully expected this to go south pretty quickly, and the bullet that slammed into his left hand, entering through his palm and burning a hole right the way out the other side, was evidence that it might.

But he'd been right.

They didn't expect him out in the open so soon. They might have imagined he was going to try to use the table as cover, but that would have been an insane plan. All they'd have to do if he did that was walk around the table and kill him.

No, Nathan had one chance as the table went up on the thrust of his desperate heave, and that was to go underneath it, out into the open, and into the gnashing, snarling maw of their weapons.

He crashed into Brant's belly, pushing him back into Perry, reaching up with both hands, and ignoring the pain and the spattering blood, he grabbed the Magnum and twisted it around. Brant's finger breaking and tearing in the trigger guard also had the effect of sending a round directly into Sergeant Perry's face.

Perry's head deformed and collapsed, his body spinning away to crash to the floor.

By the time the other soldiers had their weapons trained on Nathan's new position, he had both of his knees on Brant's chest, and had the barrel of the Magnum stuffed into his mouth, having knocked two of the mayor's front teeth back into his throat in the process.

"You pull that trigger and Brant dies, too."

The soldiers kept their weapons pointed at Nathan, but they didn't pull the trigger.

"Get out. Both of you," Nathan hissed at them.

They didn't move.

Nathan rammed the Magnum deeper into Brant's mouth. "Tell them!"

A mess of noises came out of Brant's mouth and he vigorously nodded his head, waving his hand at them.

They got the message. The door opened on a blast of snowflakes and bitter wind, and then it was shut. Nathan pulled the gun from Brant's mouth and hauled him to his feet. He propelled Brant across the room, keeping his corpulent frame between him and the only window in the room, just in case some joker decided to fire through the glass from outside. Nathan reached up with his bleeding hand and extinguished the oil lamp. There was still light bleeding in from the floodlight the FEMA troops had set up outside.

This was still, as far as Nathan could tell, a no-win situation for him. All one of the soldiers had to do out there was to bring Tony or Brandon to the window, with a gun to his head, and he was pretty sure he'd buckle. But he wasn't letting Brant know that right now. And Nathan knew he had to get this over with before the soldiers outside had time to take stock.

"I'm going to take you to the door, Brant, and with your gun stuck in the back of your head, you're going to tell the soldiers to get back in their APC and drive the hell back to Denver, or so help me God, I'll kill you where you stand."

Brant's mouth was full of blood, and his missing teeth made his voice hiss and lisp, but he got his point across with alarming alacrity. "You think they're going to stop hunting you? Even if you do kill me. You think you're going to be able to rest for one second?"

"I'll take my chances."

"You don't have a chance. Let me live and I let your kids live. That's the best deal you got right now, Nathan Tolley, the very best."

Nathan pushed Brant toward the door, holding onto his shoulder, shoving the barrel of the Magnum hard into the back of his neck. Nathan's shot hand hurt like hell, but he could still grip the material of Brant's shirt as he pushed him forward, past Sergeant Perry's crumpled body. This was the last roll of the dice and he knew it. To have come this far, with this much pain and hurt, to have it all end here, was not the life Nathan would have chosen for himself. If he could reboot it all, and be back in Glens Falls, he would do it in a heartbeat.

I'm not a killer.

I don't want to be a killer.

I don't want to be what people like Brant have been turning me into.

"Open the door."

"Last chance, Nathan. I'll let the boys live."

"Open it!"

Nathan positioned himself close in behind Brant as the door opened and the Big Winter flooded back into the room. Flakes swirled and blew, the wind tangled their hair, and it all made their clothes flap and shiver. It was like standing on the prow of a ship powering through the huge seas of the Arctic. A whole sky of killing weather thrown at them with the force of the gods.

Tommy, Free, and Dave had been separated from Lucy, Syd, and Carmel. The men had been pushed against the wall of the house, their arms on the bricks, their legs kept wide. They were being covered by two FEMA soldiers with M-16s. Two others were covering the women on the other side of the yard. They were huddled together, shivering.

Of the two soldiers Nathan had sent outside after Perry had been killed, one was holding Tony by the arm and the other had Brandon in his arms.

"Get my boys out of the cold! Put them in the truck!"

The snow fizzed and swarmed in the wind, but no one moved.

"Tell them," Nathan said, screwing the barrel of the Magnum into Brant's neck.

"Do it!" Brant called, and the soldiers moved.

"I love you, Anthony Tolley!" Nathan yelled over Brant's shoulder.

"I love you, Daddy!" Tony called back.

The soldiers put Tony into the crew cab of the F-350, then dropped Brandon into his arms before slamming the door.

"Tell them what I told you," Nathan hissed into Brant's ear. "Get them out of here."

He could feel Brant stiffen against him. Perhaps he didn't want to give Nathan the satisfaction. Perhaps he was preparing himself to die. But if he didn't give the orders Nathan wanted, they would be standing here until they all froze to death.

Nathan knew then he'd made the threat on Brant's life too many times. When you say the same word over and over again, eventually it loses all meaning and starts to sound lame. It was the same with death threats. Ultimately, they were useless if the person you were threatening wasn't afraid to die. He imagined Brant was making his peace with the fact that his life was going to end. Maybe he wanted to go to his death safe in the knowledge that Nathan would see his children die before his eyes.

"Say it."

"Go to hell," Brant whispered. "Kill me. Go ahead. Then watch your boys eat bullets. Shame I won't see it, but man, *I* can imagine it, and it's giving me a good thought to go to meet my Lord with…"

Brant began to struggle and try to pull away, but Nathan put his elbow around his throat to hold him steady. Nathan knew there was no way now that the soldiers would withdraw, not now that Brant had communicated to them that he was willing to die.

Brant's confidence that the balance of power was changing was clear in his voice as he spat through broken teeth. "Go on, you coward! Shoot me! Go on! Say goodbye to the boys for me."

Nathan felt his finger tighten on the trigger; it had been a desperate idea that had been bound to come to nothing, but he'd had to try. He'd at least owed that to his boys. That he'd gotten this far in this desperate situation was more due to luck than judgment. Now that Brant had regrown his backbone, he didn't have anywhere else to go with it. The soldiers were now just waiting for the order to shoot them both. Nathan couldn't let that happen. But there was nothing more he could do.

So, now it was up to Tony.

Preparation.

"I don't get it."

Nathan sat with his son in the F-350. The others were making camp, with Free and Lucy off hunting in the woods. The day was gray, but at least it wasn't snowing. Dave and Donie were working on the laptops and Syd was playing with Rapier near the campfire.

"Uncle Tommy and I showed you how to fire it. Now we need to hide it."

"But why are we hiding it? Don't we need it?"

Nathan pulled a roll of insulation tape from the pocket of his winter coat, and then he laid the Colt on the seat between them in the crew cab. "We're hiding it in case we need it. There are people after us; there are bad men on the road. There might come a time when I can't help you, or you're in danger, or... well... when I can't get to you."

Tony shook his head. "That's not gonna happen, Daddy. You're too smart."

Nathan ruffled the boy's hair and smiled. "Mom was the smart one, kid. I just learned some stuff from her. And one of those things was to prepare. You can't prepare enough, but if you don't prepare at all, there's nothing you can do to change the situation —any situation you're in."

Tony cuddled Brandon and nodded, and Nathan hoped he understood what he was getting to. "Every vehicle we have from now on is going to have one of these, with a full magazine taped under the driver's seat. All you'll have to do..."

"Me...?"

"Only if the situation gets so bad that I need you to do it."

Tony's face was confused and awkward, taking it all in, but Nathan could see his eyes filling up with a million questions. The boy had had to do a lot of growing up since Cyndi's death, and Nathan felt bad about putting this level of responsibility on him, but all it was was preparation. Just in case. A situation that he hoped would never happen, but if it did…

"All you have to do, if you're not in a position to fire it yourself, is throw it to the nearest person who can. Trust me, they'll be waiting for it."

"How will I know?"

"Know what, son?"

"That the situation is so bad that you need me to do it?" Tony asked.

Nathan thought. It was a good point. How would he know? It might not be possible to give the boy a direct order.

"We need a code!" Tony said, warming to the idea. "A code. That's preparing, too, right? That's what Mom would have done, yeah?"

"Great idea. What shall we use?"

Tony thought. And Nathan thought. As he did so, Nathan finished taping the gun to the underside of the seat.

"Got it!" the boy exclaimed. "It's perfect."

"Go on."

"You never call me Anthony. *Ever*. If you call me that, then I'll know. Yeah?"

Nathan smiled, and he hugged his sons.

Yes.

Yes, it really *was* the perfect preparation.

No one was watching the F-350. The Big Winter was, at last, giving Nathan and the others a break. Something positive to use to their advantage.

As Tony moved toward the open car window, Nathan fired the Magnum past Brant's ear. The mayor flinched and yelled, but now every soldier in the yard was focused on Nathan. Brant was bitching about his ear while Tony was throwing the Colt from the widow, and Lucy caught it.

The two soldiers near her were down in the snow before anyone realized what was happening.

By the time Syd reached the F-350 to open the door and reach inside, Free and the men had overpowered the distracted soldiers covering them and were relieving them of their weapons.

Nathan pushed Brant forward onto his knees.

"Please! Please! I'm sorry! Don't kill me! Please! I'm sorry!" Brant's brief show of backbone had melted completely. He was down in the buzzing, insecty snowflakes, collecting snow on his head and on his shoulders, snow silting up across the bloody handprint where Nathan had held him.

Oh man, how far we've come, Nathan thought. From a thrown together band of mechanics, runaways, millionaires, and lone star Texans. How they'd drawn together in all this adversity, which he thought had changed them irrevocably.

The Big Winter had turned them into hunters, survivors, widowers, fathers, and now mothers. It had turned them inside out, and it had shaken them down. This would not be the last danger they faced, and Nathan was sure it was not the last time they would be in a situation which brought them within a hair's breadth from death.

But Nathan was also sure that the Big Winter hadn't changed at least one thing about him.

It hadn't turned him into an executioner.

"I'm not going to shoot an unarmed man on his knees, Brant. You would. You'd do that without thinking, and you'd be smiling while you did it. But you and this damned winter haven't turned me into *you*. And it never will."

EPILOGUE
ONE YEAR LATER

"It's them, Daddy! They're coming!"

Tony, half a foot taller, ruddy-faced and building muscles that Nathan would never have thought possible on his once thin frame, came running down the trail to the Cliff Palace.

Nathan was keeping an eye on both Brandon and Hope, Lucy and Free's daughter, while her parents were heading out on a three-day hunting trip into the mountains with Carmel and Syd. A fire was burning in a round stone hearth, but it really wasn't meant to provide heat today—just to boil water for coffee.

Brandon was running hither and thither within the wooden compound Nathan had built. Hope, a beautiful, round-faced, blonde-haired child was gurgling in her sprung chair, looking out over the valley. Their camp lay in the ancient Puebloan sandstone dwellings, which in later years had become part of the Mesa Verde National Park in southwest Colorado.

Nathan and the others had been led there by Tommy eleven months before. And although it was still cold and snow would continue to fall, there was a softening of the climate to be felt here. Perhaps it was to do with the favorable positioning of the caves, the depth of the valley, or the natural shelter provided by the surrounding landscape. Since the crust of the Earth was no longer shifting around the mantle, stopping any Coloradan earthquakes, and the Big Winter had retreated a little—north and east of Denver—they had found a place that was almost temperate. As the New Year had turned, there had been an actual spring. The first Nathan could remember for three or four years.

Tony came bounding around the corner of the Square Tower and bounced up to Nathan. "Two A1s. Fifteen soldiers, I reckon. Be here in five. You want me to lead them down?"

Nathan stood up and brushed the dirt from his hands. He'd been sowing winter lettuce and onion seeds, to see if they could catch up with the unexpected spring. He thumbed at the aching back of his left hand where the ragged scar of the gunshot was lumpy and red, and then pointed back to the trail. "Sounds like a plan."

Tony ran back up the trail to meet the soldiers, and Nathan walked over to the sandstone block which contained the cell.

Tommy was watching over Brant.

Brant had known today would come, and had had eleven months in captivity to either plan an escape or find a way to end his own life. Since they'd heard the soldiers were coming for him, Nathan had put a round the clock baby-sit on the ex-mayor. That Nathan and the others had managed to keep him chained up, relatively healthy, fed but not entirely happy, had been a huge bone of contention with the others. Keeping Brant alive was a waste of resources, said some of them, others warning that he'd get away and bring hell down on them. *I'll kill him myself*, had said one more.

In the end, it had been Tommy who'd really gotten it and understood where Nathan was coming from.

"You have to be better than them, right?"

Nathan had nodded. "What's the point of resisting them, if you become just like them? What's the point of surviving all this if you give in to everything that makes a mockery of being human? Of being civilized?"

And so, they had kept Brant alive.

When they'd reached Mesa Verde, and the Cliff Palace they'd converted into homes for all of them, they'd also made a cell. It had a bed, a chemical toilet, and some books. Brant was chained by the ankles on a halter line riveted to a wall plate, and he was kept handcuffed unless someone was watching over him.

For months, he'd just spat insults through his broken teeth at anyone who came close enough to hear, but when no one had given him the satisfaction of responding, after a while, he'd just given up. He'd even asked for more books to read, which Nathan had gladly supplied from their trips down into libraries in the nearest towns.

Brant and Tommy looked up as Nathan approached. "They're here."

Brant's eyes fell. "You know they're going to kill me, don't you? You might not get blood on your hands, but it's there by proxy."

Nathan sighed. "Justice is what justice does, Brant. I don't know what they're going to do to you. Maybe you'll hang; maybe you won't. I hope you don't, precisely because I think hanging's too good for you."

Brant's eyes cut the air around Nathan. His lips thinned and drained of color.

Nathan met the hatred in the gaze and plowed on. "I'd rather you lived out your life regretting every single thing you've done. Seeing the face of everyone you've had murdered and killed yourself every time you closed your eyes. That's my idea of justice. But it's not in our hands anymore."

Brant got to his feet and Tommy pulled his hands behind his back. "It'll never be the America it was before, Tolley. You've lost everything, too. It'll never be the same again."

"I really hope it isn't," Nathan said truthfully.

Brant blinked, his face confused.

"I want it to be *better*," Nathan said, and together, Tommy and he walked Brant out of the cell and into the Cliff Palace courtyard.

"Mr. Tolley! Or should I say Mr. Grieves? Great to see you again." Lieutenant Toothill, fully recovered from her Carmel-inflicted wound, greeted Nathan as they came into view. Knowing that Toothill had been coming here today was another reason that Carmel had lit out in the morning with Lucy and Free. Carmel had been shocked to find out Toothill and her men had not been the bad guys she'd thought they were when she'd brought down her extreme form of vigilantism on them last year.

Toothill was now part of a conglomerate of military and militia forces who were trying to regain control of the country. She had been contacted by Dave and Donie two months ago. They'd been setting up solar-powered printers to make copies of Elm and Cyndi's ledger of remedies for distribution, and seen on the recovering internet how Toothill was making a name for herself.

Toothill's forces had been fighting the vicious gangs, robber barons, and corrupt FEMA forces in Denver, Detroit, and Chicago for the last eight months, and they were getting results. It would take a while for it all to come to fruition, but Nathan knew that if people like Toothill were out there fighting for what America *should* stand for, then maybe there *was* hope.

And not just a child named for it.

After the introductions were finished, and Brant, deflated and silenced, was put into custody, Toothill stayed for a simple meal with Nathan, Tommy, and the children before heading out again.

When it was time to end their visit, Toothill turned back to Nathan. "We'll be in touch. I think men like you are exactly what we need right now. I think you could do great things."

Nathan didn't know what to say, so he just shook Toothill's proffered hand and waved as she and her soldiers pushed Brant up the steep slope toward the plateau above the cave.

Later that evening, when everyone was back—and the hunting had been good, so the deer was fresh—Tony cornered his father in the roaring firelight, out of everyone's earshot. His face showed extreme concern.

"What's up, son?"

"Lieutenant Toothill was offering you a job."

Nathan thought about it. "Yeah, I guess she was. In a way."

"Don't leave us, Daddy. We need you here. Let someone else be a hero."

Nathan put an arm around his son's shoulders. "We've all gotta be heroes now, Tony. You, me, everyone."

"I know… but not yet, yeah? Not now."

Tony's eyes were glittering with what might have been tears, and he wiped at his eyelids before the water had a chance to roll over his cheeks.

"I'm not going anywhere, son. Not at the moment. Not while there's so much to do here."

"Promise. Really promise?"

Nathan took his son's cheeks in his hands and looked deep into his eyes.

"Really promise, Tony."

Tony sighed and smiled.

"Family first," Nathan said.

END OF BLACK ICE
AFTER THE SHIFT BOOK THREE

Freezing Point, September 13 2018

Killing Frost, November 8 2018

Black Ice, January 10 2019

PS: If you love EMP fiction then keep reading for exclusive extracts from ***Dark Retreat.***

ABOUT GRACE HAMILTON

Loved this book? Share it with a friend, www.GraceHamiltonBooks.com/books

To be notified of the next book release please sign up for Grace's mailing list at www.GraceHamiltonBooks.com.

Grace Hamilton is the prepper pen-name for a bad-ass, survivalist momma-bear of four kids, and wife to a wonderful husband. After being stuck in a mountain cabin for six days following a flash flood, she decided she never wanted to feel so powerless or have to send her kids to bed hungry again. Now she lives the prepper lifestyle and knows that if SHTF or TEOTWAWKI happens, she'll be ready to help protect and provide for her family.

Combine this survivalist mentality with a vivid imagination (as well as a slightly unhealthy day dreaming habit) and you get a prepper fiction author. Grace spends her days thinking about the worst possible survival situations that a person could be thrown into, then throwing her characters into these nightmares while trying to figure out "What SHOULD you do in this situation?"

It's her wish that through her characters, you will get to experience what life will be like and essentially learn from their mistakes and experiences, so that you too can survive!

BLURB

Three months after life as she knows it was decimated, Megan Wolford has only one goal: protect her daughter, Caitlin, at any cost. When a mysterious illness strikes Caitlin down, Megan is forced to forage for medical supplies at a remote lodge. The last thing she wants is help from her fellow survivors when so many in her life have let her down—but soon she'll find herself with no other option.

Ex-Navy SEAL Wyatt Morris is doing everything he can to hold his family together after the tragic death of his prepper Dad, so when Megan enters their lands, he is mistrustful at first despite feeling drawn to her. He won't turn away an ill child though—no matter how deadly the world has become. The arrival of another stranger named Kyle soon gives them all a new reason to be suspicious. Wyatt knows he'll have to forge alliances in order to keep his family safe, but trusting the wrong person could be a deadly mistake.

When Megan and Wyatt discover her daughter's illness may be linked to Kyle's arrival, it sets off a race to discover the truth before it's too late to save Caitlin—and the rest of the Morris clan. Can they work together for survival . . . and something more?

Grab your copy of *Dark Retreat* (EMP Lodge Series Book One) from www.GraceHamiltonBooks.com

EXCERPT

Megan Wolford stumbled over a rock and nearly dropped her daughter before she quickly regained her footing. The sight of a log cabin through the trees had given her a boost of adrenaline and she found she was practically running through the damp forest despite her heavy burden.

She'd fallen several times, bruising her knees and twisting her ankle. Her arms had deep cuts from tree branches that showed no mercy. There wasn't exactly a trail to follow, which meant she was cutting through the heart of the forest and its unforgiving terrain. She was making her own way, as usual, which always seemed to be far harder than it had to be.

"Caitlin, hold on, baby. Hold on," she whispered to the lifeless seven-year-old in her arms.

Megan was doing her best not to panic, but Caitlin had collapsed a couple miles back and she'd been carrying the sleeping child ever since. Carrying her where she didn't know, but now that she saw what appeared to be a hunting lodge of some sort in front of her, she had a destination in mind. She had a goal.

It gave her something to focus on other than the agony that was tearing through her entire body. Another tree branch slapped her in the face, making her wince in pain. Her physical discomfort was nothing compared to the emotional anguish she felt at the thought of losing her daughter. Caitlin was the only thing she'd left in this world. She couldn't lose her.

Her arms were burning and her lungs felt like they would collapse, but nothing would stop her from getting her daughter to what she hoped would be medicine. Without it, Megan knew her only child would die.

She didn't have a clue what had made her so sick, but Caitlin was gravely ill. In the past twenty-four hours, her daughter went from bubbly and energetic to lethargic and weak. Megan had left their most recent camp in the hopes of finding something to help her. They'd walked through one small town yesterday and found nothing. Every single place she checked had been emptied already forcing them to travel for miles.

She was afraid to walk through the city streets overrun with looters. Megan knew it wasn't safe for her and definitely not for Caitlin. It wasn't as if she could leave her daughter alone while she went on a scavenging mission. She had to do it with Caitlin or not all. Common sense told her she didn't have the strength to fight off the hundreds and thousands of other people vying for the same basic supplies. Instead, she'd decided to head out of town in the hopes of finding clinics, stores, and homes in more rural areas that weren't as likely to be quite so dangerous.

Megan took long strides, slightly shifting her daughter, as she kept moving forward. Her sweaty hands were making it difficult for her to hold on to Caitlin. Gripping her hands together under her daughter's backside, Megan pressed on.

She tried to protect her daughter's head as best she could from the branches and sharp twigs that seemed to be jumping out and stabbing the intruders in the forest. Another branch hooked her sleeve, scratching painfully at the skin beneath and she could feel blood trickling down her arm, towards her fingers. She wanted to scream at the trees and order them to stop their assault.

Her back was killing her with the awkward posture of leaning back to keep her daughter secured against her chest. The weight of her pack helped pull her backwards, but also put more strain on her hips. She was grateful to have had an old hiking pack in the closet. The internal frame made it easier for Megan to carry it and allowed her to carry a lot more without much additional strain. She didn't know if she would have been able to carry her daughter and her supplies without it. Right now, she was grateful the pushy salesman had persuaded her to spend the extra money on the pack.

Regardless, everything hurt. She could feel dried blood on her bare arms pulling the fine hairs whenever Caitlin's body rubbed against the cuts, further adding to the misery. Each twist tore open the dried wounds, causing them to start bleeding again.

She'd fallen several times, catching herself with one arm and holding her daughter with the other. She could tell her left knee was swollen. It was stiff and difficult to bend. It didn't matter. Her daughter's life was all that mattered.

"A few more steps," Megan chanted more for her own benefit than her unconscious daughter.

She was thankful the weather had been mild. It was early spring in the northwest, but there were still little piles of snow in the shady areas. Climbing steadily uphill, her overused muscles screamed at her to take a break but she knew if she did, she wouldn't be able to get back up again. The cabin ahead was growing steadily larger as her strides ate up the distance. Because of the harsh winter storms, mountain residents were prepared to outlast storms for weeks at a time, which meant they would have supplies, including medicine.

If it'd been more than the mild seventy degrees that it currently was, Megan wasn't sure she could've walked as far as she did. As it was, she was sweating and the growing fatigue was partly dehydration. Her daughter's feverish body was like carrying a giant lava rock. In addition to finding shelter and medicine, they needed water. The little water she had wouldn't last long; especially if Caitlin woke and needed it.

She'd eaten the last of the food she'd managed to scrounge up at an abandoned home earlier that morning. Megan was now running on empty and knew her collapse would mean her daughter's life. *Push, Megan. Push.*

When she got within three hundred feet of the cabin, she stopped to survey the property, staying partially hidden in the surrounding trees. If someone was here, it could go either way. Unfortunately, the new world was not kind. You didn't simply knock on a stranger's door to beg for food and water.

Not now.

Not after the EMP had plunged the world into the biggest blackout, humankind had ever experienced.

At least those who'd grown up with electricity. Pioneers would do okay in this world, but for those who'd never learned how to work with their hands or hunt for food, this was a form of population control that no one wanted to face. Those who didn't know how to perform some of the most basic skills were suffering.

Megan had seen more dead in the past few weeks than the living. After the first dozen or so, she thought she'd grow immune to the horror of death and could simply move quickly past but the smell reminded her of what it meant to be alive as her gag reflex kicked in.

This new world meant that only the fittest, strongest and most prepared would survive.

**Grab your copy of *Dark Retreat*
(EMP Lodge Series Book One) from
www.GraceHamiltonBooks.com**

WANT MORE?
WWW.GRACEHAMILTONBOOKS.COM

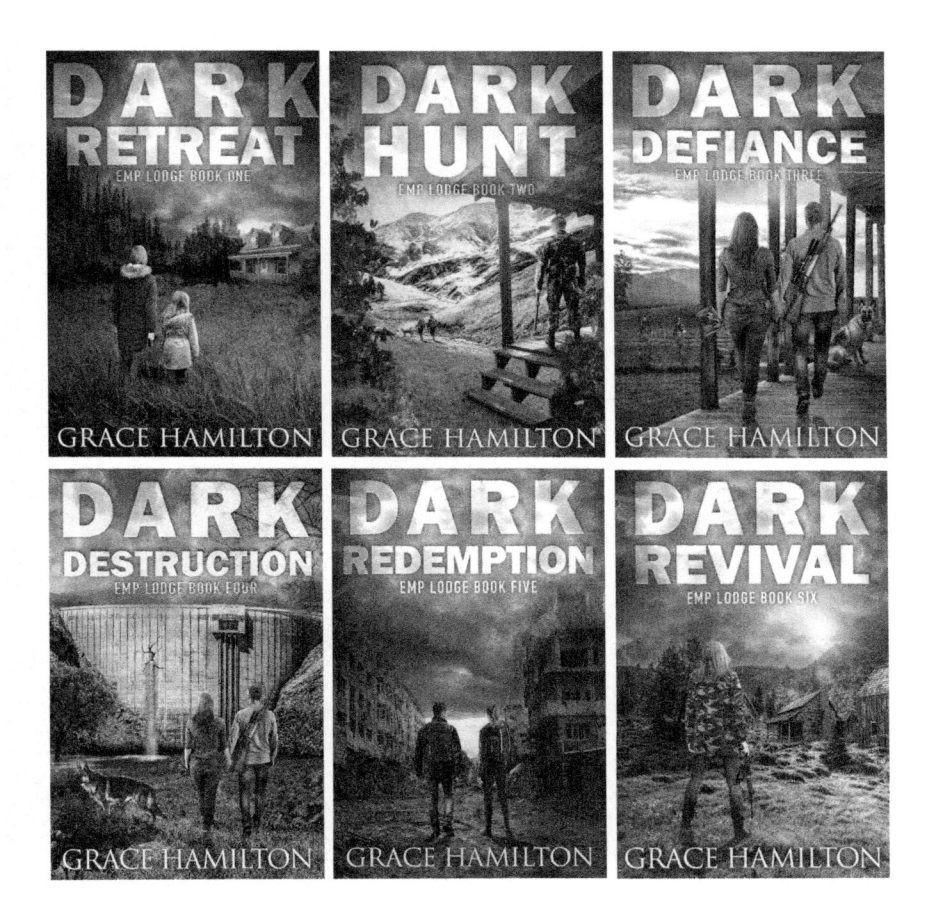

Printed in Dunstable, United Kingdom